D1187747

THE GUILD TRILOGY

BOOK I

OPERATION RED JERICHO

JOSHUA MOWLL

WALKER BOOKS
AND SUBSIDIARIES
LONDON · BOSTON · SYDNEY · AUCKLAND

*For Victoria, whose kindness guided me
to London some years ago*

*In memory of David, oldest friend,
who left the party far too early*

CONFIDENTIAL
KEEP UNDER LOCK AND KEY

INTRODUCTION

A NOTE TO THE READER

In the early spring of 2004 Walker Books received a package and letter from Joshua Mowll. In his letter he claimed to have uncovered the history of a mysterious secret society whose existence and purpose had remained hidden from the world for centuries. The information that led him to this astonishing discovery had been sealed for decades in a vault deep below the home of his late great-aunt, Rebecca MacKenzie.

Joshua's adventure began when he inherited his aunt's estate in February 2002. He received a letter and an unusually worded legal document from her solicitor which elected him *President of the Honourable Guild of Specialists* and charged him to dedicate himself to its *solemn Purpose*. Joshua had only met his aunt on a few occasions and had never heard of this organization. He was naturally both mystified and curious.

The letter from his aunt began: *Dear Joshua … if my solicitor, Melvin, has done what I asked and you are reading this letter, I must be dead.* After referring to some kind of archive, it continued: *I would like you to edit my papers and finish the project Doug and I began.*

I have left Cove Cottage to Emily and you. Use it to prepare my memoirs, if you like… It has an Internet connection and a serviceable office. Some of the artefacts won't travel well, so I suggest you leave them there. Melvin should have given you a bunch of keys which will open the door to the vault where my archives are stored. You are now responsible for the contents.

During my adventures, I was lucky enough, more by chance than

design, to see some of the most ancient cultures and tra-
ditions of human civilization. The second great
war washed away most of that, of
course, and afterwards noth-
ing was ever quite the same.
But China, the subject of the
first folder (No. 116143), was
a place I have never forgotten. I
dream about it often, even now. You
will also read about the Honourable
Guild of Specialists. My life has been
bound to it ever since I was born; it was
my destiny. The Guild itself was impossibly
old, even back then. I do not intend to
explain that great institution here – all will
become clear when you read the papers.

Almost at once, Joshua visited his aunt's
Devon cottage and began to explore the
secret archive for himself. Within minutes of
unlocking the door he realized that he had
come across something of startling importance.

The archive contained an extraordinary variety of
original material: letters, maps, sketches, photographs,
ancient artefacts and – most revealing of all – every
volume of his aunt's personal diary. Through months of
painstaking research and investigation, Joshua pieced
together the adventures of the young Rebecca and Douglas
MacKenzie, and here he finally tells their story – and the part
they played in the remarkable Operation Red Jericho.

Rebecca MacKenzie's final letter and will, in which she bequeathed
Joshua Mowll the contents of her archive. (MA 941.37 RM)

COVE COTTAGE, PERENPRITH, SOUTH HAMS, DEVON

TELEPHONE: (PERENPRITH) 452390

Thursday 10th January, 2002

Dear Joshua,

I do not wish to be melodramatic - a trait I've never admired
in anyone - but if my solicitor, Melvin, has done what I asked
and you are reading this letter, I must be dead. Don't be upset.
I'm writing this after ninety-seven years on the planet, and
I've enjoyed every single one of them.

Some years ago (about thirty in fact - how time flies!) I
started to compile the first few folders of my archive into a
publishable form, with the help of my brother Doug, who could
draw a little. Unfortunately we just spent a lot of time arguing
about minor details, as brothers and sisters tend to do, and the
project fizzled out. It needs a fresh eye to see what is of
interest and what is just sentimental nonsense. Bad luck. You
are the relative I have chosen.

I would like you to edit my papers and finish the project Doug
and I began. You might wish to know why I've chosen you rather
than your sister in America. You and Emily are the last of the
family line, and although Emily is in my view more capable of
executing my wishes. As an additional obstacle, she lives in New York.
to look after. As an additional obstacle, she lives in New York.
you, I understand, are idling around London posing as some sort
of artist, pleasing no one but yourself. You have my permission
to rework some of the drawings, if needs be - I believe that's
your line. I saw some of your work recently and your style is
not dissimilar to Doug's.

I have left Cove Cottage to Emily and you. Use it to prepare
my memoirs, if you like. I shouldn't sell the house - I'm told
by my accountant that something called the "capital growth" is
<able. It has an Internet connection and a serviceable
< the artefacts won't travel well, so I suggest
<in should have given you a bunch of
vault where my archives ar
<ents.

OPERATION RED JERICHO

LOCATOR MAP

THEATRE OF OPERATIONS – CHINA

(MA 389.109 CHINA)

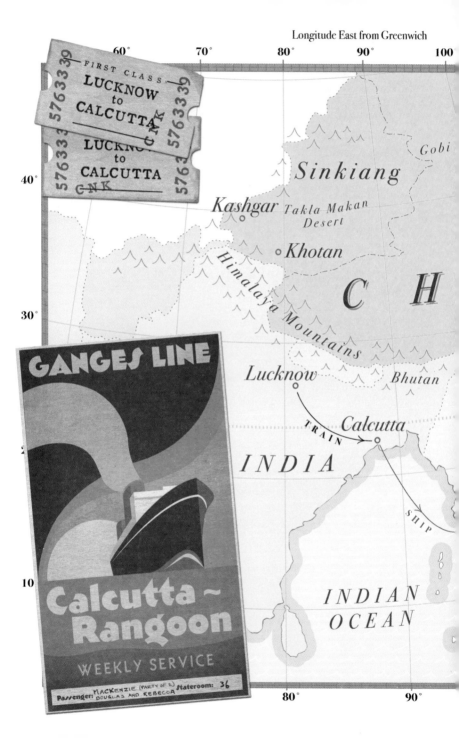

OPERATION RED JERICHO

*Those who have taken upon them to lay down the law
of nature as a thing already searched out and understood ...
have therein done philosophy and the sciences great injury.*

Francis Bacon, *Novum Organum* (1620)

CHAPTER ONE

Cutting from the 29th March 1920 edition of the *Shanghai Post*.

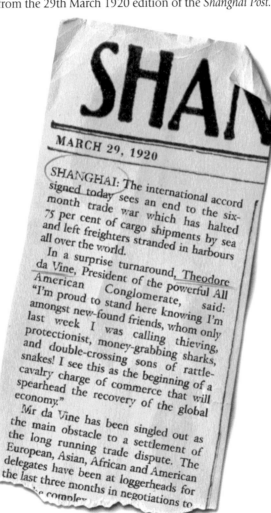

SHAN

MARCH 29, 1920

SHANGHAI: The international accord signed today sees an end to the six-month trade war which has halted 75 per cent of cargo shipments by sea and left freighters stranded in harbours all over the world.

In a surprise turnaround, Theodore da Vine, President of the powerful All American Conglomerate, said: "I'm proud to stand here knowing I'm amongst new-found friends, whom only last week I was calling thieving, protectionist, money-grabbing sharks, and double-crossing sons of rattle-snakes! I see this as the beginning of a cavalry charge of commerce that will spearhead the recovery of the global economy."

Mr da Vine has been singled out as the main obstacle to a settlement of the long running trade dispute. The European, Asian, African and American delegates have been at loggerheads for the last three months in negotiations to

Becca's diary: 2nd April 1920
In taxi from Nanking to Shanghai

I have solved the mystery of the savage stink in this taxi. It's my brother Doug's lucky socks. The heat of China has given them a new and remarkably pungent smell. He's snored his way through this afternoon and keeps trying to stretch out and take up the whole back seat. I've only given ground because I don't want him anywhere near me. In case I should die of asphyxiation, here is everything I know about the lucky socks, so he can be brought to justice.

DESCRIPTION: *heavy knitted walking socks, grey, with red band at the ankle.*

CONDITION: *huge hole in one heel; a yellow talon (possibly his big toe) hangs out of the other.*

SMELL: *curdled milk on a hot summer's day.*

HISTORY: *a Christmas present from Father four years ago for our trip to Bhutan and the Himalayas. They have never been washed. Doug wears them for sporting activities (where they gain their so-called luck, apparently) as well as taking all exams in them. Today he is wearing them to meet our uncle, Captain Fitzroy MacKenzie, who is to be our new guardian.*

BANG! An incredible explosion shook the taxi.

"Is it the engine?" Doug asked. "Is it the crankshaft?" He looked anxiously at Mr Ying, their Chinese driver.

"No, no. Please, please," the driver jabbered, waving and pointing towards the night sky over Shanghai. "Fireworks party, bang, bang!"

"Is it a Chinese holiday?"

"No, no. Shanghai Shipping Syndicate celebrate because international shipping treaty signed. No cargo move for weeks. Very bad time. Ships stay tied up. Then big conference! Big talking! Then this man, how you say … T-he-o-dore…"

"Theodore?" deciphered Doug.

"Yes, yes! The-o-dore da Vine arrive. Big cigar! Big so he can't turn corners easy. Anyway, he solve argument. Then ships start moving again. We all friends now … so big party to match big cigar!" Mr Ying laughed and slapped the steering wheel. Becca rolled her eyes and wished the journey would end.

A second explosion shook the cab; Doug wound down the window and peered out. They were nearing the centre of the city and ahead lay the sweep of the Bund, a broad thoroughfare that fronted the Huangpu River with fine European-style buildings. Across the river a shimmer of light caught his eye and he watched a third firework flare up and explode in a flash as bright as the sun, showering fountains of burning scarlet and azure earthwards.

"Lethal!" he shouted. "Double lethal!"

DOUGLAS MACKENZIE

His school reports stated that "Douglas's undoubted intelligence sleeps under a blanket of idleness." Doug was an artist and lazy scientist, but above all a freethinker. He never let rules or regulations get in the way of his quirky quest for knowledge.

Doug, his dark hair tousled and in need of a cut, had the same high cheekbones as his sister, Rebecca. At thirteen he didn't really fit the clothes he was wearing and what's more he didn't really care. In the last six months he'd become idle and awkward. But Doug was, by his very nature, enquiring and inquisitive and much concerned with getting to the root of things he didn't understand. At the moment it was crankshafts; last week it had been the mystery of where all the rubber from car tyres vanishes to when it wears off; and the week before that, why bricks at the bottom of tall buildings don't crack. These subjects had the ability to consume him utterly until he encountered the next unfathomable problem, and he could display knowledge on some extremely obscure topics. The trouble was that these pet interests were as erratic as his washdays, and seldom crossed into any of the formal academic curricula. For a person with so little direction in life, it was surprising that his most cherished possession was a compass set within a silver pocket-watch case; he carried this gift from his father at all times.

His sister, Rebecca, was two years older than him to the day, but apart from sharing a birthday they had little in common. First of all, Rebecca cared very much what she looked like, and owned three matching suitcases, whereas Doug had only a tatty canvas kitbag. She was known by her family nickname of Becca. She liked Becca; Rebecca sounded too formal to her. If Doug had grown wild in the last year, she had become withdrawn and serious, largely confining herself to diary-writing, practising ancient German swordsmanship techniques and indulging in her growing passion for music. Her dark hair was cut as short as Doug's had grown long, but despite her natural reserve, her eyes were alive with a burning spark of interest that marked her out as a thinker.

REBECCA MACKENZIE

A formerly first-class student who had become "Ungovernable, unruly, obstinate and mutinous" after the disappearance of her parents. Her chief interests were music and fencing.

Doug pushed his fringe back and waited expectantly for another rocket, but none came. He hoped there would be more. The Bund started to fill with people looking skywards, chattering and pointing. The taxi driver slowed and tooted his horn as the numbers swelled, surging towards the river. Soon there were so many bodies that the queue of cars, rickshaws and trams could barely move.

Mr Ying pumped the accelerator and shouted for the crowds to clear the way, but nobody took any notice. Excited faces pressed against the windows. Grinding into first gear, the taxi had no choice but to limp behind the throng at a crawl.

"Mister, miss," Mr Ying urged. He pointed towards the ships and junks moored on the opposite bank of the river.

Suddenly dozens of rockets were launched into the sky and exploded simultaneously with a noise like the crack of Doomsday. Then more rockets, then more, erupting in a perfect sequence of bangs and cascades of colour. The noise was deafening and smoke hung heavy in the night air. Doug had seen large fireworks displays before – indeed, he prided himself on his understanding of gunpowder-based rocketry. But there was something altogether different about this: something majestic, grand and unique.

The percussive effect was so strong that with every deafening thunder-crack the taxi seemed to tremble like a nervous dog. The fireworks rose twice as high as Doug had ever seen fireworks go before, bursts of vivid vermilion, gold and sapphire blue exploding in perfect pinpricked spheres of light. The rockets burst into myriad shapes and patterns: extraordinary star constellations, then a snake wriggling and changing colour as it fell to earth. Monkeys performed acrobatics; tigers

Fireworks over Shanghai DM 1920

From Doug's sketchbook[1] (DMS 1/14)

prowled through a jungle of green light; crocodiles circled and snapped their jaws at one another; a strutting peacock unfolded a fan of blazing feathers; a procession of dragons, each more beautiful than the last, appeared to consume the one before in great flashes of orange and blue flame.

As the taxi squeezed through the crowds, Becca and Doug could see every detail of the ships moored alongside the Bund, lit up by searing splashes of colour. Gradually the display built to a final crescendo. The fireworks rumbled and rolled, vibrating every fibre of their bodies. Despite his excitement, Doug felt a pang of fear – the fireworks were so big, so loud, that he grabbed tightly at the torn seat to steady himself. He noticed that Becca too was bracing herself, clutching the door handle as the cab began to rock with an

1 The picture above is from one of Doug MacKenzie's sketchbooks. Most of Doug's sketches were drawn from memory, and consequently may not be accurate representations of the people and events in this account.

uneasy motion. She was shouting something, but he couldn't hear a word.

Then, as abruptly as the display had started, it stopped. The last rumblings echoed away, leaving the city silent. The night faded back to its natural darkness, but the crowds lingered, hopeful there would be more. Mr Ying had completely given up. He had stopped the taxi and had his fingers stuck in his ears.

After half a minute one final rocket surged up trailing a lazy amber tail and erupted with an astonishing tearing boom far louder than the rest. It formed into the shape of a ram's head with downturned horns. Mr Ying roared with laughter, hit the ignition button on the dashboard and inched the car forward once more. "Su–jing. They crazy!"

The ram hovered, changed colour from crimson to cyan and back to crimson again, winked its right eye, then burst into the four points of the compass and was gone. Raucous cheers and laughter echoed from the crowds. At almost the same moment, with the guidance of one or two sailors, Mr Ying drew to a halt by the side of an ageing ship. Doug peered up at the smooth pearly stern of the vessel and could just make out the rust-streaked words high above him: RESEARCH SHIP EXPEDIENT. They had reached their destination.

"Welcome, Miss Rebecca; welcome, Master Douglas," came a very clean-cut English voice. "My name's Ch-Char-Charlie. The captain sends his … compliments and asks you come aboard ship im-im-immediately."

The door to their left swung open and Charlie offered his hand to Becca. She brushed it away. "I don't need any help, thank you."

Doug scrambled out behind her, eager to get a better look

at the *Expedient*. The dark hull loomed over him. The vessel was a steam-powered freighter with a long cargo hatch forward. The superstructure – boat deck, wheelhouse, bridge and funnel – rose from the halfway point and ran all the way back to the poop deck at the stern. Although she had two sizeable masts, these were in fact nothing more than derricks for lifting cargo in and out of the holds.

Becca looked up with disapproval. "Is that it?"

A stream of white-hot sparks from a welder's torch sprayed out from high on the ship's bridge.

"Is the ship damaged?" asked Doug. "Is it the crankshaft?"

"The … the crankshaft?" repeated Charlie with incredulity. "Up there?"

"Ignore him," said Becca. "He's been obsessed with crankshafts ever since our aeroplane force-landed four days ago in Indo China."

"We nearly came down in the jungle!" Doug explained. "We limped into Saigon on one engine, throwing out seats to lighten the plane. Since then I've decided to make certain—"

"Why can't you just shut up?" hissed Becca.

"You'd better a-a-ask the chief engineer," laughed Charlie. "The c-c-crankshaft is usually k-k-kept in the flag locker after dark."

"In the flag locker? Are you sure?" wondered Doug, almost to himself. He could sense the presence of others on the deck and overhear a muttered conversation. But suddenly the world seemed eerily silent; the crowds were melting away from the quayside in twos and threes, and Doug realized that he was about to board a ship commanded by an uncle he'd never met, bound for destinations yet to be revealed.

"Is our luggage safe?" asked Becca rather haughtily, trying

to hide her nerves. "There should be three suitcases, a kitbag and my mother's correspondence box."

"Your luggage is being shipped and stowed this minute." Doug recognized this sailor's accent immediately: he was a New Yorker, his voice low and breathy as a foghorn. "Get our new passengers aboard, Charlie. Hurry now, the ship's about to sail."

As they climbed the steep gangway Doug felt a rush of panic at the thought of stepping into this new and unknown world. Below them the dark, oily river looked as unsettled as he felt, and he hesitated for a second as he saw Mr Ying drive away. Becca gave Doug a rare sisterly smile and encouraged him up the last few steps. When they reached the deck the ship proved to be reassuringly solid underfoot.

"Lethal!" whispered Doug, taking in all the equipment and hawsers around the fo'c'sle.

He was distracted by an impatient jangle of bells as an ambulance swerved through the thinning crowds on the quayside and screeched to a halt beside the gangway. The rear doors were thrown open and two sailors jumped out.

"S-stand clear," Charlie advised them in a friendly tone.

They watched the sailors pull out a stretcher and carry it up the gangway. The casualty was so heavily bandaged that it was impossible to see his face – but he appeared to be handcuffed to the stretcher.

"A most impressive fireworks display," boomed a voice from above, making Becca and Doug spin round and gaze up in unison. "I thought the gates of hell had opened. I am your uncle, captain of this ship. Welcome aboard."

The dark silhouette crowned the bridge, the welder's sparks lending him an alarming, fiery aura. His face was difficult to discern in the half-light, the collar of his heavy sea coat curving up to his bearded chin. Doug shielded his eyes from the glare of an arc lamp and saw that their uncle had a patch over his left eye and carried a walking stick in his left hand. Were the two injuries related? he wondered.

"It would appear that the SSS know how to throw a party. You will dine with me at luncheon tomorrow, when we can meet properly. At present I am organizing our departure from Shanghai. Mrs Ives will look after you. I'll bid you good evening. Is all a-taut down there?" This to the deck. "All aboard. Ship the gangway and stand by to slip!"

"Who are the SSS?" asked Becca.

"The Shanghai Shipping Syndicate, the outfit the taxi driver told us about," said Doug. "I'd like to know how they do all that tricky stuff with their fireworks. Those rockets weren't gunpowder-based; couldn't have been."

CAPTAIN FITZROY MACKENZIE

With eyepatch and walking stick, Fitzroy MacKenzie was noted for his piratical appearance. He was as enigmatic as the research ship he commanded. Picture caption reads: Aboard *Expedient.* Approaching Antarctica, 1919.

"How do you actually know that, Doug?" said Becca scathingly.

"Well, the smell was wrong for a start—"

"Oh, please, not another one of your ridiculous theories."

A plump woman wheezed down the starboard bridge ladder, muttering to herself. "Filthy racket a-wakin' the dead." She was wearing a large flowery apron and sensible shoes scuffed at the toe. Her face was friendly, if a little flushed. Mrs Ives clutched the gunwale and blew her cheeks out. "Evenin' to you both."

Doug looked up again, but the

captain was bellowing more orders at the crew. "Ship that hawser, and look lively about it. Stop waltzing with it, man! This is an ocean-going vessel, not a blasted tea dance!"

"Come along, you two. It's best to go below when we're leaving harbour," said Mrs Ives, ushering them in the direction of the poop deck. "The deck's like a cat's cradle with ropes a-going this way and that. Trip over one of them and it'll 'ave your leg off."

"Can we go directly to the engine room, Mrs Ives?" asked Doug.

"Whatever for, my love?"

"I'd like to discuss the state of the engines with the chief engineer, particularly the crankshafts."

"I should keep that sort of talk stowed, my lad," scoffed Mrs Ives, hustling him towards a watertight door.

Becca's diary: 2nd April 1920
On board *Expedient*

Our new home is better than I'd imagined. We have cabins five and six; Mrs Ives describes it as a suite, but it is just two small rooms connected by a narrow door. She thought we'd like to be close to one another. I think when I know her a bit better I shall ask for a different cabin as far away from brother Doug and his lucky socks as I can get.

My cabin is self-contained, and I rather like it. I felt a small pang of homesickness for my bedroom in Lucknow, but this will be fine until Mother and Father return from their expedition to the Sinkiang. A mahogany bunk curves along one side. Underneath it are three drawers for clothes. There's a small desk beside the door, which is where I'm writing this, with bookshelves jutting out above. All the fittings are beautifully finished and the wood gleams in the soft glow of the oil lamp (there is no electric light in this part of the ship). Doug's cabin is the mirror of mine, but he's furious because I have a brass plaque on my door which says GUNNERY OFFICER!

We both have a present from the captain. Mine is a gramophone and some records. Doug has got some paints and watercolour paper, which he's mucking around with now. Our interests are known to our uncle, it seems – I suspect via the dreaded Aunt Margaret. Perhaps life aboard ship won't be as bad as I feared.

We are housed in what used to be the officers' quarters. It's a small corridor with eight cabins off it, all polished to an astonishing sheen. Mr and Mrs Ives occupy the cabins opposite ours. The rest of the crew are in the mess deck at the other end of the ship, so it's quiet down here – just the steady heartbeat thump of the engines.

Mrs Ives is the ship's cook and is married to the ship's coxswain. She's left us an enormous tray of pies and puddings.

MRS IVES

After the captain, Mrs Ives, the ship's cook, considered herself the highest authority aboard ship – she was certainly the only member of the crew allowed to argue with the captain without fear of reprimand.

Unfortunately this heat has made me thirsty rather than hungry, but Dustbin Douglas has made light work of his share and is eyeing up mine.

Before leaving us on our own, Mrs Ives repeatedly warned us that we are not allowed to wander off, as there are many dangerous parts of the ship. I think she couldn't wait to get her hands on the bandaged man we saw being stretchered aboard, who, she told us, was now resting in the sickbay. So we've been left to unpack and settle in. One small triumph is that we at least

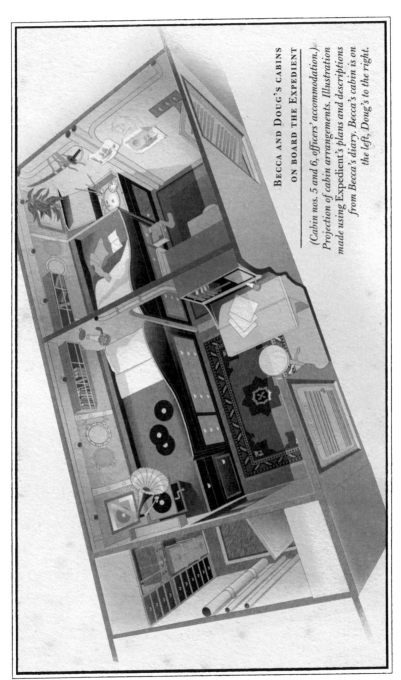

BECCA AND DOUG'S CABINS
ON BOARD THE EXPEDIENT

(Cabin nos. 5 and 6, officers' accommodation.)
Projection of cabin arrangements. Illustration
made using Expedient's plans and descriptions
from Becca's diary. Becca's cabin is on
the left, Doug's to the right.

Nautical terms and expressions

ABAFT: *behind*

AFT/AFTER: *section of ship towards stern*

BELAYING PIN: *wooden pin used to secure ropes*

BILGES: *very lowest part of hull*

BOAT DECK: *deck where ship's boats are stowed (only referred to as lifeboats after captain has given order to abandon ship)*

BOSUN: *crewman in charge of setting sails and efficient running of ship*

BOW: *(rhymes with* now*) front of ship*

BRIDGE: *where ship is commanded from; located above wheelhouse*

BULKHEAD: *solid partition within ship*

BUNKERS: *compartments for stowing coal or oil*

COAMING: *raised boundary around a hatchway or door; prevents sea water flowing in below deck*

COXSWAIN/HELMSMAN: *crewman who steers ship*

DEADLIGHTS: *steel covers that block scuttles from inside*

DERRICK: *crane for hoisting cargo*

FO'C'SLE: *(pronounced* folk-saul*) space at furthest forward part of ship (from the old term* forecastle, *when ships had a crenellated tower built over the bow, from which sailors could fight)*

FORE/FORWARD: *(pronounced* forard*) area near bow*

GUNWALE: *(pronounced* gunal*) planks directly above deck level on either side of vessel*

HALYARD: *rope for hoisting or lowering*

HATCHWAY: *opening in deck allowing passage from one deck to another*

HAWSER: *strong rope of hemp or steel; secures ship to mooring*

INBOARD: *inside ship*

JUNK: *Chinese sailing vessel*

KEDGE ANCHOR: *light anchor*

MIDSHIP: *centre section of ship (*midships: *order to centre rudder and so straighten course of a turning ship)*

MOORED: *having two anchors set; secured head and stern to harbour quay*

POOP DECK: *raised deck at stern of ship*

PORT: *left-hand side of ship when facing bow*

RUDDER: *hinged flat steel frame positioned at stern of ship below waterline; connected to ship's wheel, allowing it to steer vessel*

SAMPAN: *small Chinese boat*

SCUTTLES: *round holes in ship's sides, also known as portholes*

SHELTER DECK: *main upper deck of ship*

STANCHION RAILS: *safety rails around edge of deck*

STARBOARD: *right-hand side of ship when facing bow*

STERN: *rear of ship*

STOW: *to bring equipment or cargo aboard ship and secure*

TRANSOM: *vessel's stern timbers*

VOICE PIPE/SPEAKING TUBE: *pipe network within ship enabling communication by voice*

WHEELHOUSE: *enclosed cabin from which ship is controlled; located on boat deck*

WIRELESS TELEGRAPHY OFFICE: *archaic term for radio cabin*

now know where we are headed – Mrs Ives told us we are bound for the South China Sea on some sort of research expedition. Researching what exactly, she wasn't clear. Suddenly I realize how little we know about our uncle and his curious ship.

Through my scuttle I can see the twinkling lights of Shanghai slipping away as we steam downstream for the Yangtze and the open sea.

I can't stop thinking that our expedition should be heading towards western China and the Sinkiang, not the South China Sea. The precise whereabouts of our parents has been uncertain for a year now. Doug doesn't say it, but I think he has decided that Mother and Father are dead.

A little after midnight, Doug woke Becca with a gentle shake. For a moment she was confused, wondering where she was, but Doug's excited face made her sit up promptly.

"Shush," he whispered, pointing at the door.

"What?" But then Becca heard voices in the corridor and knew that something was happening. They opened her door a fraction and peeped out.

Captain MacKenzie stood in the open doorway of the cabin next to the Iveses', talking to a man slumped on the edge of the bunk. It was difficult to make out much detail, as the cabin had only a single oil lamp and the man's face was obscured by the captain's arm. Their new neighbour had a bandaged hand, and from his posture he looked haggard and ill. Becca tuned into their conversation.

"…and your other wounds are healing. The ambulance ride wasn't too rough?"

"No, Captain. Mrs Ives is an excellent nurse. She re-dressed this wound, but it is not as bad as she has made it look." The new guest had a soft voice with a French accent.

"Is that the man who was stretchered aboard?" whispered Becca.

Doug nodded, his suspicions growing. "It must be."

"But he couldn't walk a few hours ago. He was bandaged from head to toe. Look at him now."

"A surprisingly fast recovery," agreed Doug.

The Frenchman's voice suddenly rose in desperation. "I didn't do it, Captain! I swear to you, I did not murder him. I did not murder the professor!"

"The newspapers have convicted you, that's for sure. However, I read through the evidence at the time and was far from convinced of your guilt. I apologize for the handcuffs, but I was unaware of your exact condition and under instruction to treat you with … care. To my mind the only suspicious thing you did was to disappear so soon after Zorid was killed."

"I was kidnapped, Captain! Kidnapped in Paris, taken to China and compelled to create monstrous torpedoes for that … that venomous cobra Sheng-Fat! I was framed. Set up!" The Frenchman's voice became muffled as he buried his face in his hands.

"You are still unwell."

"The opium Sheng-Fat forced on me to break my spirit has weakened me; it played tricks with my mind. But, Captain, I insist I am innocent of Zorid's murder. You have to believe me."

"I do believe you."

"It gives me hope to hear it," said the Frenchman, slumping

forward out of view. "Has Madame Zing Zing forwarded to you my drawings for the towed magnetometer? It is a new design – much more powerful than the one your ship is currently equipped with, as you described in your letter."

The captain nodded. "For the last three days my men have been building it just as your diagram instructed. The electrical apparatus is nearing completion in the ship's laboratory. Watts says the guts of it will be ready by lunchtime tomorrow. The lab is strewn with wires, valves and switches, but he assures me they will fit together and not endanger the ship."

"Excellent … excellent. I should like to see…" The injured man faltered.

"You should rest now," said the captain. "We will speak in the morning. Mr and Mrs Ives are in the cabin next door if you should want anything."

Captain MacKenzie turned and shut the door behind him. He paused in the corridor

RUSSIAN SCIENTIST "MURDERED"

ZORID BELIEVED DEAD
TERRIBLE DESTRUCTION OF SWISS LABORATORY
LUC CHAMBOIS NAMED AS CHIEF SUSPECT
(FROM OUR CORRESPONDENT)

ZURICH: A massive explosion tore through the laboratory of Professor Zorid, the Russian émigré scientist, early yesterday. The blast was heard shortly after one o'clock in the morning. The fast-moving investigation has switched to Paris, where police are searching for the French scientist Luc Chambois, named by an undisclosed source as the murderer. Several threatening letters found by detectives at Zorid's house confirmed the Frenchman as the prime suspect. Chambois is a known associate of Professor Zorid and has "disappeared" according to the French police. Luc Chambois, aged 25, is five foot eleven with dark brown hair. He was last seen running

Cutting from the 3rd March 1919
edition of the *International Dispatch and Review*   (MA 632.11 ZORID)

From Doug's sketchbook: The view into the Frenchman's cabin. (DMS 1/21)

to straighten his tie. Unnoticed, Becca closed her door, only releasing the handle when their uncle had walked past.

"Kidnap? Murder? Torpedoes?" gasped Doug.

"I think, Douglas, our uncle may turn out to be a rather more interesting guardian than Aunt Margaret ever was."

CHAPTER TWO

I went back to bed knowing I'd seen the bandaged Frenchman somewhere before. But where? I awoke again much later with a start – I'd remembered. What had given him away was his Parisian accent: it was Luc Chambois, expert in metallurgy and theoretical physics.

We met Chambois when Mother and Father took us to one of his lectures two years ago in London – "Strengthening the Molecular Bond of Steel by Electrical Invigoration". Dull, dull, dull!

I remember Chambois not for the subject on which he spoke (a curious experiment which involved trying to squash two football-sized steel spheres), but for the gentle, witty and amusing manner in which he made the hour go by. Plenty of jokes at the stodginess of the subject, finishing off with a superb trick whereby a blue spark shot out of the end of his nose.

Douglas took everything in, of course. While I enjoyed the comic performance, Doug absorbed every detail of Chambois's demonstration. At the end he flashed out some superb question which astounded everyone there, especially Father, who turned to check it was his own son sitting next to him.

Afterwards we met Chambois briefly. He congratulated Doug on his question and grasp of the subject. Then Father handed the Frenchman a wax-sealed envelope marked FIRENZE, *telling him to "keep up the good work". Chambois gave Doug one of the steel spheres from the experiment (which I think Doug lost in Lucknow*

LUC CHAMBOIS

Wounded in the trenches of Verdun during the First World War and invalided out of the army, this brilliant young scientist conceived the idea for a steel-strengthening machine as he recuperated in hospital. His theories were taken up by the French military and he had almost perfected his "molecule invigorator" when funding dried up. Convinced of his invention's worth, he was forced to seek private financial backers to complete the project.

attempting some "deadly" experiment of his own that broke a window and ruined a weekend). Chambois thanked Father and we parted.

I'd forgotten about the lecture until last year when I read in a newspaper that Chambois had mysteriously disappeared. He had immediately been linked with the murder of a Professor Zorid, who had been killed in a terrible explosion at his laboratory in Switzerland (this fits with the conversation we overheard last night). The finger of suspicion pointed at the Frenchman because the two were rivals. Incriminating letters were discovered, and a railway porter said he'd seen Chambois near the laboratory on the evening of the disaster. I was intrigued because I didn't think he looked like a murderer.

This morning we've been given a tour of the various decks by "Posh" Charlie, the sailor who greeted us last night. Basically, we are banned from most areas because they are "too dangerous". He is as reluctant as Mrs Ives to tell us what exactly those dangers are.

"Doug, please. Just behave when we meet him," pleaded Becca. "We have to make a good impression."

"Lady Luck rides with us, sister," replied Doug with a mischievous grin.

Becca paused for a second. Doug's overconfident air was making her suspicious. "You're wearing those socks, aren't you?"

"I might be." He sniffed, wiping his nose on his sleeve as he pushed open the captain's day-cabin door. "Don't worry, my manners will be … impeccable."

The door was only half open when a huge roaring, fanged mouth lunged at them. Becca grabbed her brother's shoulder and bundled him to the floor. The creature landed in the corridor with a rolling thump. It was an immense tiger with ice-white fur and black stripes. It turned towards them, snarling and flashing razor-sharp teeth.

From Doug's sketchbook: Becca and Doug meet the Duchess. (DMS 1/29)

THE DUCHESS

As a cub in the forests of southern India, the Duchess was wounded by a hunter's poorly aimed shot. The captain nursed her back to health by staying up three nights in a row, hand-feeding her bread and mince soaked in whisky.

Found in central and southern India, the white Bengal tiger is extremely rare and is known as a solitary animal. Excellent swimmers but poor climbers, they can grow to ten feet in length.

"Duchess! Duchess! Lie down," ordered the captain.

Doug and Becca scrambled into the cabin and slammed the door behind them.

"That thing's deadly. It should be in a cage!" Doug panted.

"Let her back in!" barked the captain. "Why didn't you knock? Do you have no manners?"

"Is it yours?" Doug asked in surprise.

"It? *It?*" the captain exclaimed indignantly. "*She* is a Bengal tiger. The Duchess. She is trained to deter anyone who enters my cabin without knocking. She assumes, quite rightly, that I will not wish to speak to anyone who does not have the courtesy to do so."

Doug opened the door a fraction. The tiger was waiting outside stock-still, her huge eyes blinking in time to a deep, slow growl that made the wood shiver. He held his breath as he pulled back the door and the animal paced in, flicking her tail menacingly.

The captain motioned for them to sit at the oval dining table, which was set for three. He straightened his waistcoat and took his seat. Although Doug was still shocked, he grinned at Becca and pulled up his socks. The Duchess circled him, her nostrils twitching. After a final

subdued roar the tiger settled well away from Doug and
began to delicately lick her front paws.

"Has she killed many people?"

The captain ignored Doug's question and pulled his chair
in closer to the table. Becca and Doug were positioned far
enough away from him to feel that this was more of a formal
interview than a cosy chat.

"Your reputation precedes you," began the captain. For
the first time Doug noticed his uncle's soft Scottish burr. The
captain pushed a pile of letters and school reports to one
side, his expression serious. "Hardly a recommendation, are
they? Three branches of the MacKenzie family have looked
after you during the last year and not one of them has a
good word to say. What's more, you've each been expelled
from three different schools during the same period. Can
this be true?"

Becca and Doug nodded.

"Rebellious, disaffected, disobedient... Now, where is it...?"
The captain dug out a report from Doug's last biology teacher.
"'Douglas's undoubted intelligence sleeps under a blanket of
idleness. "Why Monkeys Are Funny" is not the kind of essay
I expect to receive from one of my students.'"

Becca couldn't help catching Doug's eye.

"Oh, you find this amusing, do you, Rebecca? Well, what
have we here? 'Ungovernable, unruly ... obstinate and mutinous' – *mutinous*! That word sends a shiver down my spine...
The headmistress of your last school received a call saying
your talents as a swordswoman had just secured you the part
of Robina Hood in a forthcoming *moving picture*" – he spat
the words out with incredulity – "about the adventures of
Robin Hood's youngest cousin..."

Becca tried to explain. "It was a—"

But her uncle interrupted her. He was clearly in no mood for discussion.

"It's all written down here in black and white. You displayed great dexterity with a sword ... impressed the film's director with your acting skill. Mm, you revealed a few other talents too – criminal tendencies even. Forged a letter from your Aunt Margaret ... sprang yourself from school for a week." His eye scanned the page. "My, my. Quite the adventuress too – travelled four hundred miles to the audition. Set yourself up in an expensive hotel under a false identity."

"I used my mother's maiden name."

"I fail to see how that makes the matter any less odious. Apart from showing a complete lack of respect for authority, you have also thrown my sister Margaret's kindness back in her face. Do you have any idea of the trouble you have caused? What would your parents think?"

Becca gulped at the mention of their mother and father.

Without waiting for a reply, the captain walked over to the scuttle and gazed out at the East China Sea, deep in thought.

Doug filled with rage at the unfairness of this tirade. In that moment he hated his uncle with a deep black fury. What right did he have to tell them off? They'd never even met him before! He clenched his teeth so tight his jaw muscles stuck out.

"So you've been passed from pillar to post until you've both ended up here on my ship. As I'm the last relation left, we'd better make a go of it, hadn't we? As a matter of fact, this is what your parents would have wanted, so by default you've arrived where you should have been sent a year ago."

"You speak as if they're dead," said Becca sharply.

"They are only lost, sir," corrected Doug. "Lost in the deserts of western China. Their expedition remains unaccounted for."

"If I'd known of this unfortunate situation regarding your parents, I would have intervened sooner."

"If we were meant to be here, as you say, why did it take you so long to send for us?" accused Doug.

Becca scowled at him.

"We have been trapped in a southern ice pack." Their uncle's one-eyed gaze made Doug shiver. He adjusted his eye-patch and continued. "When a ship's trapped in ice, nephew, there is no chance of sailing anywhere. Have you ever experienced a winter at latitudes south of seventy degrees?"

"You know very well I haven't, so why do you ask?"

"Don't take that tone with me, nephew!"

An uncomfortable silence descended on the cabin.

"Uncle?" ventured Becca, trying to draw fire from her brother. "Can I ask where we will go to school if we're living on board ship?"

"School?" The captain cracked his walking stick down on the pile of reports and letters, making Doug and Becca flinch back in their seats. He slid the stack of papers slowly across the polished table until they toppled and fell into a waste-paper basket below.

His angry face relaxed. "Fair weather follows foul, as a rule. You were first-class students before the disappearance of your parents. Douglas was even up for a science scholarship. I cannot ignore the connection between the two."

Becca was confused. "I don't understand."

"Simply put, your rebellious attitude seems to have developed only in the absence of your parents. Perhaps we can restore some order and balance to your lives while you are aboard my ship."

The door opened and Mr Teng, the captain's ancient Chinese steward, wheeled in lunch on a small trolley, setting the food down on the table with measured, precise movements. The captain nodded an acknowledgement and the steward retired without a word.

"Did your parents ever mention Italy?" their uncle asked.

"We were meant to spend last summer in Firenze, but the holiday never happened because they raced off to China."

"So you were bound for Firenze." The captain nodded. "I wish I knew more of your parents' intentions for you both. Happily, this small clue gives me some direction as to how we should proceed from here."

Becca felt as if a difficult decision had been made – one to which they were not party. But they were getting used to that. She glanced at Doug, who could clearly make no sense of the captain's words either.

"Well, we'll see how you get on. Yes, we'll give it a few weeks and see how we rub along, shall we?" He paused, drawing in a long, deep breath, then his look of concentration changed into a broad smile. "Well, welcome aboard, then. Welcome aboard, both of you!"

As the captain served the meal, some sort of bony fish, Doug looked around at the cabin. A series of complicated old-fashioned maps decorated with dolphins, sea monsters and suns and moons hung along the wall in front of him, as well as a large reproduction print of Hans Holbein's painting *The Ambassadors*. Doug knew it well; whenever their parents had moved home, their own copy of this painting had accompanied them. The other walls were given over to a library of hundreds of ancient books and scrolls neatly shelved in glass-fronted cabinets.

"I was in Lucknow once," the captain said suddenly. "I believe that is where you used to live."

"Father was stationed in Lucknow. We've lived in London and New York too," replied Becca.

"I've travelled to those cities as well, many times. Your mother's from New York State, of course. Interesting – an interesting dilemma. Which do you see yourselves as: American or British?"

"Neither," said Becca abruptly. "We were born in India and lived there just as long as the other countries. I liked them all. I see myself as a sum of all these places – Britain, America, India. I belong to nowhere in particular."

The captain raised his eyebrows. "A precocious answer, but one which shows spirit. An internationalist. You should fit in well aboard this ship."

Doug wasn't much interested in nationalities. He wanted to know if the captain had ever seen grotesque sea creatures and wondered if he dared ask how he had lost his eye and hurt his leg – perhaps he'd fought a death maul with some giant squid … *several* giant squid. And a shark for good measure.

The ship lurched to starboard and the last sprout rolled across Doug's plate. He zeroed in with his fork, but missed, sending the vegetable arcing over towards Becca, where it hit her square on the forehead before bouncing into her glass with a plop.

"Doug! You…!" she exclaimed, kicking him under the table.

"Good shot, sir!" The captain roared with laughter. "Oh, good shot! Some of Mrs Ives's veg can be a little underdone. Your brother didn't hurt you, Rebecca, I trust?"

Becca glowered at Doug, and threw her uncle a mocking half smile.

"No," muttered Doug, catching his breath, "but she got me all right."

"Fate chooses your relations, as the French poet Jacques Delille once said, and you've ended up with your brother and me." The captain banged the table in mirth. "Bad luck!"

"It isn't ideal," snapped Becca. "But unless I'm mistaken, Uncle, the full quotation is: 'Fate chooses your relations, and you choose your friends.'"

For a terrible moment Doug thought she'd gone too far. He knew Becca in this mood, and he could see that the grilling over the school reports and the captain's raucous delight at the sprout attack had triggered something deep inside her.

"Quite right," declared the captain with surprise. "I stand corrected. And I hope you will make friends aboard this fine ship."

"Now, back to your education." The captain started to serve the thickest treacle pudding Doug had ever seen. "I am above all else a sea captain, and I have no experience of being a father and none as a schoolmaster, but I expect we'll muddle through somehow. Until your parents find their way out of the Sinkiang, and it's my certain belief that they will" – he paused and looked Becca squarely in the eye – "I propose we sail the globe and I'll have a crack at educating you while we travel. There are some examination papers that I would like you to try, papers your parents have both taken themselves, but the subjects are tough, and science based. We will start with certain elements of the quadrivium."

"Quadrivium?" repeated Doug distractedly. It had made him feel better to hear his parents mentioned as if they were still alive.

"I can assure you that there'll be no questions relating to the comedic tendencies of jungle primates, Douglas. What's more, you will be aboard my ship and you will see all the natural wonders the world has to offer – and they are many, mark my words. Have you ever dived in a submarine?"

"No," said Doug.

"Then you must. A journey to the seabed is the most extraordinary experience, and a teaching occasion second to none. We have a small submarine aboard for research purposes. I shall organize it as soon as possible."

"Does the sub's engine have a crankshaft?" asked Doug, casually wiping the edge of his plate with his finger. Becca glared at him.

"What an unusual question. No. The engines are electric."

"Electric engines don't have crankshafts? That can't be right."

"Now, your lessons will be conducted by myself, Mr Teng, my steward, and Charlie. Do not let Mr Teng's quiet ways fool you. He is a walking encyclopedia, fluent in a dozen languages. His grasp of mathematics and physics is remarkable too.

"I also give you this warning: as a sea captain I will not stand for any mutinous behaviour from either of you. I'm a

THE TRIVIUM AND QUADRIVIUM

From classical times through to the late Middle Ages, the academic subjects traditionally known as the liberal arts were arranged into seven disciplines and divided into two distinct branches. The first, the trivium, related to grammar, logic and rhetoric. The second, the quadrivium, encompassed arithmetic, geometry, music and astronomy.

fair man, but I warn you not to misbehave or it will jeopardize your future. You will follow my orders to the letter or leave
the ship. Do you understand?"

Doug could see that Becca was still seething at being
laughed at, and wasn't really listening.

"Your first class tomorrow will be on the subject of Morse
code and semaphore. We will take the lesson from *The
Manual of Seamanship, Volume I*. There is a copy on the shelf
over there. I have also found you each a copy of *Nares* to add
depth to the nautical palette. I expect every sailor aboard this
ship to be able to send a distress signal or message. We can
worry about arithmetic, geometry, algebra and gravitational
physics later."

This could be interesting, thought Doug.

"What of sport?" asked the captain, standing. He unlocked
a cupboard behind him and took out two fencing helmets.
"Your father told me he started you both young with swordsmanship, as is the tradition in the MacKenzie family. Can
you handle a blade with the feather touch of your father,
Douglas?"

"Becca's the one you want for all that stuff," Doug admit-
ted reluctantly. "She's deadly with a rapier. Lots of obscure
moves that frighten the life out of people. Father used to teach
us but since they ... we haven't..." He stumbled over his
words.

"I'll give you the choice, Rebecca. Sabre or rapier?"

The captain opened a second cupboard that housed a
glittering collection of ornate swords. Becca scrutinized the
dazzling array of blades.

"Rapier," she said, fixing quickly on a rare Bavarian weapon.

"I see you know your swords, Rebecca."

Taking the handle, she flicked the blade with the nail of her thumb and held it close to her ear to listen to the tone.

"In the handle you will find—"

"—a parrying dagger which ejects when I press the hand guard like this." Becca finished the sentence for him.

The short dagger pinged out and she caught it in her left hand, flicked it around and immediately clicked it back into place.

"Oh no," sighed Doug. He knew that he was about to be paid back for the sprout incident, but would she also risk taking on the captain in some way?

"I shall affix wine corks to the ends of the blades, of course. I merely wish to assess your grasp of the basics. Besides, this cabin is too low for a proper match."

With some trepidation Doug pulled on the fencing mask and assumed the *en garde* pose. His sister did the same.

"Posture not too bad, either of you. My, I can see your father taught you both. Knees bent a little more, perhaps, and sword hand down a fraction, Douglas. Now, Rebecca, you shall attack, and Doug, I should like you to demonstrate these parries. Quarte, quinte, sixte, septime, octave!"

Doug delivered the parries to Becca's effortless attack. They'd practised these moves many times with their father.

"Good … good… Keep that sword hand down, Douglas. Your turn with the attack."

"I'm much better with a sabre," muttered Doug, who hated the flimsy rapier. He liked a good heavy cavalry sword with its curved blade.

"Don't argue. Now, *en garde*."

But at the point where Doug engaged, Becca countered his blade in such a way that the sword flew out of his hand and he

A page from the actual book used by Becca and Doug during their first lessons aboard the Expedient. *The captain expected the young MacKenzies to learn how to tie knots and send a distress signal in Morse code. Doug's notations of the knots' names can just be seen.*

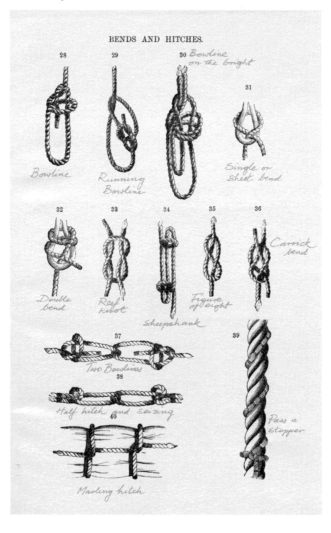

BENDS AND HITCHES.

28 — *Bowline*

29 — *Running Bowline*

30 — *Bowline on the bright* / Bowline on the bight

31 — *Single or Sheet bend*

32 — *Double bend*

33 — *Reef knot*

34 — *Sheepshank*

35 — *Figure of eight*

36 — *Carrick bend*

37 — *Two Bowlines*

38 — *Half hitch and seizing*

39 — *Pass a stopper*

40 — *Marling hitch*

tripped, accidentally standing on the Duchess's tail. The tiger rolled over and gave a deafening roar that shook the cabin, her terrifying jaws wide open. Becca tore the wine cork off the end of her blade and flung her clumsy fencing helmet to one side.

"Stop immediately!" insisted the captain.

But Becca didn't trust the animal. She levelled the blade at the tiger's throat. Doug struggled up and scrambled for his sword, backing away towards a red velvet sofa.

"Settle down, Duchess," ordered the captain.

The Duchess ignored him and paced forward, deciding which of the young MacKenzies to go for first.

"Over here!" shouted Becca, attracting the animal's attention.

Doug grabbed his rapier and made a lunge. He was foiled by the captain, who disarmed him with his walking stick and pinned Doug's sword to the deck with his foot.

"Do you two always behave like this?" snapped the captain. He barked a command at the Duchess in Magadhan, the Bengali dialect, and the tiger immediately turned and sloped away to lie down behind the sofa.

Becca's blood was still up. She lowered her sword and pressed the button on the hilt. The parrying dagger sprang out.

"Becca, don't do anything stupid!" cried Doug.

She twirled the dagger in her fingers until she held it by the blade, then narrowed her eyes. A moment later the dagger was spinning through the air. It lodged, twanging, in the reproduction print of *The Ambassadors* hanging on the bulkhead, piercing the distorted skull at the base of the painting.

"Hell's teeth – knife-throwing?" exploded the captain. He looked insulted not by the damage but by the very act itself. "You are not in Sherwood Forest now, niece. There is no honour in knife-throwing! Now hand me your weapon."

From Doug's sketchbook: Becca throws the dagger. (DMS 1/38)

"That tiger nearly killed us. Twice!" she retorted. "It should be in a jungle or a zoo."

"You brought it upon yourselves. You will be quick to discover that living aboard *Expedient* will be nothing like staying with Aunt Margaret."

Becca turned the rapier around and offered the handle to the captain.

"And you will be quick to discover that we are getting very good at looking after ourselves, Uncle."

CHAPTER THREE

Becca's diary: 10th April 1920

I have this empty, floating feeling in my stomach which has nothing to do with being on board a ship. I get it whenever I'm settling into a new place, but I don't like it. I'm not used to the routine yet, and I haven't worked out where everything is. I hate having to ask for the simplest things, as I usually receive replies in elaborate nautical terms that seldom make much sense. I long to be back home.

Doug, as usual, has settled in and seems to have befriended everyone. He knows all the crew's names and even their nicknames. He treats them like old friends, hailing them with a smile and a wave. Other than the fight with the tiger, I would say that he's having the time of his life aboard Expedient.

I keep wondering what's happened to Mother and Father. I can't get it out of my mind that they have died of thirst somewhere in the desert wastes of western China after walking for days without a drink. I have no basis in fact for this, but last night I dreamt it vividly. The strange thing was that in this dream there was plenty of water about, as the desert seemed to melt into a river. This morning I realized that I had been dreaming of the River Arno in Firenze. It is a place that seems to haunt me – the name Firenze was on the envelope that Father gave to Chambois. We had been planning to go there last summer, and our uncle seems to think it has some bearing on our lives. But what? Can it have anything to do with Mother and Father's disappearance?

I asked Doug if he could remember Chambois's lecture in

London. Apparently all that steel sphere stuff was a demonstration of something called a molecule invigorator – a device which increases the strength of steel by as much as twenty-five times.

We met Chambois at dinner last night and he vaguely remembered us, though he couldn't recall giving Doug the metal sphere. Chambois explained that his mind is still "much out of order". Some of his old charm has returned and he tried a few jokes, but he looks drawn and his skin is sallow. He ate very little and retired to his cabin before pudding. I hope he will return to his normal self soon. What I can't understand is why a Chinese criminal would be in Paris kidnapping a scientist!

"Seventy feet, Monsieur Chambois. You may engage your marvellous invention now," instructed the captain, who was seated at the controls of the *Galacia*, the *Expedient*'s small submarine.

Chambois swivelled the red leather navigator's chair and adjusted the controls on a box of electrical apparatus festooned with valves, dials and switches. The submarine's hull began to hum with a low electrical murmur, making everything metallic tingle to the touch.

"It's the molecule invigorator!" exclaimed Doug.

"But of course," replied Chambois, glancing up to meet Doug's questioning eyes.

"So you've worked out all the problems you spoke about at the end of your London lecture? The fall off of current, the difficulties of resistance…"

"Absolutely."

"So what's it invigorating?" asked Doug, tracing the line of

Pour obtenir un acier 25 fois plus résistant

Découvrez le révolutionnaire

Multiplicateur de Molécules

Utilisations industrielles multiples

Nous recherchons des investisseurs privés pour financer la réalisation de cette merveille de la science

Profits guarantis à 99%. Preuves fournies

Merci de nous contacter à l'adresse suivante:
Monsieur Luc Chambois, 176 Rue du Cardinal, Paris, France.

THE MOLECULE INVIGORATOR

Despite initial interest from the French military, Luc Chambois's theoretical work on reinforcing metals by strengthening their molecular bond was derided as madness by the scientific establishment. The advertisement above is taken from a Parisian magazine, and shows an early prototype of his idea. Chambois believed this publicity attempt had failed to find a sponsor, but in January 1918 he received a letter from a Hamish MacKenzie Esq. inviting him to demonstrate his invention before an audience in London. (See appendix 3.)

wires to the point at which they joined the steel bulkhead. "But" – he stumbled over his words – "but, of course, the hull! The invigorator is strengthening the steel hull, just like the sphere in the experiment!"

Doug pressed the palm of his hand to the steel bulkhead. After five seconds a sensation like scalding heat forced him to snatch his hand away. He clenched and unclenched his fingers several times to get the feeling back, then grinned with utter respect and tried it again.

"The captain was the first to test if my theories held water, so to speak." Chambois chuckled, banging the hull with his fist. "A dive beneath the Ross Sea's massive ice barrier, if I remember your report?"

The captain nodded. "Correct. Chambois's invention allows the submarine to dive much deeper and resist the enormous forces pressing in on the hull. It is remarkable. Unfortunately, it does not help our four divers seated outside. They cannot be included on dives below two hundred feet."

Doug peered out and saw the divers being transported to the seabed through the dark waters, fine streams of bubbles escaping from their pressure helmets. Slippery Sam, Ten Dinners, Posh Charlie and Fast Frankie all rode on the outside of the hull on special seats with handholds that made them look like horsemen. Doug wished he were out there with them in one of those elaborately engineered suits and weighted boots. He gave them a wave, and through the murk Posh Charlie gave him a thumbs up.

"We could dive to the seabed much more quickly, but the divers must adjust to the depth or suffer the dreaded bends. Their air lines are connected to a pressurized tank built into the stern of the submarine. This allows them to breathe."

"Captain," interrupted Chambois, peering into an aperture in the invigorator which bathed his face in green light. He scanned the controls, scribbling down notes and muttering to himself. "I should like to make some modifications when we surface."

"As you wish, Chambois. Now, Rebecca and Douglas, we shall continue with our lesson. You will see that the population of fish and other marine animals decreases the deeper we descend. The sunlight begins to fade…"

The *Galacia* continued its steady progress. It was the most unusual feeling; there was little sense of speed or depth. As the engine was electric, the loudest sound was the hum of the invigorated hull. Neither Becca nor Doug was paying much attention to the captain; note-taking was difficult in the darkness of the cabin, lit only by the soft glow of the dials and the shielded bulbs above their seats.

Chambois spun round and peered forward into the velvet blue gloom. He rubbed condensation off the glass instruments and checked the chart. "Come a little to starboard, Captain."

"How far do you estimate the wreck is?"

"Not much further. The readings were almost off the scale around here."

"What wreck?" asked Becca. This was the first they'd heard of any wreck.

"The magnetometer apparatus we've been towing behind *Expedient* since we left Shanghai has guided us to the wreck of the junk from which Chambois escaped."

"What do you mean?" demanded Doug.

"The Chinese warlord Sheng-Fat kidnapped our friend Chambois here and forced him to construct twenty-five

48

Shanghai 2nd April 1920

Name		Age	Quality	Place of Birth
Mackenzie	F	45	Capt.	Florence, Italy
"	E	15	Able	Lucknow, India
"	G	13	"	"
Watts	W	27	N/t Officer	Canterbury, New Zealand
Charlie	P	39	Able	Cape Town
Leo	E	53	Boatswain	New York, USA

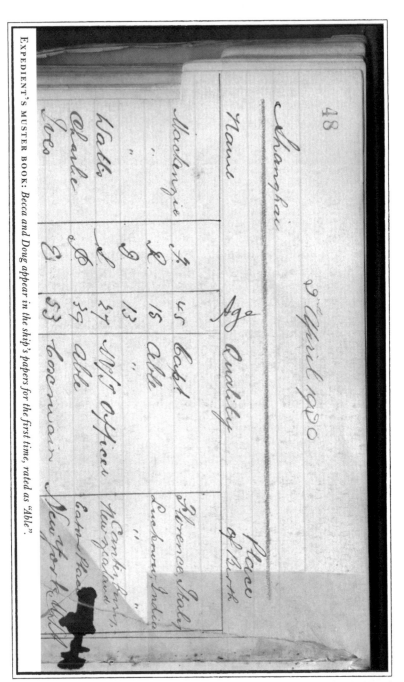

EXPEDIENT'S MUSTER BOOK: *Becca and Doug appear in the ship's papers for the first time, rated as "Able".*

torpedoes using zoridium as the explosive element for their warheads. These are abhorrent devices with huge destructive potential."

"*Zoridium?*" said Becca slowly. "Isn't that what was used to kill Professor Zorid and blow up his laboratory? It was also his great discovery."

"Well, yes…" Chambois trailed off as he glanced at the captain for reassurance.

"You can tell them, Chambois. I think we had better start trusting them with some of our secrets."

"I have been framed. The police will never believe me. They think I used zoridium to kill Professor Zorid. It's true that I vanished shortly after his death, only to reappear months later on the other side of the world in Shanghai. But I was kidnapped, incarcerated in Sheng-Fat's island fortress and compelled to build those infernal torpedoes!"

"So how did you escape?" pressed Becca.

"Well, I thought of a little trick—"

"Nonsense!" interrupted the captain. "There's no need to be modest. Chambois brilliantly designed a technical flaw in the prototype torpedo so that it circled back directly to where it was launched. Isn't that right, Monsieur?"

"Indeed. Nothing more than a desperate measure. It was an escape plan I formulated during the long months spent constructing Sheng-Fat's torpedoes. Chance and luck were my allies for the first time in a long while. I was taken aboard the junk chosen to test fire the first torpedo, and left unguarded because there was nowhere for me to go. I escaped through a gun port, and jumped into the ship's wake just minutes before they fired the torpedo at a defenceless Japanese freighter. My design worked and the torpedo returned to sink

the junk. If I'd taken ten more minutes to escape I would not
be sitting here today."

"Lethal," said Doug, trying to imagine the size of the
explosion.

"How have you managed to find the exact site of the wreck?"
Becca queried.

"According to Zorid's research, as well as being a highly
volatile substance, zoridium has some other very interesting
properties," answered Captain MacKenzie. "Exploded zoridium
fragments become highly magnetic after the intense heat of
detonation. To detect the site of the wreck we used *Expedient's*
new magnetometer. We've been cross-referencing any new
magnetic anomaly with a map of known magnetic anomalies
in the South China Sea. In fact, the new magnetic anomaly
created by the exploded zoridium torpedo is so large, it was
remarkably easy to locate."

"Lethal. Truly lethal," mumbled Doug, scribbling down
location by magnetism in his sketchbook for further investigation. He'd managed to organize an unofficial tour of the
engine room with the chief engineer, Herr Schmidt, and he
now fully understood the theory and construction of crankshafts. Magnetic location sounded like fascinating new
territory.

The captain pressed a button on the panel above his head
and a powerful beam of light cut through the twilight gloom.
Some distance below them lay the shattered stern of a
Chinese junk.

"Is that her?" the captain asked.

Chambois was already leaning forward, his breath misting
the glass of the scuttle.

"Undoubtedly. There is a section of her transom. Do you

see? I can just make out Sheng-Fat's dragon's tooth motif."
Misery clouded his face as he slumped back in his seat. "I
hoped I would never see it again."

The captain was busy taking a depth
reading. Chambois rubbed his eyes as if
to clear the dreadful vision of devastation. "How can I have been in such a
condition as to have conceived of creating
such a … such a catastrophe? I am
ashamed – ashamed of everything I have
done here in China."

**THE DRAGON'S
TOOTH MOTIF**

*This symbol was used by the
pirate warlord Sheng-Fat
to identify all his ships and
property. It was a sign
universally feared in the
South China Sea.*

"Then why did you do it?" asked Doug
unsympathetically. "I'd have refused."

"Believe me, Douglas, I tried to resist."
Chambois's agonized expression hinted
at the unspeakable traumas he'd endured.

"I would've held out. Nothing would've
broken me," asserted Doug.

Chambois fixed him with a solemn
stare. "All I will say is this: I hope you never find yourself
in the hands of Sheng-Fat. So ingenious are his methods
of twisting a man's mind that, against all moral judgement,
against all that I hold dear, I constructed a weapon for him that
is more powerful than anything mankind has ever seen! Look at
the pitiful remains of that junk. I am the only survivor. And yet
zoridium has the capacity for explosions a hundred times as big.
My deepest regret is that Sheng-Fat wasn't on board that ship."

"What's more, using zoridium as an explosive is criminal
misuse of a unique resource," added the captain. "If Sheng-
Fat ever discovers its true potential as—" He stopped
himself abruptly.

"So how did you get back to Shanghai?" Becca asked the Frenchman suspiciously. "Once you were over the side and swimming?"

"When Li-Fat, the youngest of Sheng-Fat's two brothers, fired the torpedo, it steered itself in a beautiful big circle, right back to where it was launched. I'd been swimming for a good ten minutes by then. The shock wave was quite extraordinary. When I'd jumped, I'd grabbed a small barrel for buoyancy. That kept me afloat until the tides carried me to a nearby island. My escape was made with nothing more than a barrel and an extremely large diversion."

Doug looked thoughtful. "You don't seem very proud of your getaway, Monsieur Chambois."

"I saved my own skin, but I also gave Sheng-Fat the most powerful torpedoes known to man. I cannot be proud of that. And I should not have been the only one to escape. I should have found a way to get the other ransom hostages out with me."

As he spoke, Chambois pulled from under his shirt a fabulous diamond necklace and ran his thumb over the gems. He looked lost for a moment, then, realizing that his companions were staring at it with some confusion, he hastened to explain. "This belongs to a friend I made on Sheng-Fat's island. Liberty. I fear she is probably dead." With a deep sigh, he kissed the necklace and slipped it back inside his shirt.

"But why have we come back here to the wreck?" asked Becca. "The junk is destroyed."

"We're not here for the junk; we're here for the remains of the torpedo," explained the captain.

"Seems like a lot of trouble to go to for some scrap metal," reasoned Doug.

"The zoridium-enriched steel of the warhead is not scrap metal," insisted the captain. "It has remarkable scientific properties, and since the destruction of Zorid's laboratory, what lies hereabouts is of immeasurable value and rarity."

He manoeuvred the submarine until it came to a stop with a gentle shudder beside the junk's stern. Through the scuttle, Doug could see the divers dismounting. Ten Dinners' inelegant bulk jumped forward, his heavy boots scattering a cloud of sand as he landed. He pulled his air line, leant into the weight of the water and walked towards the junk like a man struggling into a gale.

"We are … er … removing the … um … electromagnet from the aft stowage locker now," crackled Posh Charlie's voice from a speaker inside the *Galacia*.

The sound was harsh after the quiet of the descent, making Becca jump. "We can talk to the divers, Captain?"

"Of course. Is there something you wish to say to them?"

"We are attaching the electromagnet now," Ten Dinners informed them.

"Very good," replied the captain into his handset.

Slippery Sam loomed up at Becca and Doug's scuttle, blowing out his cheeks to make a fish face. They laughed, and as he moved away they could see the magnet being bolted onto the bow of the submarine. It was circular, about the size of a car tyre, and angled down to the seabed. A collection bucket hung underneath, hinged so it could swing back and forth as the submarine moved without the catch falling out.

"Now, if Zorid's research is correct, zoridium is so highly magnetic that we can harvest the scattered torpedo fragments with this electromagnet," announced Captain MacKenzie.

"Lethal," Doug whispered.

"Magnet attached and power lines connected," reported Ten Dinners.

"Excellent. All divers return to the submarine. For our first pass, we will circle the junk's stern."

The divers could be heard climbing back onto their seats, lead boots clanking against the hull.

Ten Dinners' voice cut in. "All set, Captain!"

"Chambois, engage the electromagnet, if you'd be so kind."

The captain steered around the wreck several times at varying depths, but when the divers left their seats to inspect the catch, they reported that the electromagnet had collected nothing more than three tin cans and a rusty sword. During these circuits, Doug had observed a strange phenomenon that defied understanding. In the harsh electric light something on the seabed seemed to be moving away; he imagined small creatures, startled and scattering before the submarine. But he couldn't see any bodies to these animals, just a lot of scurrying trails kicking up clouds of mud and sand.

Finally he understood. He shook Becca's shoulder. "I know what's wrong."

"No you don't," snapped Becca, paying him scant attention.

"I do. I've worked it out."

The captain and Chambois were animatedly discussing the possibility that Zorid's research could have been flawed.

"Captain..." ventured Doug.

"Doug, shut up!" said Becca sharply. "How could you possibly know what's wrong?"

The Galacia

Mark IV submersible craft

CONFIDENTIAL MATERIAL

Accurate scale drawings – Passed for publication

Doug ignored her. "Captain, I think I know what the problem is. I've been observing the pieces of zoridium, and they're being rejected by your magnet, not attracted to it."

The captain and Chambois turned to look at Doug.

"Zorid's research was very specific on the polarity. Explain yourself," said the captain in a measured tone.

"I've been watching what I thought were small animals darting away from the submarine. But now I think they were actually pieces of Chambois's torpedo rejected by the magnet. They must be of the same polarity."

Silence.

Doug looked to Becca for support. Becca looked over at the captain. The captain looked at Chambois, eyebrows raised. Chambois nodded. They disengaged the electromagnet and the Frenchman quickly set about rewiring the controls.

"Well done, Douglas. An excellent observation. Zorid predicted a positive polarity, but could it be that the explosion has reversed it?"

"It's possible, Captain. Zoridium is a highly unstable material," said Chambois. "Ready to activate electromagnet."

"Very good. Switch on."

As power surged into the electromagnet once more, small pieces of broken steel from the torpedo sped out of the gloom towards the submarine, leaving streams of cavitation bubbles in their wake. The hull came under immediate attack: there was a terrifying sound of metal striking and ricocheting off it as a hailstorm of shards bombarded the *Galacia*.

The torpedo, which had been scattered into thousands of pieces over a half-mile radius, was now being drawn back in an almost exact reverse of the explosion. The submarine began to rock alarmingly. A large fragment of the torpedo casing caught the submarine's control fin and snagged on the starboard propeller, stalling the engine.

"Curses!" shouted the captain as the *Galacia* rolled out of control and hit the bottom with a juddering crash. The hull bounced then sank back down into the seabed, ploughing along with a forty-five-degree list to starboard. There was an ominous bang and a flash from a box above the battery compartment. Acrid smoke filled the interior, making them splutter and choke.

"Chambois! I've lost the starboard engine!"

But Chambois lay sprawled unconscious in a tangle of pipework, blood trickling down his cheek. The captain tried to pull him back into his seat, wrestling with the control column at the same time. The submarine lifted and bounced with three more shocking crashes. Becca and Doug clung on desperately.

Ten Dinners' voice crackled over the speaker. "Captain, Captain! Switch off the magnet; the shards will cut us to pieces. They're like bullets. Stop it now, for the love of God."

"The divers!" yelled Doug, looking out. "Sam's been hit on the arm!"

Outside, Sam crumpled to his knees, clutching his wound as the water around him clouded red.

"My air line! I'm hit!" cried Ten Dinners, his panicked voice distorted over the speaker. Doug could just see him to the rear of the submarine. His air line was punctured. Bubbles jetted out of the rubber hose, making it dance and snake.

"Chambois! Chambois, damn you!" roared the captain, fighting to regain control of the submarine. "Cut the power to the electromagnet. *Chambois!*"

But the Frenchman was still too dazed to respond.

"Leave it to me, Captain," shouted Becca, clambering forward. She stretched over Chambois and flicked off the electromagnet with a sharp kick from her boot. The metallic din outside died away, leaving an eerie silence. The captain cut the power to the port engine and they ground to a halt.

"Frankie," he barked. "Get the spare air line plumbed into Ten Dinners' suit immediately and check Sam's arm."

"Charlie's already doing it, Captain. There are torpedo fragments trapped in the propeller housing and rudder controls." His voice came through in gasps as he struggled towards the propeller.

"A thousand curses!" cried the captain.

"If the engine is put into reverse it should clear," said Fast Frankie.

"I'll need to reset the starboard engine overload circuit-breaker before I can try that. It's burnt itself out. Clear the debris away from the rudder. We don't have much time."

"Aye, Captain," answered Frankie.

"Do we have the zoridium?" asked the captain.

"Now the electromagnet has been switched off, it's fallen into the collection bucket."

The captain climbed out of his seat and started to make his way aft. "Rebecca – take the helmsman's position. Don't touch any of the controls unless I tell you to. See if you can help Chambois. Douglas, I'll need your assistance with the circuit-breaker. Grab that toolbox and torch there. Look lively."

Becca struggled towards the control panel and slid onto the red leather seat. She looked at her unconscious co-pilot,

Chambois, and tried to rouse him, but he was still out cold. She hauled him upright and inspected the wound on his forehead, using the silk handkerchief in his top pocket to stem the flow.

Doug, meanwhile, was at the stern of the submarine, shining the torch into the burnt-out circuit box and handing tools up to the captain. Wisps of smoke still drifted from it, but his uncle set to work regardless. "Screwdriver ... wire clippers..."

Doug glanced enviously at his sister, who was tentatively checking over the controls.

"The rudder is clear now," reported Ten Dinners. "I've loosened the piece lodged around the propeller. It should come free when you put her in reverse."

"Acknowledge him, Rebecca," ordered the captain, tearing out a melted wire.

She picked up the handset as she'd seen her uncle do. "Er... Hello, Becca – I mean Rebecca here... Acknowledged, Ten Dinners."

As she replaced the handset the submarine groaned and floated off the bottom. Within seconds the bow had lifted and they were pointing vertically upwards. Doug's box of spanners clattered backwards and crashed against the rear bulkhead. He reached out and grabbed some pipework, kicking his feet around to find a foothold. The captain was doing the same, struggling to keep a grip on a vital connection in the circuit box at the same time.

Becca panicked. "What did I do?" The controls in front of her seemed to be operating themselves, the steering column moving of its own accord.

"I said not to touch anything!" bellowed the captain.

"I didn't!" Becca shook Chambois by the shoulder. "Come on, wake up!" she urged.

He stirred, and after a few seconds became aware that they were ascending. "Is it the buoyancy, Captain?" he shouted, eyes widening with fear.

"What does the pressure gauge to your starboard say, Rebecca?" mumbled the captain, a screwdriver clenched between his teeth.

Becca looked to her right at a confusing array of gauges. "Which one?"

Chambois pointed. "That one."

"One hundred and fifty-four p.s.i."

"It's not the buoyancy. Any other theories, Chambois?"

"Stop," cried Ten Dinners over the speaker. "For pity's sake, we're not aboard!"

Doug swivelled round to his scuttle and saw the seabed disappearing as the submarine picked up speed towards the surface. The four divers were waving frantically. They'd had no time to scramble into their seats.

"Stop, or we'll be dragged to the surface by our air lines!" screamed Fast Frankie.

"Douglas, keep that torch shining at my hands."

"But we must do something!" implored Doug.

The captain bristled. "Rebecca, tell them the submarine is out of control and that they should brace themselves."

The divers were trying to coil their air lines around their bodies in a desperate attempt to protect the vital connection to their diving helmets. As the submarine ascended and the final kinks in their lines straightened out, they were wrenched from the seabed, limbs flailing, like fish caught on a line.

With his arm still pouring blood, Sam soon lost hold of his air line, and swung round so that he was being dragged upwards by his diving helmet. It was a desperate scene, his pleas for help gurgling through the speaker.

"What is pulling us up, Captain?" yelled Chambois.

"I cannot understand it! This is without precedent. It makes no sense."

Doug was horrified. Would the connection on Sam's diving helmet be strong enough, or would it rip out and leave him without air? And what about the bends?

"That's it," declared the captain, slamming the circuit-breaker's cover shut. "Rebecca, pull that green lever all the way back. It will put the engine into reverse, and should shift the debris. Do it now."

Becca grabbed the lever. The engine gave a strained whirring noise followed by a thud as the debris cleared, then settled down to a sweet hum that sounded normal to her. Instinctively she returned the throttle to neutral and looked questioningly over her shoulder at the captain.

"Excellent. Now put both engines into reverse. That's it. The red and green levers together."

Both engines cut in, louder this time. Becca moved the dual engine levers back to half power, but the submarine continued to rise. She glanced at Chambois for reassurance, then pushed them right back to full astern. The submarine began to rock and buck.

"Push the control column forward. See if she'll level off," ordered the captain.

But this made no difference either – if anything they were rising even faster than before, and the submarine was now corkscrewing, a further hazard for the divers.

"It's no use," said Becca, releasing the controls.

"Captain, what about the molecule invigorator?" asked Doug.

"What about it?"

"Could it be invigorating the zoridium as well as the hull?"

"You can produce some remarkably astute scientific deductions when you can be bothered, nephew. What do you think, Chambois? Could it be invigorated zoridium?"

"Yes ... yes... It is possible." Chambois nodded as he considered Doug's latest theory.

"I don't care if it's possible or not. My men are about to drown out there. Make a judgement. Is it happening?"

"But I have no idea what the invigorator would do to zoridium-enriched steel."

"Think back to Zorid's research!"

Chambois shut his eyes as he concentrated, a thousand formulae and equations racing through his tired mind. "Yes, of course!" He smiled as inspiration came. "The *Expedient*!"

"The *Expedient*?" snapped the captain.

"Yes, the *Expedient*," continued Chambois. "If the molecule invigorator acted upon the zoridium-enriched steel, it could conceivably make it highly magnetic."

"The collection bucket under the electromagnet is steel, Captain, and connected directly to the hull ... which is connected to the molecule invigorator," added Doug.

"The entire hull of the submarine could have become like a huge magnet of incredible strength," Chambois speculated. "We would then be attracted to the largest metal object in the area..."

"Hell's teeth," swore the captain. "The answer is in front of

From Doug's sketchbook: The Galacia *speeding towards the surface.* (DMS 1/43)

our very eyes. See how the collection bucket has swung round to point directly at the *Expedient* on the surface."

"The junk was constructed out of wood, the *Expedient* from steel. We are being dragged to the surface by the temporary magnetic field generated by the invigorated zoridium!" finished Chambois.

"What is our depth?"

"One hundred and ten feet and climbing fast," called Becca, trying the engines again.

"Then the solution is simple," said the captain.

"Oh, good," whispered Becca to herself.

"When we reach seventy feet, the hull will be able to resist the pressure without the molecule invigorator. We will switch it off, thus killing the magnetic field being generated by the zoridium. With luck, we will then be able to control our ascent."

When the depth gauge needle touched seventy feet, Chambois flicked the switch to deactivate the molecule invigorator. Immediately the bucket of zoridium dropped back down and the submarine began to level off. Becca wrestled with the controls and at last they responded.

Captain MacKenzie moved forward to resume command. "Thank you, Rebecca. A first-rate job. You too, Douglas. Well done."

Doug was keeping an eye on the divers, especially Sam and his wounded arm. He was struggling with the help of the others to climb his air line up to the submarine.

"Not quite the lesson on magnetism I had envisaged," said the captain wryly, sitting back.

Doug slumped down in his seat; it had been the longest few minutes of his life. Becca too was exhausted and sat with sagged shoulders, breathing deeply.

"Once I have adjusted the trim tanks, we will rest and recuperate at this depth," announced the captain. "We must ensure the divers do not suffer the bends by a too hasty return to the surface. Pass me that copy of Dr Haldane's decompression tables, Douglas."

Outside, they could hear the lead boots of the divers as they clambered across the hull to retake their seats. Doug shut his eyes and longed to breathe some fresh air.

Becca's diary: 11th April 1920
South China Sea, 110 nautical miles
south-south-east of Hong Kong

While we waited underwater, our uncle wanted us to return to our lessons, but I barely heard his lecture. My mind raced.

As I sat in the helmsman's seat of the submarine I had seen the magnetic anomaly chart of the South China Sea that the captain had used to locate the junk. I was immediately struck by the familiarity of its style. The map had been surveyed and drawn by my father ten years ago and marked HGS FIRENZE. What a strange coincidence that my uncle is using his map. Or perhaps it isn't a coincidence at all. Of course, I've always known that Father is a cartographer, but who or what is HGS? And why is Firenze mentioned again? My uncle seemed to think it significant that our parents were planning to take us there before they went off to the Sinkiang, and now suddenly its name has appeared on a map drawn by Father. Something is going on, and I can't help wondering if our parents are involved in some way. Is the mystery of their disappearance connected to the kidnapping of Chambois and the murder of Zorid? And what of my uncle's involvement? How is it that Chambois is aboard this ship as a welcome guest, and why is Uncle helping him recover this zoridium?

Up until now I have always focused on how *Mother and Father went missing and not* why. *Why were they in the Sinkiang in the first place? I suddenly have a feeling that the answers may be much nearer than I first thought.*

Perhaps the Expedient *holds clues to at least some of these questions. Why are we not allowed access to all of the ship? What is the captain keeping on board that is so secret? I must find out. We must find out. I shall need Doug's talent for getting into places he shouldn't, and put his boundless inquisitiveness to use. We're going to explore this ship till we find out exactly what is going on.*

CHAPTER FOUR

"What's the maximum size explosion zoridium could make, Monsieur Chambois?" asked Doug, idly fiddling with the collar on the Bunsen burner and sending a bubble of flame flaring up towards the ceiling with a satisfying *whoompfff*.

"Stop that, please, Douglas," protested Chambois, shutting off the gas tap. "This is a laboratory, not a playground. You are not a child any more." He spoke softly, but in such a way that made Doug feel stupid. The Frenchman was surrounded by a delicate web of wiring that had been the submarine's molecule invigorator. "Where's your sister?"

Doug tapped out an answer in Morse code with a screwdriver, then switched tack. "Was it all moats and drawbridges?"

"Was what all moats and drawbridges?"

"The fortress Sheng-Fat imprisoned you in."

Chambois didn't answer immediately, as he was about to execute a particularly tricky solder. Through habit, Doug took out his silver pocket compass and flicked the cover open and shut a couple of times. He was disappointed at how inaccurate it was at sea: the steel hull of the ship upset the earth's magnetism, giving ludicrous readings. Since they'd recovered the torpedo fragments, however, he'd noticed that *north* seemed to be fixed in the direction of the captain's quarters.

"It was a crumbling ruin," said Chambois. "I wasn't imprisoned by the fortress so much as by the island. I was allowed to wander freely during the day, because it was impossible to escape."

"I thought you were kept in a dungeon?"

"At first, yes. But once Sheng had broken my spirit, I was permitted to walk around within sight of the walls. I made maps in my head." He tapped his temple with a finger and smiled. "I measured everywhere, pacing out the walls, tunnels and towers."

"But you said Sheng-Fat had broken your spirit. So why were you making maps?"

"My spirit was broken, yes. But then … then I found hope. A ransom prisoner called Liberty arrived. I wanted to find a way out for us both."

"Your friend? The one with the necklace?"

Chambois did not answer. "You asked me about moats and drawbridges," he said instead.

Doug's eyes lit up. He wasn't very interested in the necklace, and was glad Chambois was back on the more fertile ground of ancient fortifications.

"There was no moat, and no drawbridge that I ever saw. The only way off the island was by boat from the small harbour at the base of the gatehouse. We would've had to escape the dungeons at night, find a passage through the tunnels, sneak past the guards, make our way to the surface, steal a junk and sail it to safety. The harbour was always heavily guarded."

Doug appreciated the enormity of the problem. "Couldn't you have sneaked aboard a boat disguised as a pirate? You could've picked the lock to your cell door. Locks are easy once you know how."

"Impossible. Sheng-Fat has three hundred armed guards, each marked with a V-shaped chin scar. He cuts their faces – marks them for life in a barbaric initiation ceremony. We would have been identified within minutes."

C. refused to pose for this, so his likeness is from memory

D.M. 12–15th April 1920

From Doug's sketchbook: Chambois at work in the laboratory. (DMS 1/47)

"Tricky," considered Doug, rubbing his chin. "I'd have made a survey of the tide and currents and built a bamboo raft, I think."

"That wouldn't have worked. We were many miles from mainland China. Liberty and I decided that the only way out was to sabotage the torpedo at the test firing, and then I would go for help. But now I fear she is dead. By the time I reached Shanghai her father, Theodore da Vine, had given in and signed the international shipping treaty. Sheng vowed to drown Liberty in his tide cages once her father had done that. By my escape I saved but one life – my own."

Doug wasn't sure what to say, but he realized that Chambois had changed from the broken man who had been stretchered aboard in Shanghai. He was calm as he spoke, his voice steady – but with a cold, vengeful resolve that was a little frightening.

"I cannot understand..." mused Chambois, perplexed. "The strength of the magnetic field generated by the invigorated torpedo fragments was quite unexpected. I observed no such reaction during my construction of the warheads. The answer to the mystery must lie in some chemical change activated by the heat of the explosion."

"It's powerful stuff," said Doug, sensing he'd get nothing more on the fortress. "What if you made a really huge zoridium bomb using a ton of it?"

"What a question! It's all bang, bang and destruction with you, Douglas. Don't you see that zoridium's true potential is not as an explosive? You make the same fundamental mistake as Sheng-Fat."

"If it's so explosive, why did Sheng-Fat have to kidnap you to make his torpedoes? I mean, couldn't he just have popped some zoridium in any old torpedo and fired it off?"

"Zoridium is not like a high explosive. To make it into a viable explosive for a torpedo warhead, Sheng-Fat needed to contain the initial chain reaction within a steel chamber. It was all in Zorid's papers. That was why Zorid was communicating with me before his death. He was fascinated by the concept behind my molecule invigorator, as he saw that it might lead to a successful containment of zoridium's power."

Doug looked blankly at the scientist.

"Look. A zoridium torpedo would have to be huge..." Chambois wrestled the words out in frustration. He stood up and walked over to the blackboard, drawing the outlines of a torpedo and a steam train. "To generate a large zoridium-based explosion, the chain reaction has to be, at first, contained. You'd need a containment chamber the size of a steam train's boiler and five feet thick to get any sort of result. Sheng-Fat needed an immensely strong containment chamber that would fit within a twenty-one-inch diameter torpedo to make his warhead work. Obviously, a steam train does not fit inside a torpedo—"

"But molecularly invigorated steel would!" exclaimed Doug.

"*Et voilà*," said Chambois with relief. "Sheng-Fat kidnapped me and forced me to produce a smaller, more powerful and far more advanced molecule invigorator to strengthen a football-sized containment sphere inside his torpedoes."

"And you built more than one of these?"

"I became so dependent on Sheng-Fat's opium that I built twenty-five of the deadly things. He has an arsenal of the most powerful explosive devices known to man hidden in the tunnels beneath his fortress."

"But I don't understand, Monsieur Chambois. How much zoridium does each containment chamber hold?"

"Oh, you need only a tiny amount. Here…" Chambois grabbed a handful of sand from a fire bucket hanging on the wall. He shook a small pile into the palm of his hand, licked the end of his finger and picked up a grain. "Look at this, and look closely. I promise you that a single grain of zoridium – combined with the reactive chemical holmium – would sink a ship of this size."

67

Ho

164.93032

HOLMIUM

For zoridium to detonate, the presence of a reactive chemical was required. Chambois specified holmium, atomic number 67. Holmium is a metallic rare earth element noted for its magnetic properties; it records the highest magnetic moment of any known naturally occurring element.

"But the junk was virtually vaporized."

"In the prototype I used seven grains," said Chambois with a quiet smile. "Just to make sure of my escape."

"So you could build more of these torpedoes and counter Sheng-Fat's threat! If we all had them—"

"Douglas, you don't understand. There *is* no more zoridium. Neither Zorid nor Sheng-Fat ever revealed where it came from. The only known quantity of zoridium outside Sheng-Fat's control is on board this ship – the zoridium-enriched steel from the prototype torpedo's warhead. Which is why the captain went to such lengths to recover it from the seabed."

Doug was beginning to understand. The pieces of scrap steel were unique.

"If the source of zoridium could be located and harnessed with the molecule invigorator into something other than a torpedo," continued Chambois, "we could change the world for ever. It would be the very seed of a new Industrial Revolution! The potential is infinite – cheap energy to power everything from light bulbs to steel foundries, an alternative to petroleum and gas … the end of world hunger and starvation, even the possibility of space flight!"

"Space flight? That's better than a bomb."

"Bravo, Douglas! At last you've realized that there's more to life than blowing things up!" exclaimed Chambois, slapping the laboratory bench. As he did so, the loose bandage around his hand came away.

Doug gasped. "Monsieur Chambois, what happened to your finger?"

Chambois lifted his hand and gazed at the stunted digit with its vivid scar. "My contribution to Sheng-Fat's favourite necklace. It is made of the bones of all his victims' little fingers."

THE ZORIDIUM TORPEDO

Chambois was forced by Sheng-Fat to miniaturize his molecule invigorator so it would fit inside the confined space of a torpedo warhead. The steel containment chamber can be seen in the forward section of the device. The explosion was initiated by firing holmium at the zoridium using a small fulminated mercury detonator. The resulting chain reaction was contained within the invigorated sphere for 0.3 of a second, generating an explosion 1,000 times greater than a standard 21-inch torpedo.

Doug drew back in horror, his eyes fixed on Chambois's hand. "Sheng-Fat is wearing your little finger?"

"Quite so. Now, you have interrupted my work long enough, Douglas." Chambois clenched his injured fist and gently tapped out GO AND HELP YOUR SISTER WITH HER MORSE CODE on the workbench.

Doug sauntered off in the direction of his cabin, his brain buzzing with the possibilities of zoridium-based space flight.

CHAPTER FIVE

Becca's diary: 16th April 1920
Approaching the Formosa Strait

I'm learning Morse code for the captain's test tomorrow. Doug, of course, learnt Morse last year during a spate of interest in radio and telegraphy. How could I forget his ceaseless knocking on any available surface like some crazed drummer, day and night! Now he's sending me titbits of crucial information from his chat with Chambois by tapping it out with a paintbrush on one of the pipes that run between our cabins.

MORSE ALPHABET		MORSE NUMERALS	
A .—	N —.	1 .————
B —...	O ———	2 ..———
C —.—.	P .——.	3 ...——
D —..	Q ——.—	4 ....—
E .	R .—.	5 .....
F ..—.	S ...	6 —....
G ——.	T —	7 ——...
H	U ..—	8 ———..
I ..	V ...—	9 ————.
J .———	W .——	0 —————
K —.—	X —..—	
L .—..	Y —.——	
M ——	Z ——..	

THE EXPEDIENT

Monarch class Q ship built for British Special Service
Registered in Queenstown, Ireland, August 1915
Transferred to private ownership 10th August 1916

Expedient *was a Q ship, built to counter the German submarine threat during the First World War (1914–18). These armed fighting vessels were disguised as cargo freighters, intended to lure attacking submarines to the surface by sailing unescorted. Such isolated targets were usually sunk by a submarine's deck gun. Once the submarine's crew was on deck firing, a Q ship would lower her lifeboats to draw the enemy closer, then drop her disguise and fight back. By 1916, however, the German navy had become wise to Q ship tactics and seldom bothered suspicious vessels.*

It is thought that around 200 Q ships were built, some of which fought in famous actions throughout the war. Many were simply converted fishing trawlers and merchant vessels pressed into service. The Q prefix is in itself a mystery, but may stand for Queenstown Naval Base in Ireland.

(MA 556.24 EXP)

Expedient *was the most powerful manifestation of her type – the main armament of two 10-inch "disappearing" guns put her in a class of her own (see pages 100–1). She was capable of shelling submarines, warships and shore installations from great distances. Other refinements included twin torpedo tubes, mine-laying gear, a rear 12-pounder quick-firing gun, a spotter plane, and armoured decks and hull. She cost seven times her original budget to build and was immediately frowned upon by high-ranking officers at the Admiralty (described in one report as "neither fish nor fowl – a colossal and ruinous waste of taxpayers' money").*

After just twelve months in service, Expedient *was sold into private ownership to recoup some of her astronomical construction costs. She sailed to Brooklyn, USA, in August 1916, where she was refitted to her later configuration. Mine-laying equipment was removed to allow for the submarine deckhouse, and her engines were converted from coal to oil-fired.*

scrapes from clambering through the ship, felt like a criminal.

"Do you think this is sensible, Doug? I mean…"

"If it were sensible, I wouldn't be doing it." He grinned. "We need to get into these lockers for the good stuff. I examined the locks last week and they're almost identical to the ones on our cabin desks. They're simple to open."

He took out two of Becca's hair grips and set about unlocking one of the cupboards beside the desk. Becca was caught between telling her brother to behave, and her need to know more about her uncle and his ship. Doug bit his lip in concentration as he made minute movements with the ends of the hair grips, first one way then the other, until the lock sprang open with a crisp click.

"See what you can find, Becca. I'll start on the lower cupboard."

Becca took out a thin pamphlet, one of a set numbering about thirty arranged in neat order. She opened a page and scanned the top margin: *HGS Code Book Cipher B (Triple)*. Row upon row of numbers and letters crowded the pages. It made no sense to her, so she pulled out another entitled *Cipher F*, but it was as impenetrable as the first.

SHIP'S WATCHES

A ship's day is divided into seven watches:

AFTERNOON WATCH *noon to 4 p.m.*
FIRST DOGWATCH *4 to 6 p.m.*
SECOND DOGWATCH *6 to 8 p.m.*
FIRST WATCH *8 p.m. to midnight*
MIDDLE WATCH *midnight to 4 a.m.*
MORNING WATCH *4 to 8 a.m.*
FORENOON WATCH *8 a.m. to noon*

The dogwatch is split to make an uneven number of watches during the day. This means the crew will work different watches each day.

After the Titanic *disaster, international maritime law was changed so that larger ships had to keep a continuous 24-hour distress-call watch.*

1915 — [PART 46]—1

HGS CODE BOOK CIPHER B (TRIPLE)

A Z G F R

CODE BOOK
CIPHER
F

TRIPLE
ENCODED

TOP SECRET

HGS

To destroy:
Immerse in salt water

"That's got it." Doug sniffed and swung open the door of the lower locker. It was crammed with books and papers. "Here you are," he said, passing her up a sheaf of papers from a cubbyhole marked DUPLICATE MESSAGES. "Don't get them out of order. It'll be a dead giveaway."

"Don't start lecturing me on tidiness, Douglas MacKenzie."

Becca began to flick through the papers, unaware that Doug was tackling another smaller compartment built into the top shelf. "These are really dull. Weather reports ... more weather reports ... distress signal from oil tanker *Calcutta Maid* with broken crank—" She stopped herself. "Reply from *Calcutta Maid* saying problem fixed and proceeding to destination. This isn't going to tell us where Mother and Father are."

"Try this lot."

Doug dumped another set of messages on the desk. They were written on blue paper with the word SECRET stamped across the top. Becca looked at the first.

"*Funds cleared by board for* Expedient *to refuel at Shanghai...* When is this dated? Yesterday. Did anything happen yesterday?"

Doug thought for a moment. "Not really. Nothing special."

"We altered course. We'd been heading southwards. Now we're heading north-east for the Formosa Strait and then back to Shanghai, I suppose. Why would we be going back?"

She leafed through three more messages, then saw something that made her blood run cold.

"*From Bergstrom, HGS relay station, Lucknow, India.*"

"I'm sure there isn't a radio station in Lucknow that can transmit this far," stated Doug with some authority.

Becca opened the message, drew the lamp closer and began to read.

"Triple encoded. Cipher F. Sub code D4464. Signal strength 4.
Message reads:
To Captain MacKenzie, Expedient. After long deliberation
the board of the Honourable Guild of Specialists, Firenze—"

"Who are they?" asked Doug, his eyes meeting Becca's. His
sister's face was white, and he noticed that her hand was shaking. "Who on earth are the Honourable Guild of Specialists?
Was that who we were going to meet in Firenze?"

"We've just struck gold," she replied. Her voice unsteady,
she read on.

"...has resolved by a vote of seven to five to support your
proposed plan OPERATION RED JERICHO, and wishes to
engage the services of the Expedient under your command to
fulfil these said aims. We confirm that the objectives of the
mission are:
(1) To obtain any remaining samples of Daughter of the Sun
(zoridium) from the warlord Sheng-Fat, which will be
returned to the ancient Order of the Sujing Quantou, the
sole guardians and protectors of Daughter of the Sun, so hon-
ouring our ancient covenant and upholding our most noble
association, as laid down in the Treaty of Khotan signed in
the year 1720.

"That's odd. Zoridium must also be known by another name.
I thought Zorid had only just discovered it," said Becca pen-
sively.

"Looks like this Daughter of the Sun is much older, and
the Sujing Quantou – whoever they are – have known about
it for years," reasoned Doug. "Zorid must have stumbled on

a very well-kept secret. I wonder if Chambois knows about this? He thinks the only samples of zoridium are those we collected from the seabed."

"We mustn't be discovered. Let's read on," whispered Becca, suddenly feeling anxious.

"(2) To search for and recover or destroy the molecule invigorators constructed by our associate Luc Chambois during his imprisonment by Sheng-Fat, to protect the secrets of steel-strengthening technology.

To provide a cover story for your activities, representations have been made to various foreign powers informing them of our intention to disarm Sheng-Fat, in order to protect the recent international shipping treaty. Their thanks and offers of secret funding have, as ever, been accepted by the board.

As you are aware, this mission is bound under various ancient articles and alliances which must be represented to the Order of the Sujing Quantou in Shanghai before commencement of the operation.

On the matter of your sponsorship of Luc Chambois to become a full member of the HGS, the board feels that this would be inappropriate whilst the murder of Professor Zorid remains unsolved. He continues, of course, as an associate member and friend of the Guild and will, with your assent, remain aboard the Expedient *as your guest and special adviser.*

Both these objectives are to be achieved by any means you see fit.
Signed: The Board—"

The Duchess's roar made Becca jump so much she dropped the message. Doug leapt up, cracking his head on the top cupboard's open door. The Duchess glared at them through the scuttle for several seconds and then dropped from view with a parting growl.

"That thing can't get in here, can it?"

"Stop worrying about her and put everything back as it was," snapped Becca, scrabbling under the desk to retrieve the Lucknow message. "No one must know we've seen this stuff."

They worked fast, replacing both sheaves of papers in the lockers. Doug managed to relock the lower cupboard within ten seconds, and the one beside the desk shortly after. Becca straightened up the lamp and with a quick glance to check everything was as they'd found it, they crept into the companionway. There was no sign of the Duchess, despite some distant roars.

As they approached Piccadilly Circus Doug felt safe enough to stop and pull up his lucky socks. "Mission accomplished," he grinned.

CHAPTER SIX

I've been doing a lot of thinking since we found the message. And there is so much to think about.

Our uncle, first of all, is clearly running more than a research ship. His activities seem to be governed by this Honourable Guild of Specialists, or HGS; whoever – or whatever – they are.

Both he and the HGS seem fixated by zoridium or Daughter of the Sun. Why keep this substance such a closely guarded secret?

Then there are Mother and Father. Are they involved with the HGS too?

There is evidence to suggest they are: the chart that Father drew and the telegram from Lucknow, where we last saw them. The connection between Lucknow, Firenze, the captain and Chambois provides a strong basis for my hypothesis.

If this is the case, our whole life has revolved around a secret, and I am angry that Mother and Father never told us. I also wonder if our destiny lies with this HGS. I feel our uncle is preparing us for something with all his lessons on physics and science. But what exactly, and why?

My resolve to make further night sorties to discover what else is on board this ship has strengthened. The message we found in the telegraphy cabin was a revelation. What other secrets will we learn?

The alarm bell clattered in the closing minutes of an English literature lesson with Posh Charlie. Charlie's subject was "The use of the colour red in Thomas Hardy's *Tess of the D'Urbervilles*" – and Doug wasn't the slightest bit interested. His final comment – "So no shoot-out at Stonehenge?" – had sent Charlie into a frenzy of stuttering indignation. Becca sat in the corner with cotton wool jammed in her ears, absorbed in *David Copperfield*.

Ives put his head round the door and called, "Rebecca, Douglas. The captain wants you to go to your cabins and stay there."

"Is it a fire drill?" asked Doug.

"No. Charlie, we received a distress signal from a ship being chased by pirates. Action stations."

Becca and Doug followed Ives down to their cabins on the deck below.

"Now I want your word that you'll stay here. No wandering off, d'you understand?"

"Yes," Becca replied.

Ives turned and bounded up the ladder two steps at a time. Doug was already clambering over his bunk to the scuttle.

"What's going on, Doug? Why are we at action stations?"

"I don't know. I thought we were a research ship, not a battleship. We're turning. Pass me my binoculars. Let's have a proper look."

Expedient was steaming at full speed, leaning over as she turned. Doug focused on two ships some distance away: one was a freighter, the other a large seagoing junk with sails the colour of dried blood.

"Lethal! The junk is attacking the freighter. Men are swarming up ladders to take it. There must be sixty or seventy pirates trying to board her."

"Is it one of Sheng-Fat's junks?"

"I can't tell," answered Doug. "Wait… Yes! It has the dragon's tooth motif just like the wreck we saw! It must be. If only we could go up on deck!"

Then something quite unexpected happened. A klaxon horn sounded, followed by a curious rushing, yawning noise, and then the most astounding explosion boomed through the ship, making everything that wasn't bolted down vibrate. This was followed by a dying, whistling sound.

"What was that? Are we hit? Are we sinking?" demanded Becca.

Doug sat back on the bunk stunned, his mind working through several possibilities. "It can't be…" he said almost to himself.

"What can't be?"

Doug leant out of the scuttle just as two great splashes fell short of the junk.

"Becca!" He turned, laughing in disbelief. "We weren't hit. That was the noise of two large-calibre guns firing. We are firing at the junk! *Expedient* must have hidden guns!"

"Will they sink us with a zoridium torpedo?"

"I doubt it. They're facing the wrong way, and the captain has their range."

The klaxon sounded again and the ship echoed to another cabin-rattling explosion.

"The junk is disengaging. The captain is frightening them off. So that's what he's been keeping from us. This ship is armed to the teeth. The ship's big secret is her guns." Doug's curiosity jump-started at this marvellous deception. "They must be in the hold. But how did they get them on deck so quickly?"

From Doug's sketchbook: The junk attacking the freighter. (DMS 1/54)

"I can see smoke coming from the freighter," said Becca, peering out of her own scuttle. "Did we hit it?"

"No. Those shells are huge – it would've blown up. The pirates must have set fire to her. Becca, this is too much," said Doug. "I have to go up on deck."

"But you'll be seen! It's against orders."

"There's so much going on, I can slip up there easily. I can make it to the galley without being spotted."

Doug didn't listen to Becca's protestations. He simply ran out and up the ladders to the deck, sprinting the short distance to the safety of the galley, where he could see more through the scuttles on each side. He was amazed to discover that what he'd been told was the potato store was in fact a false deckhouse disguising an aft gun, a twelve-pounder by the look of it. It was cleared away for action, with a line of ammunition ready to fire, but was apparently unmanned. He became aware that Becca was standing beside him.

"That's not one of the main guns," he said. "They must be on the fo'c'sle."

"Where are the gun crew?"

"Busy forward. They wouldn't be able to aim at anything from this angle. If only I could get closer to see..."

"This is dangerous enough."

Expedient was closing the distance now, but appeared to be making for the freighter not the junk.

"I can see her name. She's the *Rampur Star*. The crew are abandoning ship! They're launching lifeboats!"

More smoke billowed out of the *Rampur Star*'s forward hold and a lick of orange flame burst from a watertight door near the bridge. *Expedient* had stopped firing, and her engine note dropped away.

"Why isn't the captain giving chase?" asked Doug. "We could catch the junk easily."

As if in answer the captain's voice bellowed down from the bridge. "Prepare to take aboard survivors. Scramble nets and lines. Stand by with fire hoses. We're going alongside."

"Quickly. Before we get trapped," called Becca.

They made for the galley door then ran at a crouch across the deck towards the ladder hatch. They piled down the steps and raced for the safety of their cabins. Becca collapsed onto her bunk, laughing with relief.

They'd made it. Nobody had seen them.

It was after midnight. Becca's voice made Doug jump. He'd been about to creep out of Piccadilly Circus when she'd whispered his name.

"What do you want?"

"I'm coming with you," she announced, catching her breath.

"Says who?"

"Says me. I've brought my own torch."

"It's late. Why don't you go back to bed?"

"I want to know everything. It bothers me that we're sailing aboard a ship that's pretending to be something it isn't."

"Well, I'm looking for a pair of guns, nothing else. So keep quiet and stay close."

"What about the survivors from the *Rampur Star*? They must be billeted somewhere here."

"They're right up in the fo'c'sle. I checked earlier with Mr Teng."

They slipped down a long passageway until they reached a door marked CITADEL: EMERGENCY EXIT. It was one Doug had located four days before, but hadn't had time to investigate yet.

The bulkhead was especially thick here and the door much heavier than any other they'd seen on the ship so far. It took both of them to heave it open. Once through they found a steel ladder that led three decks up. Doug clamped his torch between his teeth and started to climb; Becca followed.

They arrived on a darkened deck directly beneath the cargo hatch cover – and then they saw them. Two guns. Silent. Menacing. Majestic. Vast. Coiled down and hidden below deck on hydraulic carriages, ready to rear up and strike like a pair of deadly snakes. The guns' tapering barrels stretched out into the darkness, reflecting the weak torchlight with a blue, oily sheen, their muzzle ends indefinable in the shadow. There was a smell too – a smell different from the rest of the ship. They'd caught a waft of it when they'd hidden in the galley, but now it came again: cordite.

"Disappearing guns – double lethal!"

This was the most secret part of the ship. Becca and Doug walked slowly forward with reverence, as if in church, suddenly conscious of their footsteps. Their eyes adjusted to the darkness and they began to make out the small raised walkway in front of them which allowed the crew to load the shells. They climbed a ladder to a platform between the two guns and inspected their breeches and loading trays. The parts gleamed in the low light; it could all have been manufactured by giants.

CORDITE

A smokeless explosive used as a propellant in ammunition. When detonated, expanding gases blow the shell or bullet out of the barrel with exceptional force. Cordite is composed of nitroglycerine, guncotton and petroleum jelly.

Doug patted the cold starboard barrel, then jumped back down onto the deck, playing his light across the huge hydraulic lifting pistons and machinery. "These must elevate the guns above deck into their firing position," he said, drinking in the detail. The bolts on the pistons were larger than his clenched fist. "Lethal. Just imagine the spanners you'd need to get that lot apart!"

Becca stepped down into the gloom, and found a shape which puzzled her at first. Something large, flat and made of wood and canvas was lashed securely to the side of the hull. Walking on, she guessed it must be a wing.

"Could the captain have an aeroplane down here?" she whispered.

"Why not?" Doug replied, flashing his torch first at his sister, then at her discovery. The beam lit up the fuselage of an archaic-looking aeroplane, its engine behind the pilot's seat. "You're right. It's a seaplane. I've seen a picture of one.

EXPEDIENT'S SECRET GUNS

Expedient's armament was based on the well-established hydraulic lifting gun carriage designed for land-based shore batteries, known as "disappearing" guns. They would rise up above a fortified emplacement to fire, using the recoil of the barrel to swing back down to the loading position. The gun operators behind the emplacements were therefore never exposed to hostile fire. This system was adapted to hide Expedient's guns in what appeared to be the ship's cargo hold.

Expedient's twin 10-inch barrels were a unique and costly development, revolutionary for their time. They were mounted within a barbette – a cylindrical rotating turret that also housed the shell and cordite ammunition feeds from the magazine. Owing to problems with the weight of the barrels,

the barbette was designed to rotate only 10 degrees to either port or starboard so as not to interfere with the ship's stability. This meant that the vessel had to steer almost directly towards the target the captain wished to engage.

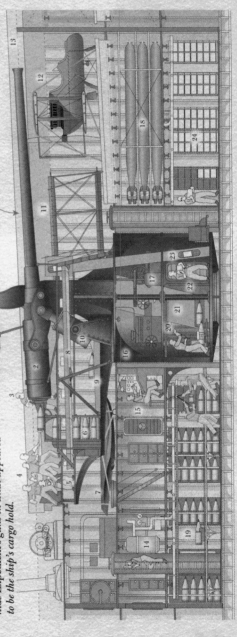

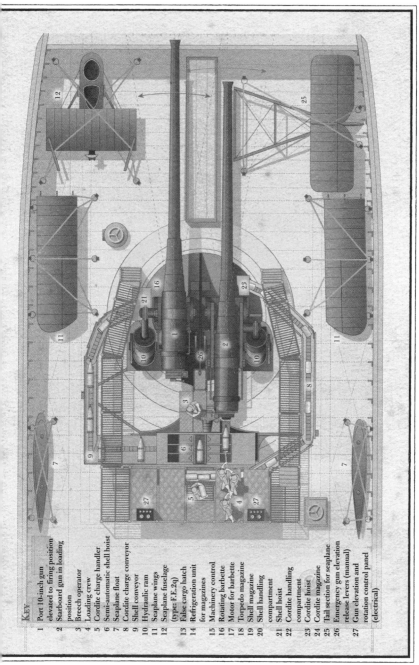

KEY

1 Port 10-inch gun elevated to firing position
2 Starboard gun in loading position
3 Breech operator
4 Loading crew
5 Cordite charge handler
6 Semi-automatic shell hoist
7 Seaplane float
8 Cordite charge conveyor
9 Shell conveyor
10 Hydraulic ram
11 Seaplane wings
12 Seaplane fuselage (type: F.E.2q)
13 False cargo hatch
14 Refrigeration unit for magazines
15 Machinery control
16 Rotating barbette
17 Motor for barbette
18 Torpedo magazine
19 Shell magazine
20 Shell handling compartment
21 Shell hoist
22 Cordite handling compartment
23 Cordite hoist
24 Cordite magazine
25 Tail section for seaplane
26 Emergency gun elevation release levers (manual)
27 Gun elevation and rotation control panel (electrical)

(MA 556.29 EXP)

Look, there are the two floats so it can land on water. They must lift her out with the derrick and assemble her on deck, then take off across the sea – although she's missing a propeller by the look of it, and some of the struts are broken. She must have landed badly. Probably on a secret mission." He whistled softly in admiration. "The captain's got some great stuff on this ship, and I bet we've only seen half of it."

Doug flicked the torch beam away, but Becca, who'd always dreamt of flying, lingered and walked slowly past the wing, trailing her hand along the canvas.

"You should learn to fly, sis."

"D'you think so?"

"Why not? You handled the sub all right. The captain said so. A plane can't be much different. Just in air rather than water."

An interesting-looking circular hatch in the deck just beside the port gun caught Doug's attention. Like the first door, it was sealed with a watertight locking mechanism. He turned the well-greased wheel, and the hatch sprang open.

"Doug, where are you going?" Becca hissed. "We've seen enough. Let's get out of here before we're caught."

"Come on. You wanted to know more about the ship, didn't you? Maybe we'll find some clues to the Guild. No one knows we're here. Let's explore!"

Becca hurried over as Doug climbed into the opening. A ladder dropped down the shaft into the darkness. A polished brass plaque at the top read: CORDITE MAGAZINE. AUTHORIZED PERSONNEL ONLY. NO NAKED FLAMES. RISK OF EXPLOSION.

"It's cold down here – like it's refrigerated or something," called up Doug, tucking the torch into his belt.

"Doug. *Doug!* This might be very dangerous!"

"Think of all the parts of the ship we've yet to see. Herr Schmidt was telling me about the electric drive."

"What?"

"The ship has electric engines as well as the triple expansion ones."

"So what?" Becca heard the metallic click of sea boots on steel as Doug dropped to the deck below.

"It means the ship can travel almost silently for short distances. There's a huge battery room somewhere down here."

"Did he tell you that too?"

"Yes. I asked him why the *Expedient* needed two sets of engines, and he said the ship had been used as a test bed for submarine engines during the war, but then he shut up. Like he'd said too much."

At that moment, to Becca's horror, the wheel on the watertight door behind her began to spin and the three locking catches crashed open one after the other. Doug must have heard too, because he bounded back up the ladder. Becca darted for the safety of the shadows between the two guns, pulling Doug after her. The door swung open and lights came on.

"They must be doing the night rounds," whispered Doug.

"If we can get up there," said Becca, pointing at the monstrous hydraulic lifting mechanism, "we'll be much higher than them."

Doug could see his sister's logic. If they were above eye level and lay still, they might get away with it. He could see Fast Frankie checking around. They had very little time.

He clambered up, trying to find a foothold. As he did so he slipped and slid back, his left foot catching a lever. He landed on the deck with a thump, knocking into Becca. Immediately the gun carriage hissed and yawned, and the huge starboard barrel started to rise with gathering speed, punching a hole through the closed cargo hatch above. The planks splintered and broke as the gun glided to a stop in its firing position. Horrified, Doug leapt up in a desperate effort to find a lever to get the gun down.

High on the flying bridge a spotlight flashed on, pinpointing him like an actor on a stage. Fast Frankie rushed over and pulled Becca from the shadows.

"I think we had better wake the captain."

"There's no need," came a voice from the deck. Their uncle stared down through the jagged remains of his cargo hatch. His next words were not what either Becca or Doug expected. "You two will dine with me tomorrow night at eight. You are excused lessons until then. Return to your cabins immediately." Then to Fast Frankie: "Rouse the gun crew. Have the gun cranked back down by hand."

CHAPTER SEVEN

Doug knocked hard on the captain's cabin door and waited until he heard him bark, "Enter!"

The captain was deep in conversation with Chambois, and barely turned to acknowledge his niece and nephew.

"...and the ruins of Zorid's laboratory were searched with an electromagnet two days ago using the opposite polarity. I received a message this afternoon. There was no trace of zoridium. Scientific analysis by HGS scientists revealed that the explosion was caused by nothing more exotic than dynamite."

"Zorid was murdered, plain and simple. But not by me."

"We will need more than just your word to clear your name, my friend. None of his research papers were found at the scene of the explosion."

"But I've told you already, Captain. Sheng-Fat has his papers. They escaped the blast, along with Zorid's phial of zoridium."

"I believe you, but a court of law would not. They'd say that Sheng-Fat must be a most ingenious warlord to have travelled all the way to Europe to kidnap you and kill Zorid."

"Whoever said Sheng-Fat did? My kidnappers were not Chinese. Two were French I think, and from the smell of his cigarette, my guess is that the third was a German. They bundled me into the back of a baker's van. We were followed by a Rolls-Royce driven by a man wearing a white linen suit, all the way to a large house in the Septième Arrondissement. I would

BOHR AND EINSTEIN

In 1920 these two scientists were at the forefront of a new generation of theoretical physicists. Einstein's revolutionary theories of relativity and Bohr's work in quantum physics transformed mankind's understanding of the structure and workings of the universe.

Einstein won the Nobel Prize for Physics in 1921 "for his services to Theoretical Physics, and especially for his discovery of the law of the photoelectric effect". Bohr took the same prize a year later "for his services in the investigation of the structure of atoms and of the radiation emanating from them".

suggest that he is the man who murdered Zorid, was responsible for my kidnap and handed me over to Sheng-Fat in Singapore."

"Then we must find the man in the white linen suit, Monsieur Chambois, and bring him to justice. We shall speak more of this later. Come, let us eat."

The meal proceeded in an uncomfortable silence for Becca and Doug. The captain barely looked at them, instead spending most of the time discussing the recent work of Bohr and Einstein with Chambois. All day Doug's stomach had been in knots as he wondered what punishment their uncle would dole out to them, but so far nothing had been said about last night's incident. This was almost worse. If he'd been given five hundred lines of *I must not play with the ship's secret weapons, especially after midnight*, he would have known where he stood. But this waiting was terrible. He hardly touched his meal, and he noticed Becca wasn't eating much either.

He was snapped out of his reverie by the captain. "Now, you two. Well, you've certainly lived up to your reputation. And there was I thinking we were making a little headway."

He leant back and took out a folder

from the sideboard behind him. Evidence, thought Doug.
This didn't look good.

"Now, let me see here. I want to make sure I've got all this
correct, you understand. I remember stating quite categorically
at our first meal together that you were to follow my orders to
the letter or leave my ship."

Becca's face was fixed as if she'd been carved in granite.
Their uncle took out a handwritten note with times and dates.

"The next day, Douglas, you informed Herr Schmidt that I'd
given my permission for you to have a conducted tour of the
engine room, paying particular attention to the crankshafts."

"Oh, Doug," hissed Becca. She'd had no idea he'd lied.

Doug gave a little sniff.

"I'm afraid I don't recall authorizing any such expedition,"
said the captain. "Still, at least you had a guide for that particular excursion. I have a report here from two nights later. The
starboard bridge lookout noted that one of the ship's boat
covers had been disturbed."

"Could've been anyone."

"Then explain to me how three days ago my radio operator
managed to get coal dust over this message, and how the
compartment containing it unlocked itself overnight."

Becca glanced at Doug. He'd only had time to relock two
of the doors.

The captain pulled out the Lucknow message, which had a
large thumbprint across one corner. "And before you say that
this smudge is nothing more than ink, I have analysed it in
the laboratory. It is coal from the ship's disused bunker,
where this very afternoon I discovered this, a woollen hat
marked with the initials DM. Here." The captain threw it
across the table. "It can keep your head warm when you next

go on deck during action stations. I saw you and your sister scrambling from the galley yesterday like a pair of bilge rats when you were meant to be in your cabins."

Chambois shifted uneasily in his chair. Doug gazed down at his feet.

"I'm not even going to mention the outrageous incident with the guns. You will both be put ashore when we dock at Shanghai tomorrow. You will return to Aunt Margaret in San Francisco."

"But can't we have another chance?" tried Doug. "We always get another chance…"

The captain glared at him from his single unflinching eye. "You slouch around this ship as if she were your own command, taking liberties with my patience and time, yawning your way through my lessons while producing an academic effort of the most shameful fatuity, and – worst of all – disobeying every order I've given you. You've lied, burgled, read papers never intended for your eyes, operated guns, trodden on my tiger. You have failed here, just as you have failed everywhere else you've been in the last year. You are a discredit to your parents. This is not a school, Douglas – there is no second chance. It is a ship. *My* ship. You endangered my ship, and my crew. Somebody could have been killed last night if they'd been resting on the cargo hatch. *You* could have been killed scrabbling about in the depths. In the cordite magazine too! I shudder to think what would have happened if you'd caused a spark down there!"

"But, Uncle, why do you keep so many secrets from us? If you would only tell us what's going on, we wouldn't have to take matters into our own hands," said Becca stubbornly. "Please tell us who the HGS are, for a start."

"You presume too much, Rebecca. There is no place here for either of you. We dock in Shanghai tomorrow morning. You will come ashore with me and the survivors from the *Rampur Star*. I shall arrange a steamer ticket to America for you both."

The captain shifted his chair so that Becca and Doug were no longer in his line of sight. There was an awkward pause. The captain's attention fixed on Chambois, who was nervously arranging a pile of breadcrumbs on the linen tablecloth with the edge of his knife. Becca and Doug remained seated, stunned by their dressing down.

"Monsieur Chambois. Do you think the idea of a fog machine I mentioned earlier would work? The fog would appear to cling to the ship?"

"I … think so," replied the Frenchman, glancing across at Becca and Doug. "We would need to build some sort of electrostatic voltage amplifier, of course…" His voice was flat.

"My laboratory is at your disposal. Please build it without delay." The captain looked over his shoulder at his niece and nephew. "Go away and pack your bags. Be ready to leave the ship tomorrow morning at nine sharp. I have nothing more to say to you."

Quietly Doug and Becca stood up and left, escorted to the door by the Duchess.

(MA 449.06 SHANG)

SHANGHAI

By 1920 Shanghai was divided into three distinct parts: the original city (whose walls dated back to 1553), the International Settlement and the French Concession. The Treaty of Nanking (1842), signed at the end of the First Opium War, had granted rights of settlement and trade to the British. The Americans and French were quick to follow. As the city grew, the Americans merged with the British, forming the International Settlement.

Shanghai's existence and prosperity was built on just one foundation – trade. World demand for exotic Chinese goods such as tea, porcelain and silk was huge. Shanghai's position near the mighty Yangtze River, one of the major trade routes through China, meant these lucrative goods flowed naturally towards it. The port's foreign merchants exported the merchandise to every country in the world. Fortunes were made and the city developed into a western-styled capital of eastern commerce and banking.

CHAPTER EIGHT

Sitting here surrounded by my cases, I'm left wondering where we'll unpack next. A few people have come down to say goodbye. Most surprising is that Chambois passed by ten minutes ago and gave me the curious diamond necklace he's been wearing. He said he no longer wanted it, and thought I might have more use for it. I was so shocked, I didn't know what to say. But he didn't want to talk and merely said he thought the captain had been a little hard on us.

I'm looking at the diamonds now as they reflect the flickering lights of Shanghai that are once again floating by my scuttle. It is an elaborate piece of jewellery, and there appears to be quite a lot of what looks like engine oil trapped in the silver setting clasps. I can't help wondering about the fate of its original owner.

Where did we go wrong? Should I have stopped Doug when I discovered he'd been clambering about the ship every night? I couldn't. I joined him because of my own need to know. And we found out more about our life in that one night than we've discovered in a year. At least now we know that our destinies seem to be controlled in some way by this Honourable Guild of Specialists.

Through circumstance, I have been made into a liar, a picker of locks, a reader of secret messages. I am the product of my situation, alone and adrift with Doug on an ocean of mysteries – guided by influences beyond our control. I was just fighting my corner as best I could.

Despite the dreadful wrench (and it is a dreadful wrench leaving the ship), I feel a strange new drive and strength. San Francisco and Aunt Margaret hold no answers to the many questions that now nag and tug at me constantly. Everything we've discovered here has simply fuelled the one burning question that I – that Doug and I – must answer: what were Mother and Father doing in the Sinkiang?

"Shanghai is like a huge pumping heart – its blood the trade and commerce flowing in and out of China," the captain explained. His rickshaw and Becca's were neck and neck, racing at a fair speed, and he was having to lean out to be heard over the din of the street traffic. "The Huangpu and the Yangtze are the main arteries. This is not like China proper, mark you. You are just as likely to hear an Indian or English voice as Chinese. It is the world condensed, and it has but a single aim – to make money. I find it a little crude for my tastes."

They had just left the steamer office where there had been a delay in securing the tickets to San Francisco. The captain was now running late for his next appointment. He had a heavy wooden box with him which intrigued Doug enormously because *north* on his silver pocket compass had remained fixed to it all morning.

"Is your brother still with us?" called the captain.

Doug was behind them in another rickshaw, standing up and urging the driver on like some latter-day charioteer.

"I wonder sometimes," muttered Becca to herself.

"So your ship leaves in a week's time, Rebecca. Until then

you will be staying at a hotel in the French Concession. It is a pleasant enough place, but I would ask you to ensure that your brother behaves himself. Mrs Ives and the Duchess will stay with you, and will see you safely aboard your steamer."

"Yes, Uncle."

"I'm aware that you now know of the Honourable Guild of Specialists. Will you give me your word as a MacKenzie that you will not speak of the Guild to anyone? If not for my sake, then for your parents'."

Becca turned to look at him. "Can you not at least tell me who they are, Uncle?"

"No, Rebecca, I'm afraid not. If you want the truth, I think you and your brother are too unreliable. Ah – I believe we have arrived."

The Sujing Quantou headquarters and fireworks factory was located deep within the Nantao quarter, to the south of the city. A pair of iron-studded red doors guarded the entrance to the windowless stone facade.

The captain lifted the huge bronze ram's-head knocker and gave it an almighty bang; after a short wait the right-hand door creaked open. They were greeted by a giant of a man over seven feet tall, dressed in a black robe buttoned tightly to the collar. His heavy features and large frame were more European than Chinese; he had dead-looking sunken eyes and an aura of detachment.

"Captain Fitzroy MacKenzie of the research ship *Expedient*. I seek the experience and expertise of the noble Order of the Sujing Quantou. I send my compliments and request an audience with your esteemed leader, Master Aa. My card, sir."

They were invited inside with a nod. As the door shut they were plunged into darkness. The doorman lit a single oil lamp that gave off so little illumination it was impossible to gauge the dimensions of the space. They were in a storeroom that had no natural light and was as creepy as a dungeon. Following the giant, they walked past long shelves of boxed fireworks that extended into the gloom. A rough wooden staircase brought them out into sudden sunlight, and to everyone's surprise they found themselves in a town house of some distinction. Glass doors opened onto a balcony overlooking a central courtyard with a graceful colonnade constructed in bright marble and embellished with gold leaf. The doorman bowed, and with a sweep of his arm motioned for them to be seated on a line of chairs arranged along the wall, then left without a word.

"I feel like I'm waiting to see the dentist," said Doug after a minute of silence. Neither the captain nor Becca responded.

Another minute ticked by.

"He wasn't very talkative, was he?" tried Doug again. "Sore throat perhaps."

"Why don't you follow his example, and hold your tongue," grunted the captain.

Doug stood up and strode out onto the balcony. Through a row of open windows on the other side of the courtyard he could glimpse rooms lavishly decorated with sumptuous furniture and silk wall hangings. On a breeze infused with incense he caught the sound of humming and a low chant which resonated through the archways, echoing off the stonework, growing stronger and stronger until it suddenly stopped and whispered away. A huge Sujing Quantou crossed the courtyard and rang a bell at its centre, chiming out four deep notes. A new smell – the aromatic waft of cooking – drifted up, making Doug's stomach rumble.

He stepped back inside to tell Becca what he'd seen just as

a door swung open and a man of the most astonishing stature – even larger than the doorman – appeared. The floor creaked under the weight of his slow, deliberate gait. He wore a red robe heavily embroidered with gold thread and his face had the same fixed, distant stare as his colleague's.

"Captain. I am Master Aa of the Sujing Quantou. Welcome to my house."

"Good day to you, sir. Thank you for agreeing to see me at such short notice."

Ignoring Becca and Doug, Master Aa bowed his head slightly and directed the captain into the room with a huge open hand, shutting the panelled door firmly behind them.

"We won't hear a thing out here," complained Becca, tip-toeing over to see if there was a keyhole. Doug started kicking the leg of his chair, utterly bored. A few minutes had passed when he heard a stifled snigger that he was sure hadn't come from Becca. His sister had her ear glued to the door and was oblivious to everything else. The noise seemed to have come from a small window high up on the opposite wall. The opening was covered with a filigree screen, but for a second he thought he saw an eye staring at him.

He sensed movement and saw some shadowy shapes. He stuck his tongue out. The silhouettes disappeared. Doug jumped up, dragged his chair across the hallway and posi-tioned it below the window. He climbed onto it and waited until he heard whispering. Immediately he banged the screen with his fist, causing a scuffle.

Becca turned to see what her brother was up to.

"What on earth are you doing, Doug? Get down."

"There was someone there!" he replied.

"Well, maybe it's their house, dummy. Maybe they have

THE SUJING QUANTOU FIREWORKS FACTORY

Sujing Quantou fireworks were celebrated as the most powerful and impressive in all China. Masters of explosive chemistry, the Sujing Quantou funded their mysterious order on the proceeds of their very profitable fireworks business. Their solemn demeanour was diametrically opposed to their remarkable combustible creations. We have only Becca's description of the interior of this fortified town house, as it was destroyed by fire in 1932. Such was the reputation of the factory's products that the Shanghai fire brigade refused to attend the blaze.

every right to be there. You haven't. Now get down and shut up; I'm trying to listen."

He dragged his chair back with great reluctance and slumped down. Moments later he heard a scraping noise, but the silhouettes behind the screen didn't return; he kept watch, barely blinking, ready to jump back up if they did. Becca was still listening at the door, but could hear no more than muffled voices.

Suddenly Doug gave a startled cry as his handkerchief flew out of his shirt pocket and shot towards the ceiling. "This place is haunted!"

"Nonsense." From where she crouched Becca could see a small hand in a hole in the ceiling, hauling up a barely visible fishing line with the handkerchief hooked on the end.

"I see you!" shouted Doug, catching a flash of the mysterious hand. The handkerchief disappeared up through the hole, and the hatch scraped back into place. "That's mine!" he complained, springing to his feet.

"Please, Doug, just sit down! Where are you off to now?"

"To get it back. I want to have a look around anyhow," he added, hitching up his socks. "You're never going to hear anything through that door."

"Oh, Doug, not again," groaned Becca. "Forget the handkerchief…"

But her brother had already reached the end of the corridor. Becca followed, losing sight of him as he turned a corner. The air was stifling, and Doug felt as though he were being watched. His heart started to beat faster and he glanced up at the ceiling to see if anyone was there.

"Doug, where are you?" Becca whispered.

Doug could hear the unmistakable Scottish burr of his

uncle. It was faint but clear, and seemed to be coming from behind a door to his right.

"Doug!" Becca hissed. "Doug! Where are you? Uncle may be finished any minute. We shouldn't be wandering around."

"Sshh, in here!" he said, grabbing her arm and pulling her through the door. "Don't say a word."

They crept into a small laboratory lit by smoke-yellowed windows and crammed with an extraordinary jumble of ancient and modern apparatus. Glass chemical bottles stood alongside terracotta clay pots that looked a thousand years old. A huge pestle and mortar sat on one end of the workbench. Bamboo pipework zigzagged from jars to test tubes to condensers in a most elaborate and complex-looking experiment, the result of which seemed to be a bubbling silver-blue chemical giving off a foul-smelling odour. They spotted Master Aa through a half-open door, seated behind a monumental wooden desk; their uncle was out of view.

"...we do not fight on water, Captain MacKenzie. Our skills are not suited to combat on board ships and junks."

"But what if I told you that the warlord Sheng-Fat may have obtained some of your Daughter of the Sun? A scientist named Chambois, a colleague of Professor Zorid" – the Sujing Quantou inhaled sharply at the mention of Zorid – "was kidnapped by Sheng-Fat to create torpedoes armed with a substance called zoridium, which appears to bear striking similarities to Daughter of the Sun."

The captain's hands came into view as he emptied the contents of his wooden box onto Master Aa's desk. Doug checked his compass and smiled: due north.

"I recovered these torpedo fragments from the bottom of the

From Doug's sketchbook: Master Aa seen from the laboratory. (DMS 1/63)

South China Sea. As you know, I am duty-bound under the Treaty of Khotan, signed between the Guild and your Order, to inform you of any incidents involving Daughter of the Sun."

Master Aa picked up a shard and turned it over in his fingers. "When detonated, what colour was the smoke from the blast?"

"Blue, I believe."

"This is a concern. Your fears are well founded, Captain. There have been reports of similar explosions from other sources."

"On behalf of the Guild I press you for an alliance to contain this threat…"

Master Aa did not answer straight away. Instead he pulled

a piece of tattered paper from his desk drawer and cast his deep-set eyes over the Chinese characters.

"I recently heard news of the Guild from our brothers and sisters in the western chapter at Khotan," said the Sujing Quantou leader calmly. "An alliance was formed with guildsmen bearing the same name as yours, Captain, for an expedition into the Sinkiang, although I am not aware of the exact nature of the mission or the outcome."

"Yes, my brother and sister-in-law." The captain's voice dropped. "We have lost track of them. What news do you have?"

Becca and Doug looked at one another wide-eyed, and strained to hear more. Master Aa's response was disappointing.

"China is very troubled at present. Communications with the west have become … infrequent."

"Any scrap of information…" pressed the captain.

"I know nothing more." The Sujing leader

SHIP SUNK BY NOTABLE AZURE EXPLOSION

ONLY ONE SURVIVOR RESCUED

SHIPPING TREATY IN PERIL

The *Mandalay Maid*, a 2,000-ton vessel carrying a cargo of rubber from Singapore to Macao, sank yesterday twenty miles south of Hong Kong in a mysterious azure explosion.

The only survivor claims the ship was hit by a torpedo fired from a heavily armoured junk. This news comes just two days after another cargo vessel, the *Perseus*, was sunk in a similar fashion ten miles off Macao. The question being asked by shipping companies around the world is: could there be a new threat in the China Seas – and is the delicate shipping treaty so recently signed in Shanghai now in desperate peril?

Cutting from the 20th April 1920 edition of the *Shanghai Post* (MA 632.43 ZORID)

examined the burn marks on another torpedo fragment. "One thing is certain, Captain – the blue smoke is unique to Daughter of the Sun, and it should not be in the hands of Sheng-Fat."

"The whole matter is most troubling. The threat to world order dictates we must take action immediately. Will you join my proposed alliance?"

"Without hesitation, Captain. There has not been such a grievous threat to our secret covenant for two hundred years. The power of Daughter of the Sun must remain a secret."

"I should like to clear up this business quickly. I plan to sail for India within the month. I ... I have pressing matters to attend to there."

"Quickly? Sheng-Fat is a formidable enemy – his growing influence over the monopolies and protection rackets in the South China Sea makes him rich. His organization – his tong – has grown strong and has a reputation for extreme violence. What do you offer in terms of equipment and strength of men?"

"A ship, well armed and fully crewed. We have ordnance enough, I believe."

"How many men do you have?"

"Twenty, including myself."

"Twenty?" scoffed the Sujing in disbelief. "Gods! Sheng-Fat occupies Wenzi Island, Captain. Have you seen the fortress there?"

"I understand it is a crumbling ruin."

"Crumbling, yes, but built by ancient warlords to be impregnable. The fortress lies up a narrow estuary, fortified with hidden gun positions. The only enemies that have ever breached its walls are earthquakes and plague. I can offer eleven Sujing Quantou fighters, including myself. Eleven plus your twenty – a combined force of thirty-one men. The odds are stacked against us. Thirty-one against three hundred!"

"But what choice do we have?"

"None. The attack must be made."

"I propose a two-pronged assault," stated the captain. "I shall sail up the river and hammer on his front door, while a raiding party gains access to the fortress over the ruined rear walls to either recover or destroy the Daughter of the Sun. Chambois has provided me with a map of the tunnel network which shows a route to the torpedo store."

"Hammer on his front door!" Master Aa laughed so loud the floor vibrated. "You mean the gatehouse, Captain. There is a huge cannon mounted on top of it. You and your ship will be blown out of the water."

"Let me worry about that. If I can get all the way up the estuary and distract Sheng-Fat, can you invade the fortress?"

"It might be possible. But I am concerned about his tong." Master Aa opened a drawer in his desk and took out a heavy leather-bound book. He flicked through the pages until he found what he was looking for. "Yes, let me see. I heard from a contact that four hundred Martini-Henry rifles were shipped to Sheng-Fat just six months ago."

"Ancient single-shot weapons of Zulu War vintage," retorted the captain.

"Four hundred guns and one hundred thousand rounds, Captain. This will be no simple task."

"My ship will take the full brunt of Sheng-Fat's onslaught. Can the Sujing Quantou storm the tunnels and recover the Daughter of the Sun from the torpedo warheads?"

"We will need to be fast. Disarming warheads is laborious.

Detonation would be more simple. I imagine you have thought of a way to get us on and off this island?"

"Of course."

Master Aa sat back. "Sheng-Fat… He is a powerful warlord, it is true. But I smell subterfuge. I suspect the malignancy here does not lie with one lowly pirate. Sheng-Fat is merely the foul soil from which this poisoned harvest of so-called zoridium weaponry has grown. You must ask yourself, Captain, who planted the seed?"

"Who indeed? What do you know of Sheng-Fat and his associates? His name is not Chinese."

"He is half Chinese. His mother was a Sea Dyak from Borneo. He uses the parang and files his teeth, as his Sarawak traditions dictate. He has a talent for bloody and brutal piracy which is second to none in the South China Sea. He takes prisoners whom he holds for ransom and he distributes his captured cargoes through a series of legitimate companies in Shanghai, Macao and Manila."

"And you think he may not be operating alone?"

Master Aa shook his head. "Sheng-Fat is nothing more than a vile criminal. To my mind torpedo manufacture and tooth-sharpening rituals do not sit easily together. This is not his natural territory. I am quite sure he does not work alone."

"You confirm my own suspicions, Master Aa."

"Perhaps our visit to Wenzi Island will give us some answers." The Sujing leader closed his eyes and began to

Master Aa
(from memory)

(DMS 1/67)

mutter under his breath as if in prayer. His facial muscles tightened, and he spoke in staccato sentences, his voice filled with pain and anguish. "The future ... yes ... the future. Is suddenly unclear... A choice must be made... The Ha-Mi ... the ancient purpose ... Ur-Can—" He stopped abruptly and opened his eyes as if someone had jabbed him in the side.

Becca and Doug could hear the captain shifting in his chair as Master Aa's face regained its normal composure.

"It is an honour to rekindle the bond between the Order of the Sujing Quantou and the Honourable Guild of Specialists."

"I too am honoured," replied the captain, bowing his head. "I plan to launch my attack on the night of the next full moon. My ship is rafted to a German tramp steamer opposite the Bund..."

Outside the window there was a slight scuffling noise against the stonework. Master Aa stood and peered out. Reaching out, he grabbed the arm of a boy of about fourteen who was hiding on the sill and dragged him into the room.

"It wasn't me, Master!"

"Wasn't you? What do you mean? You spy on me then you make an excuse? You and your brother are a great disappointment to me!"

"No, it was Xu, Master! He said I was bad at climbing, and that I couldn't even climb a fruit tree. He made me scramble up here. I wasn't listening on purpose—"

"Silence!" boomed the Sujing. "Any more of this and you will not go to Khotan. Give me just one more reason..."

"I bet he's the one who took my hanky," whispered Doug to Becca back in the laboratory.

"I'll bid you good day, sir," said the captain. "I too have family matters to attend to."

The only known photograph of Sheng-Fat.

SHENG-FAT

Conflicting accounts of this notorious pirate make it impossible to form a coherent biography. Certainly he was a warlord of brutal reknown who operated from Wenzi Island in the South China Sea. Two sources from a private library in Macao cast more light. The first, a secret report compiled by a shipping company, states:

Shing-Fat: Our Hong Kong contact reports he is the son of a Chinese pirate; his mother is a headhunting Sea-Dyak. His father died when he was seven during a pirate battle off Bias Bay (Shing-Fat is reported to have tended to dying father). His mother subsequently set up home with an English schoolteacher in Shantou. At seventeen, Shing-Fat ran away to sea with his brothers (Chung-Fat and Li-Fat) to avenge their father's death.

And from the second, a copy of a police report:

NAME: Sheng-Fat AGE: 45
PHYSICAL DESCRIPTION: Sharpened teeth. V-shaped chin scar borne by all members of Sheng-Fat's tong (see Tongs: Sheng-Fat).
FAMILY BACKGROUND: Father, English. Mother, Sea Dyak. Takes his name from his Borneo lineage.
CRIMINAL ACTIVITIES: Believed to have legitimate business interests in Shanghai and Manila. Operates several fishing-fleet protection rackets in South China Sea. Suspected ransomer, hijacker and smuggler. Listed as dangerous. Feared by criminal competitors. [Photographed landing at Bias Bay by our agent using hidden camera. Agent disappeared two weeks later.]

The young MacKenzies heard his chair scrape back on the rough boards. Becca panicked: they had to get back to their seats fast. She looked around for Doug, but he was already running. They shot out of the laboratory, belted round the corner and arrived back where they should have been just as Master Aa's office door opened.

The captain strode out swinging his walking stick like a band major. "Now, Rebecca and Douglas, to the hotel without delay."

CHAPTER NINE

From Doug's sketchbook: Madame Zing Zing's Hotel. (DMS 1/70)

Becca's diary: 22nd April 1920
Madame Zing Zing's Tea House and Hotel,
Quai de France, French Concession, Shanghai

We arrived at Madame Zing Zing's Tea House and Hotel at the same time as Mrs Ives, the Duchess and our luggage – although I was horrified to find that Mother's correspondence box had been left behind in my cabin. The captain promised to send it on, then shook us both by the hand, saying he was sorry it hadn't all worked out a little better. After the conversation we'd overheard at the fireworks factory, Doug looked for all the world like he'd just been swindled out of a large sum of money. I suppose he thought that if he'd behaved over the last few weeks he would still have been aboard a ship that was about to raid a pirate fortress. I very much doubt the captain would have taken us on the mission with him under any circumstances.

At the very least, we know a little more about Mother and Father – that they went into the Sinkiang with members of the Sujing Quantou to protect them. It's so frustrating. Just as we're getting somewhere with all this we're being sent away.

Madame Zing Zing

(DMS 1/71)

Madame Zing Zing's Hotel looks as if it has been transplanted brick by brick from Paris. I don't like it at all – it gives me the creeps. And Madame Zing Zing actually exists! She's a carefully coiffured Frenchwoman who snaps around pursued by seven poodles, issuing orders to her handful of downtrodden staff. These highly manicured pets yap in unison at guests and staff alike, biting anyone who gets in their way – all apart from the Duchess, of course, who roars with such menace that they retreat en masse behind the reception desk.

The head porter is an elderly German named Otto who looks a bit down at heel. Doug was laughing and joking with him after a couple of minutes. How does he do that? All I managed was a polite hello.

The plasterwork may be falling off the walls of this monstrosity, but what a view! From the balcony I can see the breathtaking sweep of the river all the way up to the Bund – the waterway is crowded with a thousand sampans, junks and ships. In our room the air is tainted with the smell of the river. The street below is a shifting mass of people talking, laughing and going about their business. It's an energetic city, and I think I quite like it.

Doug and I have just watched Expedient's *brick-coloured funnel edge out downstream. Doug watched through his binoculars, but I could see her well enough. Only a few weeks ago, we set sail with her on that very stretch of water. This time we were left behind, and I felt a curious and unexpected pang in my stomach. Despite everything that happened on the* Expedient, *we made some good friends there. Watching them sail away made me feel, well, homesick.*

BECCA AND DOUG'S ROOM AT MADAME ZING'S

Pages from Becca's Operation Red Jericho journal (see appendix 6) showing her rough plan of their room, next door to Mrs Ives's.

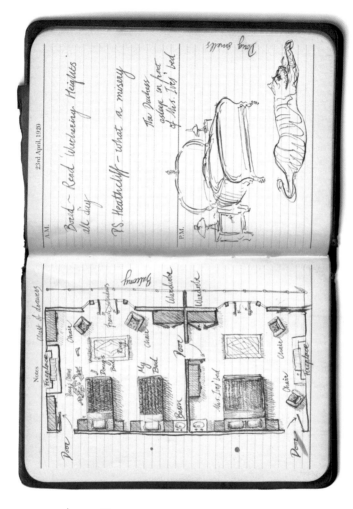

23rd April, 1920

A.M.

Bored ~ Read 'Wuthering Heights' all day

P.S. Heathcliff ~ what a misery

P.M.

The Duchess asleep in front of Mrs. Ives' bed

Doug snooze

Notes (Kept & drawers)

Door

Fireplace

Doug's trunk

Chair

Doug's Bed

French windows

My Chair

My Bed

Gallery

Wardrobe

Door

Basin

Wardrobe

Mrs Ives' bed

Chair

My trunk

Door

Just as the ship slipped out of sight her signal lamp winked back at us. The Morse message read: DON'T MUCK ABOUT DOUGLAS. BON VOYAGE TO BOTH OF YOU. CH-CH-CHARLIE.

Early on the fourth morning at Madame Zing Zing's, Becca and Doug found a handwritten note slipped under their door. At first Becca was alarmed by the letter, then intrigued, then highly suspicious, and finally mystified as to its origin.

The previous three days had been excruciatingly monotonous. Becca had read *Wuthering Heights* (twice), while Doug had spent most of the time on the balcony glued to his new binoculars, a parting gift from the crew. After two days he could list any ship moored in the harbour, and where it was registered.

What really irked Becca was that all tours of Shanghai were banned on the captain's orders, although Doug had managed to get hold of a guidebook from the hotel's library. The novelty of spotting buildings on the Bund with the binoculars and cross-referencing them against the fold-out map lasted for about eight minutes.

So the days had dragged by, until they received the mysterious message. Now Becca stood on the balcony gazing out at Shanghai's morning traffic while Doug made an "intelligence sortie" at her instigation. Mrs Ives was closeted in Madame Zing Zing's parlour downstairs. Finally alone, Becca looked over the note again:

Sheng-Fat's Daughter of the Sun comes from the Sinkiang. His brother, the ransom broker Chung-Fat, will be found in the fan-tan club at the House of Idle Delights near the junction of

The view along the Bund. (MA 449.16 SHANG)

the Pon Lai and Voo Ming roads at midnight. His table is on
the first floor beside the red birdcage. He may sell information
about the Guild mission to the Sinkiang for a price.

Doug burst onto the balcony. "The porter says it's a gambling
house in the middle of the old Chinese city."

"You didn't tell him what was in the message?"

"Do you think I'm stupid?"

"Yes."

"Do we go, Becca?"

"I'm extremely suspicious. Who can have written this? But
if there's a chance to discover anything about Mother and
Father and what they're doing in the Sinkiang before we go
back to Aunt Margaret's, we have no choice."

"Good, because I've already found a way to slip out of
the hotel."

"That's a surprise. How?"

"Well, there's this door which leads to a balcony," he revealed, digging out two of Becca's hairgrips from his back pocket.

"Is there now?" said Becca with a thin smile.

"This must be it," said Doug, checking his map again. Fabric banners decorated with Chinese script hung in long strips outside the building. A couple of well-built doormen guarded the entrance. "Ten to midnight. We're early."

"The House of Idle Delights," read Becca with growing unease. She clambered out of the rickshaw and paid the fare.

They had disguised themselves as sailors. Rather young sailors admittedly, but Doug had seen quite a few on the Bund who weren't much older than himself. They still had their sea coats from the *Expedient*, and with their collars turned up and woolly hats pulled down, they thought they could get away with it. In Shanghai, people asked very few questions.

The sound of jazz drifted out of the fan-tan club, swelling momentarily as a grotesque chorus line of dancing Russian sailors burst out of the entrance. One of them raised a vodka bottle in salute to a white Rolls-Royce Silver Shadow which splashed through a puddle and pulled up outside.

Becca and Doug watched as a man in a panama hat and a white linen suit stepped out of the car and strode forward with a nod to the doormen. The brim of his hat hid his features, but he was clearly a westerner, and walked with a distinct swagger.

"That's him!" murmured Doug, pushing Becca into the shadows.

THE CHINESE
QUARTER,
SHANGHAI

*A postcard of
Shanghai found
among Rebecca
MacKenzie's papers.
There is a note on the
back dated 21st April
1920, which reads:*
Dear Rebecca and
Douglas,
Good fortune in all
your endeavours.
Your friend,
Luc Chambois.

From Doug's sketchbook: The man in the white linen suit. (DMS 1/72)

"Who? Chung-Fat?"

"No, the man who kidnapped Chambois! Linen Suit! This is a trap. He must have sent the note. I *knew* it was too easy."

"What do you mean?"

"Chambois was kidnapped by a man in a white linen suit, driving a Rolls-Royce. It's got to be him."

"Oh, Doug, it could have been anyone. He'd hardly ship a Rolls-Royce all the way from Paris, would he?"

"Maybe it's not the same vehicle."

"Maybe it's not the same man, more like." However, the seed of doubt had been sown. "I suppose it's possible… But what would he want with us?"

"I'm not marching in the front door to find out. He's best friends with Sheng-Fat."

A dishevelled figure lurched towards them from a side alley – another drunk Russian sailor. He pushed past Becca and shouted at his eight friends, who were trying to hire a rickshaw built for one passenger.

"Where did that sailor come from?" asked Becca.

"There must be a back entrance," guessed Doug. Without a word, they slipped down the dark alleyway. It opened onto a scruffy courtyard lit by the dim glow of windows at the rear of the fan-tan house. A wheelbarrow in one dingy corner gave them some cover while they formed their plan.

"We must get a good look at Linen Suit. Maybe he's here to see Chung-Fat too," mused Doug.

The back door opened. A haggard gambler flicked a dying cigarette butt in their direction, coughed on a couple of lung-fuls of night air and staggered back into the club.

"That must be where the sailor came from. There's no doorman and it isn't locked. We can just walk in."

"Walk in?"

"Yes," sniffed Doug, "and scout around for Chung-Fat and Linen Suit. I can see a staircase through the window. We'll sneak upstairs and start looking there. Once we're in it'll be easy."

"What about the message? Finding out what's been going on in the Sinkiang? That's more important, isn't it?" reasoned Becca, checking she still had the necklace Chambois had given her safe in her pocket, as payment for information.

"Linen Suit has changed all that. Perhaps he's kidnapped Mother and Father too. We'll just have to play it by ear."

"My brain's reeling, Doug. You're making an awful lot of assumptions. We don't even know if Linen Suit is the same man who kidnapped Chambois, and we certainly don't know if he sent the note."

"Well, we'll never find the answers behind this wheelbarrow, will we, Becca?"

"What do we do if we're caught?"

"Just act drunk like the Russian sailors and run for it. Come on."

The place stank of cheap tobacco and sweat, and there was another peculiar odour that Doug realized he'd smelt once before in India – opium. They made it to the second floor without any difficulty and opened the door into the fan-tan house proper. It was laid out over three storeys with balconies on the upper two floors so that spectators could watch the

From Doug's sketchbook: Inside the House of Idle Delights. (DMS 1/79)

game in action on the ground floor, where the players were gathered around a long table.

Becca and Doug found themselves on the smarter upper floor reserved for tourists and regular gamblers. Baskets carrying bets and winnings ascended and descended on strings between floors. A heavy smoke haze hung in the air, dulling the red and gold of the embroidered wall hangings. Nobody seemed to think it strange them being there; one of the attendants, a *tangu*, smiled and offered them a table.

Doug gave the *tangu* a huge grin. "Will Chung-Fat be in tonight?" he asked casually.

The *tangu* smiled and gave a slow bow. "Chung-Fat arrives midnight. His table empty." He was pointing at a table on the balcony below with a red birdcage hanging beside it – just as the note had described.

"We'll take the one in the corner, if you don't mind." Doug headed towards a gloomy corner with an excellent view of Chung's table.

"You place bets with me," said the *tangu*, putting a small plate of watermelon seeds on their table. "I pass bets down to fan-tan table."

Doug shrugged and sat back. "We will watch for a while, my friend. How's the game shaping?"

The *tangu* handed Doug a sheet of paper covered with numbers, then walked away to serve another customer.

"Otto told me about this," enthused Doug, leaning towards Becca. "The numbers written down show the progress of the game for the last fifteen turns."

"We're not here to gamble, Doug," said Becca primly. "We're here for information."

"We must play the part, though."

"We're not gambling!"

Suddenly Linen Suit appeared and made for the table beside the birdcage. His face was still masked by the brim of his hat. He sat down, lit his cigar from the candle lamp and deliberately extinguished the flame in a cloud of thick smoke. He summoned a *tangu* and placed a bet, his cash descending to the gaming table in a basket.

"How long till midnight?" asked Doug.

"Five minutes."

Doug watched the game intently. Linen Suit won consistently, his basket ascending with a steady stream of winnings after each bet placed. It was nearly one o'clock in the morning now. Linen Suit had started to tap his fingers against the balustrade in agitation and kept looking at his watch and the main door. It didn't look as if Chung-Fat was going to show up.

"I have an idea," said Becca, tearing a page from her diary. "If we're not going to get any information from the ransom broker, we can at least satisfy ourselves of one thing. For Chambois's sake."

"What are you going to do?"

"Write a note to Linen Suit. A note that can only mean something to Chambois's kidnapper. If he reacts we'll know we have the right man. Call the *tangu* over. I'll send it down in a basket. How much money do you have?"

"I traded us up a few Mexican dollars with Otto in case of an emergency."

CURRENCY IN SHANGHAI

Two forms of currency circulated: the (much preferred) silver Mexican dollar coin weighing about 1 oz; and the tael, a weight of silver of about 1.3 oz, usually represented in the form of paper money.

The *tangu* arrived and Doug asked him to deliver the note, giving him a hefty tip. Becca wrote CHAMBOIS LIVES in bold capitals. "That should seal it one way or another."

The *tangu* bowed and walked to the other side of the atrium, where he lowered the message.

It took a second or two for Linen Suit to catch on, but he took the bait as the basket dangled in front of him. He read the note and looked up immediately. They saw him clearly. He was in his mid-forties and wore a green silk bow tie and waistcoat. His features were fixed in angry determination, his shifty eyes momentarily widening with fury as he reread the message. He muttered something to himself, then crumpled the paper in his hand until his knuckles went white. Pounding his fist twice on the balustrade, he jerked round to check if anyone behind was watching him, then summoned his *tangu*.

"Got you," whispered Becca in triumph, pulling Doug back into the shadows. Linen Suit's man called up to Becca and Doug's *tangu*, who pointed at the MacKenzies.

"Run for it!" shouted Becca, shoving her brother towards the door before their *tangu* could cut them off. Once out on the small landing they could hear the thunderous clamour of two people crashing down the stairs. Whatever was going on, the MacKenzies instinctively turned and ran up another narrow staircase, using this timely diversion to escape. There was a distant shout of "Stop those two!" but the noise seemed to be dying away, not coming towards them. Nobody was following.

"We've lost them," said Doug.

"But how?"

"I've no idea."

Doug pushed on. They found themselves at the very top of the fan-tan house at the end of a dim corridor. He worked his way along, passing several offices, until he saw a shuttered door which led out onto a rickety balcony overlooking the rear courtyard.

"Through here. They might check the offices."

Becca followed him out into the cleaner night air of Shanghai, and closed the door as quietly as she could. There was still no sign of any pursuers, but suddenly Linen Suit and the two *tangu* burst out into the courtyard far below, chasing after two smaller figures.

"They've got the wrong people – they think those two are us!" murmured Doug. "They've made it to the alley. Linen Suit'll never catch them."

The figures got clean away, running at surprising speed. Linen Suit and the *tangu* gave up the chase and turned to go back into the club. Linen Suit kicked an empty bottle in frustration.

"D'you think it was Linen Suit who sent us the message to come here?" asked Doug.

"No," said Becca. "He's got this place in his back pocket. The *tangu* would have identified us to him immediately if we'd been expected. I'd say that the sender of the note remains a mystery. And I also think our news about Chambois came as something of a shock to Linen Suit."

"Let's wait here till everything calms down, then slip away. It'd be too dangerous to try and meet Chung-Fat while Linen Suit's still here. We can head back to Madame Zing Zing's once the dust has settled."

After a slow hour huddled on the balcony, there was a slight movement in the office next to them.

Becca tensed, expecting somebody to come out and grab them, but no light went on behind the shutters.

A few heart-stopping moments elapsed, then Doug whispered, "Perhaps it was that mangy-looking cat." The animal had hissed and spat at them as they'd taken up residence earlier. "Let's get back to Madame Zing Zing's."

They crept back inside the fan-tan house and down the staircase. Both were nervous, expecting Linen Suit or one of the *tangu* to be lying in wait at every tortuous twist of the stairs. Doug had never felt so jittery on a night sortie, and when they reached the ground floor he froze. Their escape route was blocked by an unconscious gambler slumped across the exit. It was Becca who forged ahead, grabbing the man under the armpits and dragging him far enough out of the way to get by.

"Walk slowly and don't look back," she ordered, edging out into the courtyard. Once in the darkness of the alley they both ran. They reached the street and stopped to check that the coast was clear. Everything on Voo Ming Road looked normal, and the Rolls-Royce was still parked outside. It seemed they'd made it.

"Let's get a rickshaw and get out of here," said Doug.

They crouched in a doorway within sight of the fan-tan club and waited. Becca was the first to speak.

"I can't believe we missed Chung-Fat. This could be our last chance to find out what happened to Mother and Father before we leave Shanghai. If this Daughter of the Sun really does come from the Sinkiang, it's too much of a coincidence. It *must* be connected with their disappearance. Linen Suit kidnapped Chambois to make the torpedoes to house the zoridium. We know Chambois knew Mother and Father. Perhaps Linen Suit did kidnap them too."

"Now *you're* jumping to conclusions, Becca. The Sinkiang expedition might still show up. We have no proof they were kidnapped."

"Why does nobody seem bothered about what's happened to Mother and Father? You heard the captain. He's off to India once the raid on Sheng-Fat's island is over. He has no intention of searching for them. Meanwhile, we're being bundled off to San Francisco. We need to be *here*. In China. This is where the answers are. You saw Linen Suit's reaction to my note. He knows something. We must find out what, not let the captain force us back to lousy Aunt Margaret's."

Doug sniffed and looked at his sister, unconvinced.

"It's just you and me now, Doug. There is nobody else. We have to solve this. I don't want to go to Aunt Margaret's until I've found out. Once I know, I'll be happy to have her bossing me about again. Until then I just can't go back. I cannot get on that steamer. Do you understand what I'm saying?"

Doug looked uncertain. Becca normally took the sensible line. What she was suggesting was far from sensible. In fact it was downright dangerous.

"Why don't we stay and follow Linen Suit's Rolls? See where he goes."

"You know, Becca, I think you've been hanging around with me too much. That's an outrageous plan—"

At that moment the chauffeur started up the Rolls-Royce. The MacKenzies had been so busy talking that they'd missed Linen Suit's exit.

"What do you say, Doug?"

"I don't know, Becca."

"I'm going after that Rolls. Are you coming?"

The car purred by with Linen Suit sitting in the back adjusting his bow tie. He still looked furious. Doug stepped out of the doorway, took a deep breath and hailed a passing rickshaw.

"Can you take two of us?"

The rickshaw puller did his best to keep up with the Rolls, but it was an uneven contest. Judging from the guidebook, the car was heading for the Huangpu River. They swung out onto the river front, and to their relief saw the vehicle some distance away heading south. But their puller was panting hard and progress had slowed to a walk. They paid him and started to run.

RICKSHAWS

Their perseverance was rewarded; just as they were about to lose sight of the Rolls it pulled in next to a jetty. The MacKenzies watched Linen Suit carry a small suitcase up a gangway leading to the nearest junk. The chauffeur turned the car around and accelerated away.

"Whatever happens we must stick with Linen Suit," said Becca.

"That means boarding the junk."

"Exactly."

(From the Japanese jinrikisha, *meaning "man-powered carriage".)*

Common in many parts of Asia, these hand-drawn passenger vehicles can be hired like taxis. They were invented by an English missionary in Japan around 1870.

Junk

"China is the mother of boats"

from Cherish the Sea: A history of sail *by Jean de la Varende*

Sampan

JUNKS AND SAMPANS

Traditional Chinese shipping fell into two categories, both of which carried cargo:
JUNKS: with two or three masts, they could be easily converted to warships by
mounting cannon on their decks and attaching steel side armour. Recognized as
superb sailing vessels, despite having no keel, they ranged in size from river junks
to huge ocean-going ships.
SAMPANS: these smaller boats were propelled by an oar called a yuloh and could
carry a single sail for long river journeys or short trips at sea.

They looked over at the decrepit vessel, which was being loaded with a cargo of fuel barrels by an overhead crane.

"Any ideas?"

"Perhaps we could swim round to the other side of the ship."

"In that river? It stinks, Doug."

"How much money do you have? Enough to hire a sampan?"

"Yes, I think so." Becca rummaged in her coat pocket.

"There are some sampans over there. Let's see if we can get one to run us out to the junk. The river side of the ship will be dark. It's our best chance of getting aboard without anyone seeing us."

They chose an old man whose face was creased like an autumn leaf. He owned a very small, tired-looking sampan that Doug considered the best match to their meagre resources. Becca explained that they wished to pull up alongside the junk with minimum fuss. The boatman was impressed with the amount of money they were offering for such a short journey and accepted them aboard with a nod.

The sampan needed just two oar strokes to get out into the main stream of the river, and they were quickly alongside the junk. The crew were busy shipping cargo into the hold amidships, allowing Becca and Doug to board undetected and with surprising ease.

They edged along the outside of the gunwale and dropped onto the fo'c'sle, making for a hatchway which led below. Hiding in the shadows they paused, hearts pounding, to watch Linen Suit, who was now deep in conversation with the Chinese skipper.

"Apologies," said the skipper. "This delivery was late arriving. Too late to make it to the club. I am very angry."

"Rather be gambling than shipping my boat fuel, heh, Chung-Fat?" said Linen Suit in a crisp English accent.

The skipper laughed and slapped Linen Suit on the back. "Was luck with you, my friend?"

"Yes and no. I lost a couple of... No matter."

Linen Suit shook Chung-Fat's hand and went below through a low hatchway behind the ship's tiller. The skipper shouted several orders then stepped out of the way of the next load of fuel barrels swinging aboard.

"That's Chung-Fat!" whispered Becca excitedly. "We have to keep with them."

Keen to get off the deck, they quickly descended a rotten ladder beneath the hatch and climbed down into a dark, fetid forward cargo hold. Suddenly there were footsteps on the deck above, and the hatch banged shut. Doug shot back up the ladder – but as he reached the top rung he heard the sound of bolts being drawn. The hatch was immovable.

They were trapped.

Chapter Ten

The voices were muffled but Doug could just hear them through the cracks between the deck planks. It was morning now, and the junk had been anchored for about ten minutes.

"...tell Sheng-Fat he'll get his share of the money when I return from Macao." It was the Englishman, Linen Suit. A night's sleep had made him sound more arrogant. "He can kill Liberty now. She's served her purpose. News of the next torpedo attack should put the frighteners on every shipping company operating on the China Seas. With the backlog of cargoes to shift after the treaty, we'll make a fortune."

"I'll tell him," said the skipper.

"Good luck, Chung, and thanks for the lift."

What sounded like a sampan bumped against the junk.

"He's rowing away," said Doug, hearing the slap of an oar on water.

Becca stifled a yelp as something scampered over her foot. The MacKenzies had spent a sleepless night sitting on a rotting tea chest. About six inches of stinking bilge water was slopping about in the hold, so their boots were soaked. To make matters worse, they were not alone. There were rats – and plenty of them. They scuttled and swam by, occasionally scurrying over Becca and Doug's feet with a high-pitched squeak.

Suddenly the cargo hatch clattered open; brilliant morning sunshine flooded the dank hold, blinding them both for a second.

"Topside, topside!" shouted a figure silhouetted above them. "Up, up, up!"

Strong hands gripped Doug by his coat and yanked him out of the hold like a sack of potatoes. Becca received the same treatment, and they were both shoved roughly along the deck.

The air filled with the vibration of a powerful engine, building and drowning out every other noise until it sounded like the roar of a thousand cornered lions. It was a two-seater seaplane, flying so low that it only just missed the junk's mast.

"Linen Suit!" yelled Doug, catching sight of the pilot. Water rained down on the deck as it was blown off the plane's floats by the propeller backwash. Doug traced the wake back to a jetty where the aircraft must have been moored. He saw that they were now anchored in a bay somewhere near the mouth of a river. Overnight they'd sailed for about five hours at the most.

Doug shielded his eyes against the glare of the sun and watched the plane bank around. It was a beautiful biplane – red with a black dragon snaking all the way down the length of its body. The low, sweet sound of its engine hummed away into the distance. As a final touch, Linen Suit barrel-rolled the plane and then climbed up into the clouds.

Any doubts that they were now on board a pirate junk evaporated as Doug noticed the V-shaped scars on every crew member's chin. The MacKenzies were pushed further along until they were standing in front of Chung-Fat, who was stretched out on an elegant deckchair. He was dressed in loose, dark clothes, with a sunhat resting on his sizeable gut. He leered up at them with a sarcastic smile. The coldness in his eyes could have stopped a lava flow.

CHINESE PIRACY

Piracy conjures up images of the Caribbean, Blackbeard and buried treasure. But for sheer scale and professionalism, Chinese and South-East Asian piracy has a much longer and more notorious history. In 1806, for example, the Hong Kong pirate Cheung Po Tsai commanded 270 junks and a reported 40,000 men, a feat of organization never matched by the brigands sailing the Spanish Main.

For over 600 years South-East Asian waters have been troubled by hijacks, robbery, protection rackets, smuggling, kidnap and ransom; they remain some of the most dangerous sea lanes in the world.

"You have found the passenger accommodation to your liking?"

Becca tried to speak but her mouth was dry.

"You paid the sampan skipper well."

"How did you find out?" asked Doug.

"He works for me. You make a very bad choice. Very bad choice." Chung-Fat yawned. "I ask myself why... Why do you two want to get aboard my junk and hide in that half-flooded hold all night? Do we need more crew?" – this to the bosun – "Are we short-handed?"

The bosun remained silent, leaning against a halyard. Becca and Doug were terrified. This was the worst jam they'd ever been in. This wasn't a schoolteacher or a maiden aunt. This was the brother of a ruthless pirate warlord.

"We've boarded the wrong junk," began Doug. "Perhaps you could return us to Shanghai, and we will pay for our passage and any inconvenience we've caused. Please accept our apologies."

Chung-Fat gave a long, hollow laugh. "Oh, forgive me, I will turn my junk around and return to Shanghai immediately. Perhaps you would like my deckchair to sun yourself on as we cruise back, or perhaps—"

CHUNG-FAT

Doug noted that it was hard to capture the character of this vile pirate. (DMS 1/81)

A sharp scream from the bow made them all look round. A boy of about fourteen had leapt out of a hatch pursued by a pirate wielding a belaying pin. Doug recognized him at once. It was the boy from the Sujing Quantou fireworks factory. He grabbed a broom from the deck to defend himself with and spun with exceptional speed to intercept the cook's first lunge.

"I am Xi, of the ancient and noble Order of the Sujing Quantou," taunted the boy. Chung-Fat frowned in irritation. Xi used the broom handle to cartwheel around, hitting the cook with a series of lightning-fast blows and sending the belaying pin rolling harmlessly away. "You are nothing but a stinking pirate!" He backflipped up onto the gunwale, then flicked the cook's hat off with the brush and swung the handle round to jab his opponent's bulging stomach. He made it look easy, but Doug could tell by the tension in his limbs and the bright light in his eyes that it was not as effortless as it appeared.

"Come here, you little…"

But Xi was too fast: with a jump he climbed a forward halyard and swung clear. The cook lumbered towards him, giving Xi enough time to do a few mocking sweeps of the deck with his broom, whistling a jaunty tune.

"Oh, there you are. I was just brushing up some of the filth on this barge while I waited."

Meanwhile, the bosun was advancing from the other side, but Xi cartwheeled away, knocking the cook to the deck. The bosun drew his parang and made a slashing motion.

"Watch out!" shouted Doug, his fists clenched. With his swordsman's eye, Doug could see that Xi's skills with the broom were exact and rehearsed. Armed with a fighting blade he'd be lethal.

At both ends of the ship the crew began to crowd onto the deck armed with rifles. They were silent and menacing, just waiting for their master to give the word. But Chung-Fat seemed unruffled by this sudden turn of events. In fact, thought Doug, he was clearly rather enjoying it. There were about twenty crewmen and women in total. Xi had seen them, but he continued to fight, undaunted by the number of opponents that might follow the cook and the bosun. Did he really think he could take them all on, one by one? thought Doug. He certainly fought that way.

The bosun attempted a running attack, but with three quick strokes and a sweeping high kick, Xi sent him sprawling into the scuppers. "You think you can catch me, pirate? Ha! I am the Sujing Quantou prodigy, the chosen one, trained from the age of one–two–three–four." As he counted he struck each of the cook's limbs, then rubbed his face with the brush. "And you, my friend the cook, you practise your fighting style in the galley, chopping vegetables!"

"I'll chop you and feed you to the rats," replied the cook furiously.

From Doug's sketchbook: Xi fighting the cook on deck. (DMS 1/82)

Xi shimmied up a rope then somersaulted back onto the deck behind the cook, who turned and tried a series of desperate blows. Xi repelled each with expert timing.

"I do not fight lowlife like you from the backstreets of Shanghai, whose greasy, ill-trained hands look like bunches of ripe bananas," he mocked, grabbing a gutted fish from a bucket near by.

"You are nothing but an overgrown schoolboy!"

"And you are nothing but an overgrown cook, who eats too many of the noodles he fries!" shouted Xi. The cook attacked again, fists and feet flying, but Xi used the broom to vault over him and managed to plant the fish square on his head.

Doug suppressed a laugh.

"Your new hat suits you, my friend," Xi jeered. But he had gone too far. As he leant against the broom handle, he slipped on some fish guts and landed on his backside with a resounding crack. Chung-Fat, still seated in his deckchair, burst into laughter. The bosun ran forward and grabbed the young Sujing, dragging him to his feet. The cook, bent on revenge, slowly removed the fish and picked up his belaying pin.

"No!" cried Becca, unable to stop herself.

But hardly was the word out of her mouth when Chung-Fat clapped his hands. "Enough! Get back to the galley; I want my breakfast."

The cook stared at Xi for several seconds then retreated, wiping fish guts from his head.

"Another stowaway! This one is more dangerous than these others, I think. He fights like a tiger! A Sujing Quantou too. My brother Sheng-Fat will be pleased with this ripe little cargo," gloated Chung-Fat. "Show me your left hands, fingers outstretched."

Becca and Doug raised their hands. Chung-Fat's eyes narrowed. "Yes," he mused. "They are small, but not too small – excellent … excellent. My brother will be delighted to make your acquaintance."

"What shall we do with them?" asked the bosun.

"Separate the Sujing from the others. He could cause trouble. Put him in the aft hold, well away from the fuel. As for these two" – he sneered at Becca and Doug – "show them back to their cabin." He chuckled. "Three good ransom hostages before breakfast, and I haven't even left my chair."

Doug looked for comfort in Becca's eyes, but all he could see was the reflection of his own terror.

CHAPTER ELEVEN

On the morning of the fourth day, the hatch trapping Becca and Doug in the stinking depths of the pirate junk opened and Xi scrambled down, assisted by a blow on the shoulder from a rifle butt. It was the first time they'd seen him since his battle with the cook. He looked thin and pale, but he remained undaunted.

"You two are more trouble than you're worth," said the Sujing without so much as a hello. "If you'd helped me fight, we might have taken the ship or at least swum for the shore! We could have been back in Shanghai by now. You just stood there like slack-jawed fools. Why didn't you help me?"

Becca flushed with anger. "There are at least twenty of them and only three of us. And they're armed. We wouldn't have stood a chance. If you hadn't decided to show off, we might have bribed Chung-Fat to let us go. What are you doing here anyway?"

"Protecting you!" He laughed flatly. "There's the joke!"

"Protecting us?" repeated Doug. "You can't be."

Xi pulled out Doug's old handkerchief and threw it across to him. "Wipe away your idle sweat with that," he said. "We're in this mess together."

"We don't need looking after," insisted Becca.

"Look around you," Xi continued. "After your uncle left the fireworks factory we followed you to Madame Zing Zing's. Master Aa told us to keep a watch on you. He was uncertain of the captain's intentions as there is disharmony in the Guild.

After our Sujing Quantou brothers left Shanghai on board your uncle's ship, Xu and I took matters into our own hands. Who do you think sent you the note?"

"It was you? Why?"

"As a test. Xu and I thought it was your parents who had supplied the Daughter of the Sun to Sheng-Fat. We knew that if Chung-Fat treated you as a friend, then you were our enemy. Chung never showed up, as he was delayed loading his cargo of fuel barrels, but the man in the white suit did—"

"The white linen suit?"

"Yes, him. We know he and Sheng are working together. Master Aa didn't tell your uncle, but the Sujing Quantou have been looking for him for months. When you sent the message to him in the basket—"

"You saw that?"

"Of course. My brother and I were sitting at a table by the door watching your backs. When we saw Linen Suit's reaction, we knew you were on our side."

"So it was you on the stairs – you led them away," said Doug.

"They were all old men in that club. They'd never catch us. We doubled back and saw you hiding on the balcony. The club is owned by Sheng-Fat, by the way. We went back in to have a look around the offices. We saw you leaving the alleyway and hiring the rickshaw. We followed you to Chung-Fat's junk."

"And came aboard," finished Doug.

"I am still under orders from Master Aa. I slipped on board after you. Hungry?"

Doug was astonished by what he'd heard. They had never once sensed that they were being watched.

"Here." Xi threw them a fresh tomato apiece.

"Where did you get these from?" Doug asked in disbelief. The first bite was amazing, the flavour exploding in his mouth. It was the most delicious thing he'd ever tasted. They'd survived the last few days on a daily ration of thin soup and the few dried melon seeds Doug had pocketed in the gambling house.

Xi smiled and pulled out an orange from his tunic. "A Sujing Quantou fighter never reveals his secrets – that is our first lesson."

"Do you have any water?" asked Becca.

"Of course." Xi pulled a bottle of cool fresh water from inside his tunic and handed it over, saying not unkindly, "Small sips – don't drink it all."

Becca swallowed a couple of mouthfuls, then passed the bottle to her brother.

"Here, I found this in the office." Xi handed a note to Becca, who lifted it to a thin shaft of light filtering through a gap in the hatch. She read aloud:

"OK, Chung-Fat, you slimy rattlesnake, you have a deal. I'll get our side to sign the shipping agreement, but if my daughter Liberty's not handed back alive, I'll hunt you down and dig your stinking grave. T da V."

Becca felt for the necklace in the pocket of her sea coat. "So T da V is Liberty's father," she said. "Theodore da Vine."

As the ship altered course, Doug could feel the slow ocean swell ease. Half an hour later an echoing bump through the boat's timbers indicated that they'd arrived at a harbour. Men were moving about on deck; in the neighbouring hold the crew started to unload the consignment of fuel.

"What does he need all that fuel for?" asked Becca.

"It's high-octane fuel," said Xi. "I checked when they were loading it back in Shanghai.

"We have arrived at Wenzi Island," he told them in an urgent whisper. "Prepare for the worst. This tong is vicious."

Becca busied herself ripping the seam of her sea coat's inside pocket; she stuffed her diary and pencil and the necklace deep into the lining and shook out the creases. Doug did the same with his pocket compass. Moments later the bosun shouted down into the hold. "Topside! UP, UP, UP."

From the look on Xi's face it was apparent he was relishing the idea of meeting Chung-Fat again. He bounded up the ladder as if preparing to greet an old friend, but at the top he paused and gazed back at Becca and Doug solemnly. "Something Master Aa always taught me," he called down. "Never fear your enemy: it only makes him stronger."

The MacKenzies clambered up the rotten ladder with much less zeal than Xi. Outside, the dazzling sunlight made them squint for a few moments. Looking around they saw that the junk was berthed in a small harbour at the base of what looked like a sheer cliff. Deep blue water lapped at the harbour walls and large black-headed gulls with sharp beaks rode the swell of the waves and eyed them in an unfriendly way. Even though the day was already hot, a cold shiver ran down Doug's spine.

To the accompaniment of shouts and whistles, the high-octane fuel was being loaded onto small sampans and ferried across to a flooded cave that disappeared into the base of the cliff. The entrance was hollowed out of a great fissure which split the rock to a height of about eighty feet.

Doug followed the line of the crack upwards, shielding his

eyes from the sun's glare. "My God!" he whispered, unable to hide his fear.

Xi and Becca craned their necks and gasped in unison. A magnificent ancient fortress towered above them. The ornate gatehouse jutted out and tapered skywards; it was terrifying. The stone was of a strange green-blue hue, decorated with elaborate age-old carvings of fiendish design. Doug didn't know that it was the work of stonemasons driven by cruel masters centuries before, but he recognized its macabre theme: carved into the rock were images of merciless torture and death wrought by fire-breathing mythical beasts on hapless human beings. Headless bodies danced in fires stoked by cannibals chewing on human bones. Along the base ran a frieze some fifty feet in length, packed with thousands of skulls, their eye sockets hollow and jaws gaping open in an eternal stony death scream. Even Xi was silent, overawed by what he saw.

They were hurried ashore by Chung-Fat and driven up the twisting path which led to the massive bronze gates. One hung awkwardly askew, shaken loose by long-forgotten earthquakes. Over fifty feet high and three feet thick, the gates depicted more devilish scenes: huge, fanged Chinese demons and snarling dragons whose scaly tails snaked up and around to the very top.

But they didn't have time to stand and gawp. Chung-Fat issued a series of staccato commands and they were pushed into line and forced into a running march, with Chung-Fat at the head of the procession and half a dozen brigands at the rear. Through the entrance was a small courtyard. In the corner lay a mean-looking female pirate smoking an opium pipe, her chin disfigured by the V.

carving from left leaf of bronze fortress
gates,
Wenzi Island —
1796.

Detail from the bronze gates of the fortress.[2] (MA 809.114 WEN)

"Where is my brother, the esteemed warlord Sheng-Fat?" demanded Chung.

"Below, in the banqueting hall," came the answer. "He is angry. He expected you at dawn."

Doug's terror deepened. He thought of the state Chambois had been in after his stay at Sheng-Fat's fortress, and shivered. His fist closed instinctively around his little finger.

Some of the massive outside walls still stood on the estuary side, fading into encroaching trees and undergrowth, but most had been destroyed by earthquakes. There was no apparent order – a new bamboo village had been built over what

2 Drawing made during Captain William MacKenzie's 1796 HGS survey of Wenzi Island (see appendix 5).

remained of the old stone fortress. Interconnecting walkways snaked this way and that, bridging gaps in the walls and buildings. Despite all the internal damage, four of the huge towers were still standing, their Chinese roofs sweeping upwards. As they walked into the central courtyard Becca and Doug froze: four rotting heads were impaled on bamboo poles, eyes staring out and mouths hanging open, as if gasping for their last breath. The air had a sickly-sweet smell. Doug felt himself gag. He quickly turned to Becca, who looked as green as he felt.

They were urged on towards one of the few original stone buildings that remained intact. The frontage was dominated by two bronze doors carved with scenes of death by fire.

"I think I'm beginning to miss Aunt Margaret's..." began Becca, seeing the dark stone staircase that dropped downwards like some lost portal to the underworld.

"No talking," growled Chung-Fat. He grabbed them both and pushed them after Xi.

At the bottom of the stairs they reached a long vaulted stone undercroft that had been set up as a kind of banqueting hall and that was clearly the heart of Sheng-Fat's operation. It was not as dark as might have been expected. Part of the roof had collapsed, and through this fracture daylight flooded in, piercing the smoky atmosphere. They could hear the screams of someone in great pain.

At the end of the hall a shaft of sunlight shone down on a man who could only be Sheng-Fat. He sat in a gilded chair elevated on a crude stage, the light lending it the dazzling appearance of a throne. The warlord's intense menace suffocated the room. His face was without any compassion or the slightest hint of humanity; the chill of his stare could have changed summer into winter.

A woman prisoner writhed on the floor in front of him, cradling her hand and howling with pain. Some of Sheng-Fat's tong were ranged around the hall, watching the warlord's latest entertainment.

Sheng-Fat shifted in his seat and straightened up to get a better look at his brother's new prisoners. Doug focused on the jewellery hanging around his neck. Becca must have seen the ghastly finger-bone necklace too, because she thrust her clenched hands behind her back and drew in a sharp breath. One of those yellowing fingertips must be Chambois's, thought Doug.

"Listen here, mister," gasped the woman. "You're makin' a big mistake to think my father even wants me back! He hates me more than my mother!" Despite her suffering, her Texan drawl was clear. Sheng-Fat looked bored, as if he'd heard such pleading many times before. "So why don't you let me go, goddammit!" She struggled up into a kneeling position and began to wrap a handkerchief around her bloodied finger, sucking air through her teeth at the excruciating pain.

"Where is the fuel, brother?" demanded Sheng-Fat. He spat out a lump of food, coughed, and wiped his mouth on the back of his sleeve.

"Hey! Don't ignore me! I'm ... I'm talkin' to you!" persisted the woman. Her voice grew weaker as her bravado deserted her.

"It is being unloaded now, and transported to the sea cave." There was fear in Chung-Fat's voice. He shuffled uneasily, head bowed.

"Good. Who are these scrawny wretches? I told you not to waste time taking ransom hostages. I needed the fuel here at dawn."

"I ... I didn't take any prisoners. The shipment was late arriving in Shanghai. These three are stowaways."

Sheng-Fat's eyes narrowed. "They are nothing but children."

"I don't trust them," continued Chung-Fat. "This one is a young Sujing Quantou fighter."

Sheng-Fat shot a glance at Xi. "A Sujing? A surprisingly lucky catch, brother," he said suspiciously. "He may prove useful to our English friend. What of the other two?"

"They crept aboard at Shanghai. I believe they are somehow connected."

Sheng-Fat stood and walked slowly down to the captives. He pressed the rusty blade of his parang to Doug's ear. Doug felt the sharp edge biting into his skin. There was still fresh blood on the blade. The warlord smiled. Doug almost buckled when he saw Sheng's teeth – individually filed to a point and sharpened. Becca had frozen in terror beside him.

"Have you heard of Daughter of the Sun?" barked Sheng-Fat suddenly.

"No ... no," whispered Doug.

"Hey! Why don't you leave the kid alone!" the injured woman shouted.

Chung-Fat turned and kicked her. As she squirmed on the floor swearing, her face was caught in a shaft of light. She looked up at the MacKenzies.

"Liberty da Vine. Pleased to meet you. I'm named after the statue in New York, but I don't hold a torch for no one."

"Silence!" bellowed Sheng-Fat.

Chung grabbed the collar of Liberty's flying jacket and hauled her to her feet, pushing her into line next to Becca. She was a little over twenty; short, with a fringe cut as straight as Cleopatra's and of the same dark hue. The rest of her hair had

LIBERTY DA VINE

Barnstorming daughter of the oil baron Theodore da Vine, Liberty skipped her Swiss finishing school to join a flying circus as a wing-walker and parachutist when she was just eighteen. But Liberty could never be content as a passenger, and her restless nature quickly mastered the art of flying. Her natural talent in the air made her a huge hit on the acrobatic circuit, but her real interest was the purist's quest for speed and endurance.

become impossibly tangled. Her face was bruised and scratched but her eyes had a beguiling glint of danger that bordered on beauty. Her angular cheekbones were still smudged with traces of engine oil that outlined the last position of the flying goggles hanging around her neck like a badge of office. She wore a tattered silk scarf that had been a vivid red, but was now an oil-smeared ochre. Becca felt for the necklace again. It was Liberty's – and now she understood why it was so dirty.

Sheng's attention returned to Doug. "What is your name? What is the girl's name? Won't say? Can't remember? Well, I will ask you again." The pressure of the blade increased. "With this delicate ear, I want to know if you have ever heard of Daughter of the Sun."

"Hurt my brother and you'll regret it!" blurted out Becca, surprising herself and everyone else with the volume and strength of her outburst.

Sheng-Fat stared at her. "The girl has some fire, Chung-Fat. Why will I regret it?" He leant forward to examine her more closely, his voice unnervingly soft. "Tell me, girl."

Doug thought fast, his brain flashing with ideas. Their only hope was to buy time until the captain's attack. "We are Liberty's cousins, Douglas and Rebecca da Vine. We went to the House of Idle Delights to open negotiations to pay her ransom. Your brother Chung-Fat wasn't there, so our guide, Xi, a hired mercenary, took us to his junk. We boarded and became locked in the cargo hold before we could speak."

But Sheng-Fat suddenly appeared to have lost interest. He dropped the blade and returned to his chair. He lit a thick wooden pipe using a candle, then inhaled a mouthful of opium smoke. "There is an easy way to find out how much of this is truth. We will soften these three up in the usual manner. The Englishman will be keen to make your acquaintance, Sujing Quantou. He is interested in anything connected with the Sinkiang. He may even cast some light on these other two stow-aways. Turn out their pockets and search for identification."

"The boy has a key," said Chung-Fat. "That is all. Room 10, Madame Zing Zing's Tea House and Hotel, Shanghai."

"Get a message to Shanghai to investigate. These three can enjoy our hospitality until then – inside the tide cages," sneered Sheng-Fat.

"The Englishman says you can kill Liberty now. She has served her purpose."

"Kill Liberty? Her usefulness to the Englishman may have come to an end, but she is still valuable merchandise. Her father will pay a good price eventually – but I doubt a man such as he would send these children to negotiate."

"No, brother," agreed Chung.

"You two 'cousins' are a mystery. Perhaps the rising tides will cleanse your minds of the half-truths and lies you speak. We will talk again in two days' time when your stomachs are empty and your spirits broken. You will squeal the truth just like the rest. If you are from the da Vine family, I will gladly triple the ransom. Take them away! All of them!"

"Great," wheezed Liberty. "Sunshine and sea air. Just what a girl needs to recuperate."

Doug stumbled forward so he was beside Liberty as they were escorted back across the hall.

"We're friends," he whispered.

"Y'all aren't my cousins, that's for sure," she replied. "Listen, I make enemies quickly and friends slowly. What's that God-awful smell?"

"It could be my socks. They're lucky."

"Lucky for you, maybe," she said, clutching her bloodied handkerchief with a wince. "A darn curse for the rest of humanity."

"You could be right," considered Doug.

"Well, take a look around you, kiddo. Ever think their luck just ran out?"

CHAPTER TWELVE

As an instrument of torture, there were few methods to rival the barbarism of Sheng-Fat's tide cages. These savage devices were located at the estuary mouth, some distance away from the fortress, and relied on nothing more than the power of the sea to strike horror into their victims. They worked on the simple principle that although the tide level rose and fell twice a day, the cages did not. At low water each prisoner hung just above the water. At high water the sea level almost covered the top of the cage.

Doug pressed his face harder against the bamboo roof bars and gasped for air. It was around ten o'clock at night and the water was at its height. He was almost completely submersed, the small estuary waves breaking over him. Every moment was an intense battle of concentration as he tried to predict when the next wave would dip the sea level enough for him to catch his breath.

He could hear Becca and Liberty shouting encouragement, although he couldn't understand where they found the breath. Three times he almost drowned as he tried to gulp air but swallowed only choking sea water.

Then, little by little, the water subsided. Fractionally at first. He thought it was his mind playing tricks. But after an hour and a half fighting for his life, he'd survived. It became easier to breathe.

"We only have to last one more night, then we'll be safe," he said with relief.

"I don't think you've quite gotten the idea of this island, coz," spluttered Liberty. "This place doesn't get safer. Just more and more dangerous. Look at your neighbour in the next cage there." In the moonlight Doug could see the rotting corpse of a drowned man still clutching the bars. The eddies and currents were tugging at his jaw, making his mouth open and shut. "I'll bet y'all that stiff didn't die laughin'."

"Wait till tomorrow night when our uncle attacks – when Sheng-Fat's defeated we'll all have something to laugh about!"

"How's that? Your uncle's attackin' this place?"

"Yes, tomorrow night."

"Whaddya mean, tomorrow night?" There was incredulity and suspicion in Liberty's cracked voice.

"Er, well, yes."

"Doug! You weren't meant to say anything," snapped Becca.

"You want me to believe this?" asked Liberty. "How does he know about this place?"

"Monsieur Chambois told him," confessed Doug.

"*Chambois?* You two know Chambois? Goddammit, I'd given up on that French guy – thought he was a goner. Why didn't you tell me earlier? And how the hell is your uncle plannin' to tackle this joint?"

"He's going to sail up the estuary. He has a ship with secret guns—"

"Sail up to the fortress! Is he insane?"

"Well, it's a two-pronged assault…"

"What's he gonna use?" she asked, exasperated. "A pitchfork?"

"He's got some help…"

"Oh, Doug, shut up!" Becca finally cried out. "You never could keep secrets."

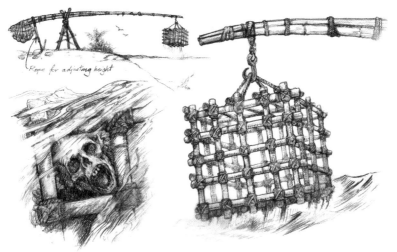

From Doug's sketchbook: Sheng-Fat's tide cages. (DMS 2/11)

"It is true," added Xi. "We, the noble Order of the Sujing Quantou, will attack with him."

"Oh, that's all right then," mocked Liberty. "You're stuck in a bamboo cage, so you're gonna be as much use as a raincoat in Nevada."

"There are many more of us."

"How many more?"

"Thirty-one."

"Thirty-one hundred. That should give Sheng-Fat somethin' to think about," said Liberty enthusiastically.

"No, just thirty-one."

"Oh, no. No, no, no. You've got to be jokin'. Thirty-one? And how many is your uncle bringin', coz?"

"No, you don't understand. The whole assault force is thirty-one people," explained Doug. "And a tigress. Although she's still in Shang—"

"No. Please don't tell me any more. It's a lot of ill-fated hokum."

"It's all true. If we can hang on until tomorrow night we can get aboard the *Expedient*," said Becca.

"Now *you* just hang on a minute. You said your uncle was gonna sail up this estuary. Does he know about the cannon on the top of the gatehouse?"

"Yes."

"So he must have thought of a way round that. But he's gonna fail."

"What do you mean?"

"He won't know about the Dragon's Teeth. There's a winch that connects to iron chains in the estuary. They pull up a set of iron spikes. A ship can sail up to the fortress, but she'll never get away. The bottom will be ripped out of her like a tin opener cuts through a can of beans. The whole plan is doomed."

"But Chambois will have told the captain. He surveyed the fortress."

"Don't bet on it! Chambois knew nothin' about them. I only found out a couple of weeks back when we were forced to grease the liftin' chains in the winch room."

Doug could just make out the splash of someone paddling towards them. At first he assumed it was one of Sheng-Fat's men and he froze, a tingle of fear running through his body at what might have been overheard.

"Xi! Xi, it's me. Xu!" came an excited whisper from the darkness.

"About time! Where have you been?" demanded Xi.

"I couldn't get off the junk until after dark."

In the moonlight Xu looked uncannily like Xi. In fact they were identical – identical twins. So there had been two of them on Chung-Fat's junk, Doug realized. That was how Xi had got supplies of fresh food and water. Xu had hidden aboard undetected.

Xi began to chide his brother. "Why didn't you help me fight the cook? You are as useless as these two!"

"We were outnumbered. You were lucky they didn't shoot you to pieces with their rifles. Even Master Aa could not have fought that many."

"Where did you hide?" wondered Becca.

"Hey, look, this is fun and all, but I'd sure be obliged if your brother there could get me out of this darned bamboo corral. We've got work to do and time's a-wastin'," cut in Liberty. "If this uncle guy is comin' here to slug it out with Sheng-Fat, we need to sabotage the Dragon's Teeth or we'll be takin' up permanent residence on this stinkin' rock."

XU AND XI

The Sujing Quantou twins had completely different characters – Xi was impetuous and arrogant, Xu quiet and thoughtful. Xi had been trained from birth to be the chosen Sujing prodigy, and never let Xu forget it.

"I will go back to the harbour and find a heavy blade to cut through the bamboo," said Xu.

"You do that, pal," yelled Liberty as Xu swam away. "And if you see Sheng-Fat, tell him I've had just about enough of this parrot in a cage routine. I ain't squawkin' pieces of eight for no one!"

"Liberty!" exclaimed Becca. "I'd completely forgotten. I have your necklace."

"What?"

"You gave Chambois a necklace. It's in my pocket."

"Well, I hoped I'd never see that pug-ugly trinket again. Don't throw it over, honey, with this river between you and

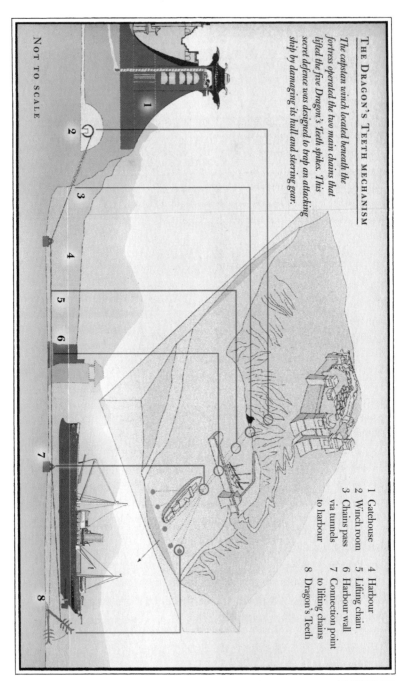

THE DRAGON'S TEETH MECHANISM

The capstan winch located beneath the fortress operated the two main chains that lifted the five Dragon's Teeth spikes. This secret defence was designed to trap an attacking ship by damaging its hull and steering gear.

NOT TO SCALE

1 Gatehouse
2 Winch room
3 Chains pass via tunnels to harbour
4 Harbour
5 Lifting chain
6 Harbour wall
7 Connection point to lifting chains
8 Dragon's Teeth

(MA 809.34 WEN)

me. But you could use it to start sawin' your way to freedom
through the vines of that there bamboo cage – just in case
our new friend doesn't come good with the blade, you
understand."

Xu didn't come good with the blade. As night turned to day,
the captives learnt the full horror of their torture. With each
passing hour the cages became more claustrophobic and the
inevitability of the next high tide gnawed at their exhausted
minds. Doug knew it would be higher than the last – the
moon had been almost full, which meant a rising spring tide.
How much higher? The last one had been a struggle. The next
might be deadly. But Sheng-Fat knew this, and as the tide
climbed towards the top of the cages late in the morning, his
men arrived to raise them just enough to prevent the captives
from drowning – so prolonging their torment.

Only two things happened during the day to distract the
prisoners' minds from these appalling thoughts, and both
were to do with seaplanes. A large cargo plane landed right in
front of them and taxied into the harbour. Ten minutes later it
took off again. Liberty described it as a "mutt of a plane" and
thought it belonged to a company based in Shanghai. The
second plane they heard but did not see, as it landed higher
up the estuary beyond the fortress. Liberty recognized the
engine note, however, and launched into a tirade of curses.

By ten o'clock that night their bamboo prisons were already
three quarters filled with water as the flood tide rose yet again.
Doug dreaded the waves as they lapped higher and higher
around his neck. The insects that had swarmed in their thousands around his dead neighbour all day were nothing; it was

the sea that terrified him. The constraint of not being able to poke his head above the height of the cage was excruciating. Worst of all was being trapped under the waves, struggling for air as the wake from a passing junk completely submerged the bars for several terrifying seconds. He rattled the hinged roof for what seemed like the thousandth time that day.

"Where have you been? Shanghai?" It was Xi, who had just spotted his brother swimming towards them. "You were meant to return last night!"

Xu drifted downstream towards the tide cages, making very little movement. He reached out and grabbed the side of his brother's cage. "Be grateful I came back at all," he retorted, wiping the water from his face and pulling a small rusted parang from his belt.

"Is that it?" said Xi in disgust. "Is that what we've waited all day for?"

"You are lucky to get this. I was forced to hide in the undergrowth. Hurry, there are armed men approaching."

Further down the estuary flaming torches danced towards them through the trees.

"There are ten of them. I saw them leave the fortress half an hour ago," whispered Xu.

"They're coming to take us to Sheng-Fat," said Doug.

"Quick," ordered Xi. "Cut the bindings. We must escape before they reach the beach."

Xu swung up on top of Xi's cage and started to hack at the vine holding one of the side bars. Becca had been working on her cage all day with Liberty's necklace. It was large as a piece of jewellery but small as a cutting tool, and progress had been painfully slow. She'd only managed to get through half of the bindings and the bar was still solid.

"How long till they get to the beach?" asked Becca, kicking the bamboo in frustration.

"Five minutes, maybe less," replied Doug.

Xi braced himself against the other side of his cage and pressed his foot hard on the bamboo bar. Xu worked fast, cutting and slitting. Finally it gave way, and Xi squeezed through the gap and swam towards Becca's cage.

"No! Time's too short," Becca said. "I have the necklace, I might still get through. Leave me till last."

Xu and Xi didn't argue, and moved on to Doug's cage.

Liberty was becoming impatient. "Those torches aren't gettin' any farther away."

Doug did exactly as Xi had done, pushing against the bar as the Sujing twins worked on the bindings. Like a rotten tooth, the bar gave, and he squeezed out. Liberty's cage was next, but almost immediately they began cutting, the blade snapped and a sizeable piece dropped into the water.

"What are you doing?" Xi snapped, as if his brother were some humble apprentice.

"Just hold your tongue and pull the bar."

"Don't tell me what to do! I am the Sujing Quantou prodigy—"

"I–am–the–Sujing–Quantou–prodigy!" imitated Xu, nodding his head from side to side.

"Come on, guys. We don't have much time."

The torches were so close now that they could smell the smoke, but the pirates still hadn't seen what was going on. Becca worked harder with the necklace, tugging at the bar. Doug swam over to help her.

"Doug, get ashore and hide," she ordered.

"I'm not going anywhere. You're getting out of this cage."

"There's no time. You must get to the winch room with Liberty or the attack will fail."

Fierce cries and wild rifle shots sliced through the darkness as the guards finally realized the prisoners were escaping.

"I'm not leaving you here," Doug insisted.

Becca was resolute. "You have to go with the others. You four have a chance of saving us all. Go with Liberty."

After a struggle and a lot of swearing, Liberty was finally free. "How're you doin' over there, cousin Rebecca?" she called.

"It's no good. Take Doug with you. Get to the winch room."

The guards were less than two hundred yards away and racing to close the distance.

Doug looked at his sister trapped behind the bars.

"You've no choice," pleaded Becca.

"She's right," agreed Liberty. "Come on, kiddo."

"Doug – just go!"

He hesitated. "I'll come and find you as soon as we've sabotaged the winch room."

There was no more time. Liberty pushed Doug into the water. "Hang on as best you can," she called back. "Remember, Becca, you're more valuable to Sheng-Fat alive than dead."

The four fugitives swam away into the shrouding safety of the night. The tide was swift and dangerous, the current carrying them fast. Liberty led the way, aiming for a spur of land that would take them into the heart of the undergrowth that covered the island. As Doug's feet touched the soft sand, he looked back at Becca's tide cage and saw it surrounded by a swarm of angry torch flames.

CHAPTER THIRTEEN

After landing on the beach, Doug and the others had slipped into the undergrowth to escape their pursuers. Xu and Xi seemed naturally skilled at this and, using their Sujing training, had diverted, frustrated and confused Sheng's guard. They'd worked their way back towards the fortress to a point about four hundred yards east of the walls, where they thought it safe to await the captain's attack. They were now quite a way up the side of the hill and had an excellent view of the estuary in the cool moonlight.

"The winch room is deep in the fortress tunnels. The only way to reach it will be under cover of the captain's attack," said Liberty. "We'll let him get in close and open fire, then we'll run for the breach in the wall." She pointed at the first of three huge cracks in the fortress wall. "Now stick close to me, coz, and don't go wanderin' off."

"Why can't we go now? Before he attacks."

"He'll need the element of surprise, and we'll need the pandemonium inside the fortress to get us in undetected. It'll be a close call."

"D'you think we can do it?"

"Hell knows, Doug. This sure isn't the night I'd have chosen. You can see for miles. I hope your uncle knows what he's doin'."

Below they could see the ribbon of water stretching out to the open sea, glinting in the full moon. Visibility was remarkably good. To their right they could see the high fortress walls and the monstrous gatehouse cannon. About a hundred feet below them was one of several carefully hidden gun positions they'd had to skirt around to avoid the search parties that had been pursuing them since their escape. The artillery piece was a breech-loader, not dissimilar in size to *Expedient*'s aft twelve-pounder, and a danger to any attacking ship in the enclosed waters below. They could see and hear the three-man gun crew laughing and joking. Doug felt increasingly uneasy. Sheng's men would have a clear shot whenever the *Expedient* came into range.

Xu and Xi, who had been off scavenging, returned with a bundle of loose grass and sticks.

"You twins sure are strange," Liberty mocked. "This isn't a nature ramble."

"We will need to help the captain with as many diversionary tactics as we can," countered Xi.

"What're y'all gonna do, surprise Sheng-Fat into surrender with a darned bird's nest?" Liberty chuckled.

Doug settled into a hollow in the boulder behind him. He thought about Becca and the last dreadful moments at the tide cages. There had been a terror in her eyes that had gripped and twisted at him ever since. Could they have got her out of the cage? Did they flee too soon? A cold, terrible realization struck him: if their mother and father were dead, and if Sheng-Fat killed Becca, then he would be alone in the world. He turned and tried to find comfort in the rock. His mind drifted to the finger-bone necklace. Exhausted, he fell into a fitful sleep.

"Bring her here." Sheng-Fat's eyes flashed with madness. He slid off his seat and drew his parang. "So you are the only hostage left. And this fat cook we found in Shanghai."

A rotund figure was pushed from the shadows towards the steps of the banqueting hall's stage.

"Mrs Ives!"

"Rebecca! What *is* going on?" Mrs Ives's smile of surprise rapidly turned into a scowl. She put her arm round Becca and said in a whisper, "You and I are going to have a little chat about all this later. Running off from Madame Zing Zing's. I've not slept a wink through worry … had the police scouring the place… Where's your brother?"

"On the island somewhere. I'm so sorry, Mrs Ives."

"Not as sorry as you'll be when the captain hears what you've been up to. He doesn't take kindly to people disobeying orders."

Becca grasped Liberty's necklace tighter in her hand and moved closer to the comforting bulk of *Expedient*'s cook.

"We should drown them both at the next high tide," spat Chung-Fat.

"Drown the entertainment?" Sheng laughed. "Where is the fun in that? We will make them dance for us first, brother. They will dance to the tune of their own tortured screams."

Sheng-Fat flashed a conspiratorial smile, baring his freakish teeth. Becca and Mrs Ives were shoved up the steps to the platform where his makeshift throne stood. Sheng's eyes were deep-set and almost impenetrably dark in the gloom; as he bent down close to Becca's terrified face, the yellowing finger bones of his ghastly necklace jangled

THE PARANG

A sword used in South-East Asia, particularly the South China Sea, Malaysia, Indonesia and the Philippines. The handle is of carved wood and the blade is sharpened on one side only. Ideal for use in close-quarter skirmishes such as boarding ships during hijacks.

in front of her. There were at least seventy of the gruesome mementoes.

"You! Who are you? Why did you stow away on my junk in Shanghai?"

Becca didn't answer because she was shocked to see the Duchess shackled to one of the stone columns. She was straining at her chain and roaring at Sheng-Fat.

"Duchess!" whispered Becca.

"Oh, you like my new pet? If her temper does not improve, I will have her made into a rug."

The Duchess fixed her wild gaze on Sheng-Fat's neck and tried to pounce, almost throttling herself as the chain cut into her throat.

"I'd like to see you try," said Becca. She turned to Mrs Ives. "How did they get her here?"

"They drugged both of us. Filled the hotel room with some foul-smelling smoke. I expect Madame Zing Zing thinks we ran off without paying our bill!" Mrs Ives wiped her eyes with the back of her hand.

"You must have arrived by cargo plane. We saw it land."

"Yes, trussed up like a roasted chicken, I was—"

Sheng-Fat grabbed Becca by the hair and yanked her head back. "Why did you board my junk?"

"I didn't—"

"Why?"

"I think I may be able to cast a little light on our mystery guest here, Sheng-Fat." Becca recognized the voice. It was Linen Suit; his words were pronounced in a tight, controlled manner as if he was restraining great anger. He stood on a crumbling balcony above the stage, half hidden by shadows.

"The face is familiar. I saw her in your gambling house the night of my departure from Shanghai. She had an accomplice."

Would he mention the note? thought Becca. Would he mention Chambois? Linen Suit strode down a ruined staircase and onto the stage.

"Gamblin' house?" echoed Mrs Ives with incredulity. "Gamblin' house? This just gets worse and worse!"

"I hear she's been masquerading as a da Vine. Well, let me tell you, she's not, Sheng my old friend. I would guess … yes … now I see her properly she looks rather like a MacKenzie to me."

"She is not a da Vine?"

"No. Definitely not."

"The name MacKenzie means nothing to me," said Sheng-Fat. "Are they rich? Will the family pay a good ransom?"

"One of the reasons I like working with you, Sheng, is that you always get straight down to business. I'm afraid that the MacKenzies have always pursued honour and duty over wealth. It is their great weakness."

"Honour and duty do not pay."

"Indeed not, old chap. Still, a remarkable coincidence that she is here."

"We were at the gambling house to find out about our parents. We had a tip-off that Chung-Fat might know something. They were on an expedition to the Sinkiang," conceded Becca.

"There's no need to tell me what your parents were up to, young lady." Linen Suit sniggered. "No need at all."

Becca's heart missed a beat. Linen Suit knew…

Without warning, Sheng-Fat flew at Becca, grabbing her arm so hard she was almost knocked flat.

"If you are of no ransom value to me, I will have your finger all the same!" he snarled. Sheng twisted her little finger free and positioned the rusty blade of his parang just below the joint, running his tongue along his sharpened teeth with relish. Becca's stomach sickened in anticipation of the agony to come.

Suddenly a terrible crashing explosion shook the banqueting hall, taking everyone by surprise. A huge block of masonry fell from the vaulted roof, sending up clouds of dust. There were shouts and cries from the pirates, and the brothers looked at each other in alarm. Sheng-Fat pushed Becca to the ground and glared up at the roof.

"You'll not see another dawn, Sheng-Fat!" shouted Becca.

Linen Suit's face creased with fury. "Fitzroy MacKenzie. It's got to be. Only he would be so idiotically bold."

"Man the gatehouse and walls!" ordered Sheng-Fat, grabbing a rifle and running for the door.

Linen Suit strode forward and took hold of Becca by the collar of her sodden sea coat. "You and I are going to the gatehouse to see what's going on, young MacKenzie. You may prove useful yet. Put the old woman back in her cage," he ordered Sheng's men. "The MacKenzie family is remarkably tenacious, is it not?" he added, returning his attention to Becca.

She glanced at him, her eyes brimming with hate and fear. She had nothing to say.

"An honourable characteristic that will undoubtedly be its downfall."

"Hey, coz. Rise and shine!"

The quiet of the night was ripped in two as *Expedient* fired. Doug blinked his eyes open.

"The big game's on and it's time we got off the bench!"

"How long have I been asleep?" he asked excitedly, rubbing his eyes.

"A half-hour or so. Your uncle's attackin'. He's doin' it, just like you said. Darn it, if I live to be a hundred… Look at the estuary. See that fog?"

"Fog? There can't be fog on a night like this. It's not possible," said Doug. But a thick white fog bank was rolling up the estuary; it had a ghostly appearance that was more than a little eerie.

"I guess you're right. You said your uncle had a plan to get himself up the estuary. My bet is he's gone and built himself a fog machine … but I didn't hear any engines."

Doug's mind flicked back to his last night on board *Expedient*. The captain had been talking to Chambois about fog-machines. And what about the secondary engines?

Wenzi Island DM. 1920

From Doug's sketchbook: Fog rolling up the estuary. (DMS 2/23)

"Not if she's using her electric drive."

"What?"

"You wouldn't hear her if she's using her electric drive. *Expedient*'s got electric engines. She can run silently for short distances. Chambois and the captain must have constructed a fog generator."

"That French guy is chock-full of good ideas, isn't he just?" remarked Liberty.

Xu and Xi were still busy with their collection of grasses and sticks; they had woven a large basket with a long plaited rope attached to one end.

"Get ready to move out. Hey, y'all can leave the shoppin' basket behind, twins." The *Expedient* rattled out another devastating salvo. "Boy, he's firin' more than just a popgun down there, coz!" The shells impacted on the rock beneath the gatehouse in an ear-shattering explosion.

"I told you he'd attack, Liberty!"

Xu and Xi hardly looked up. Xi was rubbing two sticks together, generating an amber glow which flared into flame as Xu set light to a handful of kindling grass; the woven basket positioned alongside caught immediately. Xu took the rope and began spinning the blazing basket around his head, faster and faster, then released it and sent it flying down towards the hidden gun position below.

"Sujing Quantou!" shouted Xi.

"Sujing Cha!" screamed Xu.

Liberty and Doug looked on in utter astonishment.

The fire basket circled down and landed on the shells and cordite charges. With a phenomenal explosion, the gun blew up in a scorching fireball. Smoke and flame blasted upwards just as Liberty managed to push Doug behind the cover of the rock.

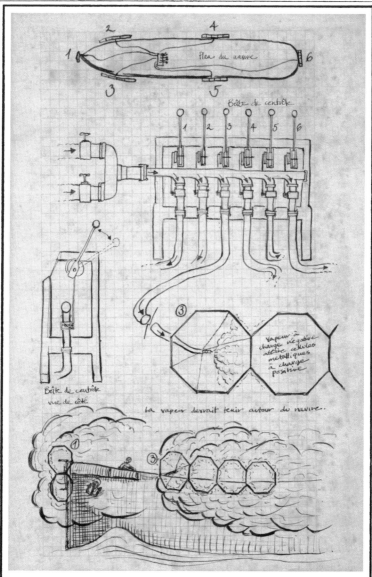

CHAMBOIS'S FOG GENERATOR

A device cobbled together from spare parts found on the Expedient. *This page from Chambois's notebook shows some of his detailed working sketches. See appendix 3 for an explanation of its working principles.*

"Don't you ever try that, d'you hear? That's just not safe."

"Not likely," muttered Doug, reeling from shock.

"Good. Come on now. We've got a winch room to sabotage."

Linen Suit and Becca scaled the last few steps to the gun platform high on the gatehouse tower. Sheng-Fat and his brother had arrived there only moments before. The gatehouse gun was silent, its huge barrel aimed hopelessly at the estuary swamped with Chambois's dense fog. The gun crew cringed away as the warlord strode towards them brandishing his parang.

"Shoot, you fools!" Sheng screamed.

"We cannot see the target, master," ventured the shaking gun captain. "Some of the men think it is a ghost ship. Spirits returned to seek vengeance!"

Becca did some quick mental calculations and reckoned Sheng-Fat's gun was about an equal match to the *Expedient's*.

"I said FIRE!" screamed Sheng-Fat again.

At that moment the *Expedient* discharged another salvo.

"There's your target! Aim at the muzzle flashes!"

"The barrel will not depress far enough!" cried Chung-Fat, kicking the gun carriage. There was hysteria in his voice.

"Keep calm, brother." Sheng-Fat's eyes narrowed. "The ship has been allowed to

BREECH- AND MUZZLE-LOADING WEAPONS

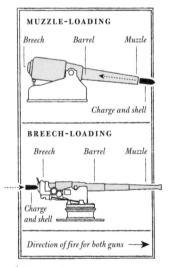

The gatehouse gun was a muzzle-loader, which was much slower than the breech-loading mechanism of Expedient's guns.

sail too near the fortress." He looked up at the hidden gun position so recently destroyed by Xu and Xi; flames danced up to the irregular drumbeat of burning ammunition. "They have men on the island too. Those idle dogs at the mouth of the estuary will answer for this outrage."

Another salvo screeched over and pounded the fortress with a force that shook the stone beneath Becca's feet. But *Expedient* was so close that, with her guns at maximum elevation, she could only hit the very base of the gatehouse tower. For a split second the bow of the ship was visible as the shells tore through the veil of brilliant white fog. Then it re-formed around her in a most unnatural way.

"How big is this ship? I cannot see the enemy!" Chung-Fat screeched.

"Neither can I, brother. The guns are of a very great calibre."

The *Expedient* ceased fire and the billowing clouds cleared from her hull. The fog machine had been deactivated.

A flare shot up from the wheelhouse and blazed into blinding light, illuminating the whole estuary as it slowly parachuted down to earth. The majestic ship was revealed in the harsh glare, every inch of her from bow to stern painted matt black. She emanated a brooding menace and power as the guns reared up, poised to fire their next shocking salvo.

The captain's voice boomed out through a loudspeaker. "Surrender your island, Sheng-Fat, or I shall be forced to obliterate you and your fortress."

Sheng-Fat wiped his mouth with the back of his hand, his eyes fixed on this curious opponent.

"It is indeed Captain Fitzroy MacKenzie," muttered Linen Suit to himself. "And so the Guild has found me."

"Will you answer him, brother?" asked Chung-Fat.

"Answer him?" screamed Sheng-Fat. "*Answer him?* I will have the fool's head skewered on a pole by dawn!"

"Yes, brother."

"Now wouldn't that ship make a lovely prize, heh, Sheng?" suggested Linen-Suit. "Why not take her as the flagship for your new fleet?"

Sheng-Fat considered. "We will trap the ship where she lies. I want those guns."

He grabbed the receiver of a field telephone and wound the handle furiously. "Unleash the Dragon's Teeth!" he bellowed. "Prepare to fire the secondary artillery but DO NOT sink her." He spun round to Chung-Fat. "Get down to the harbour and make ready to board her in the junks."

Becca watched in horror as the water began to boil. A ring of huge iron spikes reared up from the waves, trapping the *Expedient* in the estuary.

The Dragon's Teeth.

CHAPTER FOURTEEN

Xu, Xi, Liberty and Doug had found a good path to the rear of the fortress and made for the first of the breaches in the ancient wall. The captain's attack had been under way for about ten minutes, and half of Sheng's tong, about a hundred and fifty brigands, were making for the harbour ready to board their junks and counter-attack. In the confusion Liberty led her small team through the undergrowth until they found the fallen masonry marking the start of their climb. They clambered over stone blocks and rubble to a point where they overlooked the interior of the fortress. Below them lay the courtyard and bamboo shanty town, lit by lanterns and campfires.

"I sure hope your uncle knows what he's doin'," said Liberty, watching Sheng-Fat's men. "They look madder than my Aunt Bessy."

"The raiding party!" whispered Xu, pointing at a line of figures flickering through the jungle. "The Sujing Quantou. They are heading towards the second breach in the wall."

"I'm sure glad they showed. Let's get over there." Liberty set off to intercept them. The raiding party numbered sixteen – the eleven Sujing fighters in the lead and five crew from the *Expedient*. As they approached, Xi called through cupped hands. "Cha!" The raiding party stopped immediately and melted into the shadows of the ruins.

"Cha!" Xi called again.

"Sujing Quantou!" shouted the lead figure, beckoning his

comrades on. Master Aa's huge bulk came towards them. "Xi? What in the name...? You should be in Shanghai! Xu – you too? And who are these others?"

"Liberty da Vine, pleased to meet you," said the American. "Aviator and recent escapee of this here fortress. Oh, and this is Doug MacKenzie, a very distant cousin of mine."

"Liberty?" gasped Chambois, rushing forward. "My God! You're alive! You see – I came back for you!"

"Gee, thanks," replied Liberty, unimpressed. "Glad you could finally make it."

"But I thought you'd be dead!"

"Nope. Still very much alive, no thanks to you."

Chambois noticed her bandage. "But your hand – he has your finger too?"

"Yup. Didn't you hear? There's ten per cent off all manicures at this luxury island resort."

"D-D-Doug!" came a muffled shout as the rest of the raiding party caught up.

"Charlie!"

"You're meant to be on your way to S-S-San Francisco."

"We ran into a spot of bother."

"We? Where's your s-s-sister?"

"Um. Hopefully in there," said Doug, pointing at the fortress. Another salvo shook the bedrock, making them all duck. "Frankie! Ten Dinners! Ives!"

"What is it with you, Doug?" Ives caught his breath and adjusted his bulky rucksack. "I keep seeing your moon-face staring out of every puddle of trouble. The captain's gonna scuttle you, that's for sure."

"Master, we have vital information that will save the mission," said Xu.

"Save the mission?"

Liberty moved forward. "Yeah. Your captain down there's goin' no place fast. He might have snuck up the estuary, but Sheng-Fat's got a ring of iron spikes that he raises from the seabed to stop ships gettin' away. They'll rip the bottom out of the hull."

"There is no way to warn the *Expedient* now. We are committed to destroying the torpedoes," said Master Aa.

"Well, I'd say those spikes out there are our number one priority," replied Liberty. "No point in hairin' after the torpedoes until we've sabotaged the liftin' gear in the winch room. We're not gettin' out of here till we do."

"Can you find this winch room?"

"I'll give it a shot. It's close to the torpedo store in the deep tunnels."

"We have to rescue Becca too!" urged Doug. "She must be in the fortress somewhere. We saw her being taken from the tide cages."

"This was to be a swift raid," said Master Aa. "Searching for the girl may jeopardize the entire operation. We will attack the winch room first, then locate the torpedoes. If there is time we will look for your sister. We are already late."

"I'm not leaving Becca," insisted Doug. "I'll go by myself if I have to."

"To get to the winch room we'll have to swing by the prison cells," pointed out Liberty. "Becca may be in there. If we release the other prisoners they'll bulk up our numbers some. I reckon the more help we can pick up along the way for this daredevil raid the better."

"The prisoners will be a hindrance," boomed Master Aa.

"Hey, stormin' this place is close to madness anyhow,"

retorted Liberty. "We'll have to tackle the guards down there to get to the torpedoes, so it won't be any skin off your nose to have a go at rescuin' them, will it now?"

Doug was watching the Sujing Quantou warriors preparing for the attack. Each pulled a silver discus about six inches in diameter from their robes. They carefully adjusted some complex control dials at the centre and nodded to Master Aa in unison. They were ready.

"The eastern chapter of the Sujing Quantou has not undertaken such an assault in twenty years," enthused Xi.

"Do they ever speak?" Doug asked.

"Never – only our leader, Master Aa, speaks during combat."

"But you and Xu talk."

"We have yet to pass the Khotan challenges. A full Sujing Quantou fighter does not speak during battle. It is disrespectful to our traditions."

"Why?"

"Our training is as scouts – reconnaissance troops for the great army of the west. How can we hear the enemy if we are talking? And silence increases our menace."

Doug looked at the line of silent armoured figures and couldn't help but think that there was something magnificently ancient about the Sujing Quantou. Who and what they were was an intriguing mystery. Half were women. They carried no rifles or pistols, preferring to wear two swords strapped in scabbards on their backs, and a short dagger on their belts. Between the scabbards was a small bamboo box. Their headgear was as large as it was elaborate, with downturned horns and ornate curving metalwork. A light armour covered their thighs and body, and more discuses were strapped to webbing across their chests.

Chambois crawled forward to get a better view of the courtyard. "The entrance to the tunnels is in that derelict tower."

On Master Aa's signal, the Sujing Quantou all stood with their discuses at the ready. As one, they whirled around, arms outstretched, gathering speed, then released the discus bombs with a cry of "Sujing Cha!" The metal devices spun away, swift and deadly, with a strange vibrating hum. They landed in a well-spaced line and immediately exploded, smothering the courtyard with thick, choking smoke.

Master Aa nodded to the raiding party and they crested the rubble and bounded down towards the tower. Doug found himself running as well, Chambois at his side, his face a mixture of exhilaration and terror. Doug felt a little sick, but the thought of Becca at the mercy of Sheng-Fat spurred him on.

"How did you get here? I mean up the river … before *Expedient* arrived?" Doug managed to ask between breaths.

"The *Galacia*," replied Chambois. "She's moored in the estuary upstream."

They leapt up the broken steps into the tower and paused, gasping for air.

The first room was a sort of entrance hall, piled high with hessian sacks filled with rotting rice. Ives flashed his torch around, spotlighting the eyes of several rats which scattered into the shadows. He fixed the beam on a stairwell that sank straight down into the gloom of an underground tunnel system. It looked to Doug like a forgotten mineshaft; there was no light to be seen, just a thick darkness and the pungent stench of blocked drains. Were they really going down there?

"Monsieur Chambois, you are to be congratulated," said Master Aa, examining the tunnel entrance. He drew first one

Inches 1 2 3 4 5 6
mm 10 20 30 40 50 60 70 80 90 100 110 120 130 140 150

SUJING QUANTOU BATTLE DISCUS

Accurate to half a mile, this self-propelling weapon was deadly in the hands of a Sujing Quantou fighter. The upper and lower halves separated before detonation and the explosive yield was adjustable. This versatile device could also be attached to a target and set for a timed detonation, or used as a simple smoke bomb.
(See also page 193 foldout.)

sword then the other from the scabbards on his back in a single graceful movement.

"Hey, Chambois," whispered Liberty. "Feels creepy to be back in here, heh? How many fingers d'you think he'll chop off if he catches you this time?"

"Please can we change the subject?"

Master Aa climbed down the crumbling steps and dropped to the tunnel floor. Doug watched in fascination as the Sujing Quantou fighters lit small lanterns mounted on their helmets, which hissed and smoked slightly, casting long brilliant white beams. One by one, drawing their swords, they dropped down into the tunnel. Doug followed Chambois and the others. The stinking tunnel turned and descended three worn flights of steps covered with rubbish and rat droppings, then broadened out.

"Master Aa. To the right at the next fork," called out Chambois.

The Frenchman directed them into a newer and wider tunnel lit by flickering electric light bulbs. Doug was sweating profusely, expecting to meet Sheng-Fat at every corner.

"We need to go deeper, and closer to the estuary," Chambois added, wiping his forehead with his handkerchief. "The quickest way is to the right."

Very quietly they advanced in single file. As they descended further Doug noticed that the air grew more humid and the walls of the tunnel smelt even worse. The passageways looked older again, and he retched as he tripped over the lower half of a human arm, the flesh gnawed by rats. He looked away quickly, but not before he'd noticed that its little finger was missing too. He yelped, and Frankie kicked the limb aside, telling him not to look.

"We are getting close," said Chambois.

"Silence," commanded Master Aa, holding up his hand for everyone to stop. He listened intently then crouched on his haunches and rested his hand flat on the sandy floor. Doug watched his lips move. Was he counting? "Quick! The enemy is near. This way."

The approach of running footsteps made Doug's nervous system scream. They all dived into a low side tunnel and pressed against the damp wall, hardly daring to breathe. The Sujing Quantou shielded their lights with small hinged shutters and readied their swords.

Master Aa timed his attack with cool precision. He thrust his right sword out so that the first guard ran onto its blade, then sprang out of the side tunnel and lunged with his left at the second man's abdomen. Both of Sheng's men slumped where they fell, dead.

"Move the bodies into the side tunnel. Fast. There is no time to lose."

Liberty swiftly disarmed one of the dead men, taking his ancient flintlock blunderbuss. Its two barrels were half the length of a normal rifle and flared out like a pair of trumpet horns. She unclipped the powder charges and shot belt from the gun's previous owner and checked the weapon.

"That should be in a museum," commented Frankie.

"I kinda like it," said Liberty, testing the weight.

"Loose off both barrels at once and you should be able to scatter insults over a wider range than you can with your mouth," muttered Chambois.

Once the bodies were hidden, Master Aa picked up the pace again. The short burst of action had sharpened everyone's focus. Xu and Xi had been silent since the raid began, following behind their elders and never once turning to look at Doug. They moved swiftly until they reached the next bend, where they were blocked by a door with a barred window.

Doug tried desperately not to gag. The smell was atrocious: raw sewage blended with a putrid bittersweet stench that made him cough and splutter.

"We're near the prison cells," whispered Chambois, sensing Doug's revulsion. "We will be out of this maniac's paradise very soon now."

Doug knew Chambois didn't believe it would be that easy – his voice betrayed him. The words had hardly left his mouth

Attack in the tunnel DM 1920

From Doug's sketchbook (DMS 2/31)

when the door flew open and a scruffy guard burst out brandishing a rifle. Master Aa high-kicked him, sending the weapon flying, and finished him with a brief double sword stroke.

"Sheng-Fat's men might be able to hijack ships," observed the Sujing leader, "but they cannot fight."

Chambois ran forward and tugged the keys from the dead guard's belt. The Frenchman's face reddened with anger. "This man was the most brutal of my gaolers. He has the keys to the cells."

At the sound of their voices, ransom prisoners had begun to stir behind their locked doors. With horror, Doug saw roughly bandaged hands reach out through the bars and heard plaintive whispers of "Let us out!" and "Put us out of our misery." All were missing their little fingers.

"Becca!" shouted Doug. "Becca, are you here?" He ran along trying each of the doors, but there was no answer. "She must be on the surface still." He was in despair. "We *have* to find her!"

"The secret of Daughter of the Sun is more important than the life of your sister," answered Master Aa resolutely.

Chambois unlocked the doors in turn and the prisoners began to file out.

"You think this half-dead rabble can fight, Miss Liberty?" questioned Master Aa.

"What kinda animal are you? Would you just leave them in their cells while you blow the place to kingdom come? Some of these people are my friends!"

"How many are there?" asked Ives, attempting to count them.

"About twenty. Some are no longer all there, I'll grant you..." Liberty faltered as a cluster of wretched-looking prisoners staggered out. "A few of the younger ones are in better shape. They hate Sheng-Fat. They'll fight."

"We cannot take them with us," said Master Aa.

Liberty looked at the prisoners and considered. They were in a terrible state, filthy rotting clothes hanging off them, many covered in weeping sores and wracked with coughs.

"All right, boss, you may have a point. You leave them with me. I'll lead them out of here and try to get to the ship. Just remember, if you make it back first, don't you dare leave without me."

"It is the most sensible plan."

"Yeah, well, we'll see about that," she said.

"Miss Liberty. That gun you have – it is your only weapon?"

"Yeah. What about it?"

Master Aa pulled a small silk bag from his robe and handed it to her. "Put a pinch of this additive in your gunpowder and make sure all your friends are standing behind you when you fire. We will see you at the ship."

"The winch room is that way. Turn left at the fork. It's about three hundred yards."

Liberty said nothing more. She turned and waved the prisoners back to retrace their steps to the surface. The shambolic parade fell into line and shuffled away, a desperate sight. Doug noticed that some were smiling, though, and that every one of them had a glimmer of hope in their eyes.

"Something's bothering me, Charlie," said Ives. "This is too easy. And when things run too easy on an operation, I get this twitchy nose. Damn thing is positively bunny-like at the moment."

"When I'm under fire," answered Charlie, "my stammer just disappears. Strange, isn't it?"

The tunnel shook violently, followed by a low answering rumble. Fifty yards behind them a section of the tunnel roof collapsed, sending a cloud of dust rolling towards them.

"*Expedient*'s guns are shaking the foundations of the fortress," shouted Master Aa. "The whole structure is unstable."

Doug looked at the blocked tunnel. "Was that the way we were planning to get out?"

Charlie grimaced. "Not any more."

CHAPTER FIFTEEN

"Look at your uncle down there." Linen Suit thrust Becca dangerously close to the battlements. "Go on. Take a close look at the Honourable Guild of Specialists. They've dedicated their lives to a cause since 1533 and yet they've *still* not realized the true purpose of the Indus mysteries."

Becca struggled away from the precipitous edge. "I don't understand! I don't know what you're talking about."

"I remember now – Rebecca, isn't it? Well, Rebecca, I've discovered more in the last six years than the Guild has managed in four centuries." Linen Suit smirked, the expression on his face dancing between excitement and insanity. He wiped the sweat from his moustache and turned his head until his cheek rested on the stonework. His eyes were fixed on the *Expedient*. "I'm getting close now. Yes. And Fitzroy knows it. If it hadn't been for your father's untimely arrival, I would've killed the captain in Zanzibar four years ago – finished him off properly. It would have been … no bother."

"The junks are ready to attack," shouted Sheng-Fat. He grabbed the field telephone and spoke rapidly into the receiver. "Secondary artillery, on my command give covering fire as the junks approach. Do *not* sink the ship, just disable her. OPEN FIRE!"

Four guns immediately fired from their hidden emplacements along the estuary, their shells sending up great plumes of water as they exploded on the mudbanks on either side of the ship. A second salvo cracked out, finding the ship's range.

One shell hit the superstructure, landing behind *Expedient's* bridge. Instantly the wireless telegraphy office erupted in an orange fireball.

"Sparkie!" cried Becca, picturing him at his station. Then she saw *Expedient's* bow veer round as if the helmsman had just let go of the ship's wheel.

"I told you NOT to sink the ship!" screamed Sheng-Fat into his field telephone.

The *Expedient* was out of control and being dragged by the river current. But this was not the open sea – the navigable channel was extremely narrow. Her stern struck a mudbank to starboard and her rudder ran up against one of the iron teeth, halting her progress.

FIELD TELEPHONE

This field telephone is identical to that used by Sheng-Fat to command his estuary defences.

"Steer her!" shouted Becca, hoping that someone in the wheelhouse was still conscious. *Expedient* rested for a few seconds then started to pivot like the hand of a clock as the river pulled her bow until it also ran aground on a mudbank to port. The vessel had turned ninety degrees and was now stranded across the river.

The smoke cleared around the wheelhouse; the wireless telegraphy office was no longer there. A running figure could just be made out dousing the flames with the fire hose.

Becca watched wide-eyed, open-mouthed in shock. One of *Expedient's* disappearing guns reared up again and tried to swivel towards the gatehouse, but could not rotate far enough to aim. The aft twelve-pounder was engaged in a furious battle with Sheng's secondary artillery. At that moment the first crowded junk edged out from behind the harbour wall and steered straight for the immobilized ship.

"This is it – the winch room!" exclaimed Chambois, forging ahead towards a large steel-riveted door. Doug hung back. Was it a trap? Could Sheng-Fat be behind there with a hundred armed men just waiting for them to charge in? There had been precious little resistance so far.

"Xu, Xi. Stay back with Monsieur Chambois and keep watch on the passageway," commanded Master Aa. "Mr Ives, have your men cover us with their weapons. We will rig the door with our explosives."

Doug poked his head round the corner to get a better view, readying himself to make a run for it.

The Sujing fighters attached four discuses to the outside of the door using a soft putty as adhesive. They linked the charges with a single firing cord which they handed to Master Aa. He gave a sign and all the Sujing Quantou pulled down their helmet visors and stood well back.

"All set," said Master Aa.

Xu found Doug and shouted, "It's Daughter of the Sun in there. Turn away! Cover your eyes!"

Master Aa yanked the firing cord and the door was blown apart with an intense blue-white explosion. With a cry of "Sujing Cha!" the Sujing Quantou stormed the room. There were screams from the dazed guards inside as the warriors secured control of the winch room with a furious display of swordsmanship.

"Mr Ives!" bellowed Master Aa. "Move everyone in here."

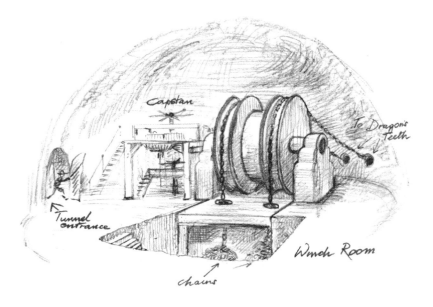

From Doug's sketchbook: The winch room. (DMS 2/35)

Doug ran past the smoking door and skidded to a halt on the loose grit floor. The winch room was a massive domed cavity carved out of solid rock. It was dominated by a huge capstan mechanism that operated the Dragon's Teeth in the estuary. In front of him two immense iron chains with links as thick as the top of his arm disappeared through openings leading to the river.

"The wheel must turn the lifting chains," Doug called out as he inspected the machinery.

"Master Aa. Charges here and here will put it out of action," Chambois informed him.

The Sujing leader made some complex hand signals and his silent comrades swarmed over the machinery, placing discus bombs as Chambois directed. Once they were set, Master Aa and his team climbed down and ran for the door.

"They are timed explosions; we have thirty seconds. We must leave immediately," ordered Master Aa.

"Hurry now, Doug," called Ives. "This thing's rigged to blow! Frankie! Ten Dinners! Get everyone out. Chambois, it's up to you to find us these torpedoes now. Then we can get the hell out of here."

"By my reckoning, if we return to the fork in the tunnel we should be able to cut back to the torpedo store," replied Chambois.

The explosions cracked out, ripping through the winch room and severing the chains. They could hear the rattle and clunk reverberating through the bedrock as the broken links ran out towards the estuary.

Chambois broke into a run. "This way!" he urged when he reached the fork. But there was uncertainty in his voice.

This new tunnel didn't look right to Doug somehow. "How's your nose, Mr Ives?"

"Twitching bad. Real bad."

"How are you going to blow up the torpedoes?" Doug asked Charlie.

"The plan's to arm them by activating the molecule invigorators, then detonate the lot with delayed linked charges. The explosion should bring down the gatehouse and that great big gun Sheng-Fat wants to shoot at us so very much. Our exit will be clear. Of course, the captain didn't know of your little advance party, so it's all got rather, er, complicated."

Suddenly, from nowhere, a solid iron door crashed down in front of them with ominous finality, showering the tunnel with sand and dust. The Sujing fighters ahead slowed to a halt; in the choking atmosphere their lamps made them look like monochrome silhouettes, reminding Doug of a Lucknow shadow theatre he'd once seen.

Doug was petrified that at any minute a vengeful Sheng-Fat would appear: the warlord had to know they were down here now after the explosions from the winch room. Master Aa's deep voice cut through his terror, saying exactly what Doug didn't want to hear. "Back to the winch room. Now!"

They retraced their steps at speed until they reached two side tunnels. Chambois paused.

"Which way?" demanded Ives.

The Frenchman hesitated for a second, his scientific mind unwilling to commit to a wild guess.

"We don't have much time. Make a decision!" shouted Posh Charlie.

"Then, to the right," murmured Chambois without conviction.

They pushed on, the Sujing running with swords drawn, until they arrived at a watertight steel door. Doug didn't like the look of it. While Ives and Master Aa examined it, another huge steel door suddenly descended a few yards behind them.

"We're trapped!" yelled Doug.

Master Aa pulled another discus from his belt and adjusted the controls, setting the weapon at the base of the door. "Keep as far back as you can."

"Close your mouth and cover your eyes," instructed Xu, pushing Doug behind him. Seconds later a dense explosion

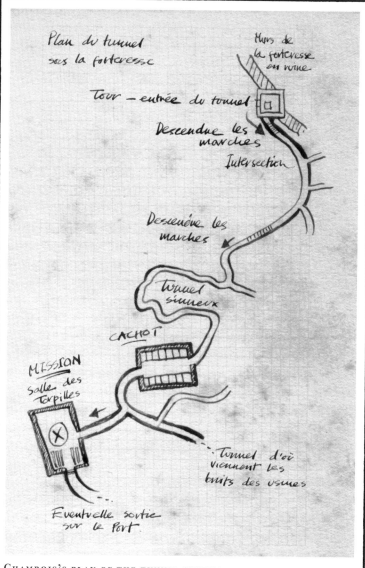

Plan du tunnel
sous la forteresse

Murs de
la forteresse
en ruine

Tour — entrée du tunnel

Descendre les
marches

Intersection

Descendre les
marches

Tunnel
sinueux

CACHOT

MISSION
Salle des
Torpilles

Tunnel d'où
viennent les
bruits des usines

Eventuelle sortie
sur le Port.

CHAMBOIS'S PLAN OF THE TUNNEL SYSTEM

Chambois used this rough sketch to navigate the tunnel system. It is interesting to contrast it with the detailed plan in appendix 5. It can be seen that Chambois made many mistakes and underestimated the size and complexity of the tunnels.

rolled around the tunnel, blasting them with grit and making their ears ring. But the door remained intact.

"All our exits are blocked. I knew Sheng-Fat wouldn't just let us walk out of here," said Doug.

Chambois banged the door with his fist. "He knows we are down here. It is only a matter of time."

Water began to drip from a pipe in the roof lining. The drip turned into a stream, then a powerful deluge. Within seconds sea water began to fill the chamber at an alarming rate.

"More tricks," shouted Posh Charlie as a second jet of water sent him sprawling to the floor like a novice ice skater.

"There must be a shut-off valve!" yelled Chambois in desperation.

The freezing water was deep enough to swim in now, and as Doug's feet floated up from the floor, he tried to calculate how much time they had before the water reached the roof of the chamber and drowned them all.

CHAPTER SIXTEEN

As Sheng-Fat's junks sailed closer to the crippled *Expedient*, the warlord rubbed his hands together, his eyes alive with the anticipation of his impending victory. Linen Suit lit a cigar and, although clearly agitated, sat well away from view at the rear of the gun platform. Becca gazed down, hoping to catch a glimpse of the captain.

The battle had not all gone Sheng-Fat's way. Shortly after the hidden estuary guns had opened fire, *Expedient*'s aft cannon replied by knocking out each one in turn with devastating accuracy. Five fires blazed in a line along the estuary, punctuated every so often by the pop and thud of burning ammunition. Although armed with two torpedoes, the ship was now lying at an angle on the mudbank which prevented her from firing at the junks. The aft gun landed a couple of shots on the first junk, then the crew ran forward to prepare to repel the attack.

"I'll write the epitaph for his gravestone," mused Linen Suit. "*Fitzroy MacKenzie. Explorer. Sea captain. Destroyed by his persistence and vanity.* Wasn't your mother a Sea Dyak, Sheng?"

"Yes," replied Sheng-Fat with suspicion.

"Could you have the captain's head shrunk in the Sarawak style of your ancestors? I should like it as a desk ornament – a keepsake to remind me of this great victory over the Guild. And could you make him look like he's grinning? Would it be any bother?"

"A great pleasure, my friend."

The captain's unmistakable silhouette moved out onto the boat deck. The crew followed, carrying rifles and cutlasses, and made a dash for the wheelhouse. It appeared they would make a valiant last stand there.

Chung-Fat's junk ran up alongside the *Expedient* and made fast. With frenzied battle cries, the pirates surged aboard, storming the crippled ship with bamboo ladders and grappling irons. *Expedient*'s men fanned out and took positions on the wheelhouse, bridge and boat deck, then took aim.

"FIRE!" roared the captain; a fusillade of rifle and pistol shots cracked out across the estuary, cutting a swathe through the first wave of pirates. But *Expedient*'s crew couldn't fire fast enough to stem their advance. As the second and third junks joined the fray, Captain MacKenzie had to concentrate his forces around the wheelhouse.

The battle was sharp and fast. Urged on by Chung-Fat, the pirates swarmed over the main deck and clambered up the bridge ladders. The crew held them at bay, but this position couldn't last for ever. Becca could scarcely bring herself to watch. There were pirates from stem to stern now. Twenty or so climbed below decks through the aft hatch to storm the interior.

At that moment, there was a deep, low rumble and the Dragon's Teeth collapsed, crashing back to the seabed behind the ship.

"The Dragon's Teeth!" cried Becca. "They did it!"

"But they play me like a fool!" screamed Sheng-Fat, pushing the gatehouse gun captain to the floor. He grabbed the firing

cord and wrenched it as hard as he could. The muzzle discharged a vast, thunderous explosion, shaking the stonework beneath Becca's feet and making the tower groan. The shell tore down the estuary and ripped into a mudbank about two hundred feet beyond *Expedient*'s stern.

The battle on the water stopped dead.

"Now I have their attention, I will show this captain the MacKenzie girl." Sheng-Fat seized Becca by the shoulder and dragged her forward.

"Wise change of tactics, Sheng. She is his beloved niece, and Fitzroy is such a family man," sneered Linen Suit.

Sheng-Fat's eyes darted at Linen Suit, suddenly suspicious. He beckoned to two guards near by. They hauled Becca up and after a swift nod from their leader they swung her over the battlements and dangled her in the air by her wrists. Sheng pulled a flaming torch from the wall and held it next to her so she was bathed in its light.

Becca's head swam and her stomach twisted as she tried not to baulk, but she heard the captain issue a "cease fire" order. The breeze from the estuary rushed in her ears and a stabbing pain shot up her arms. She could not open her eyes; she knew that nothing but fresh air and an unimaginable drop lay beneath her. A voice in her head whispered again and again, *You are going to die; you are going to die.* She kicked out instinctively in search of a foothold, but found nothing to support her.

After what seemed like an eternity, the warlord cupped his hands and called out, "Do you see the girl? She is a MacKenzie."

"I see her," came the captain's distant reply.

"You will surrender your ship, and I, the warlord Sheng-Fat, will decide your fate and the fate of your men."

The pirate's voice echoed around the estuary.

There was another silence. Becca felt herself slipping. Panic screamed inside her. Over the pounding of her heart she could just hear the captain's order. "All hands," he called. "We will surrender."

Sheng-Fat suddenly spun round and levelled his parang at Linen Suit's chest. "How stupid I have been! You knew this captain's name, this MacKenzie, but you have not even seen him until now. The girl's name is MacKenzie, and yet you did not warn me about this ship. You tell me too late that they are of the same family. So I begin to think ... perhaps it was you who told the children which junk to board in Shanghai to infiltrate my island."

"Nonsense, damn your eyes!" replied Linen Suit.

"The children were to guide the ship in by night, perhaps? Yes, you arranged this attack, didn't you, Englishman? You have been hiding behind the battlements, cowering away from the shellfire. But I suspect you double-cross me. Now I want answers, or perhaps there will be two heads to shrink. And how do you say, Englishman ... *two heads always better than one?*"

Deep beneath the fortress, the water level in the flooding chamber was now so high that barely a foot of air remained. Doug and the rest of the raiding party struggled to suck in every lungful they could. Doug thrashed against the current, clutching at the rough-hewn rock of the roof to stop himself being swept away by the water gushing in from the pipes. He was shivering uncontrollably.

"Your discuses are our only hope," shouted Ives hoarsely.

"We must risk the blast. We're all going to die at this rate, anyway!"

"It would—" Master Aa was cut off as the door at the other end of the tunnel suddenly lifted up with a squeal like a dying animal. Immediately the water burst through and Doug found himself propelled forward by the force of the torrent.

He landed gasping in the next chamber, cannoning into Xu and Xi. He struggled to his feet, water swirling around his knees.

"Give us a straight fight!" demanded Xu, striking the surface of the water in frustration. "We have no way of tackling this infernal water trap!"

The Sujing Quantou weaponry was indeed useless and their physical strength no match for the might of the water. The huge door behind them crashed back down from the ceiling as another torrent of water started to pour from a large conduit above. Then a narrow hatch opened further along the roof, funnelling in hundreds of rats that squealed and swam in every direction.

"We're being flushed out from tunnel to tunnel!" cried Posh Charlie, wiping his hair from his face. He flashed his torch around the chamber and found a ladder that climbed steeply into the darkness.

"Let's go!" yelled Doug. "It's the only way out."

The ladder was dangerous in itself. It ascended over fifty feet but became more treacherous as they reached the top: many of the rungs were rotten and crumbled beneath the weight of the Sujing Quantou. Doug moved as fast as he could, following Xi's nimble feet. He paused once to glance down at the rat-infested water below. It was as if they were in a well; the water had already started to fill the ladder shaft.

From Doug's sketchbook: Master Aa and Ives make their escape. (DMS 2/42)

The air that had been squeezed out of the chamber rushed up towards him with a haunting moan.

Doug hauled himself up the last few rungs and scrambled into the new higher chamber. It looked different from the last: perfectly cylindrical and lined with dressed stone. Ives was last to arrive, more swimming than climbing, carried upwards with the rats on the unstoppable surge of water.

"Serpent!" yelled Fast Frankie as a black and white striped sea snake fell writhing into the water beside him.

"The captain assured me that we would be fighting on land!" complained Master Aa, slicing into the torrent and beheading the animal. He grabbed the severed head and threw it to the far end of the chamber. A much larger sea snake landed on a Sujing fighter's shoulder. She grabbed its tail, shouting "Sujing Cha!" as her comrade spun round and chopped its body in half. Four more snakes slipped into the water, but the warriors were ready now: the water foamed with flashing blades, deadly serpents and squealing vermin.

More water flooded in from the roof, filling the chamber at a phenomenal rate. It reached chest height and they all began to swim. A dead snake's head bobbed up beside Doug; exhausted, he tried to punch it away. He kicked his legs underwater, trying to find the floor, but a strong vortex tugged at him and he was sucked under. He couldn't breathe. He was drowning. He tumbled and somersaulted through the depths until Xu and Xi dragged him to the surface. They linked arms and held him safe in the air pocket.

"You must be strong like a Sujing Quantou fighter, Doug," ordered Xi. "Do not let Sheng-Fat's cowardly traps defeat you. There is no honour in that."

"Think about rescuing your sister. You may be her last chance."

Doug coughed and recovered slightly. Xu and Xi smiled at him.

"You're right."

"Of course. We are the Sujing Quantou."

"Well, I'm Doug MacKenzie, and I'm not going to be drowned. Not by Sheng-Fat!"

"Sujing Quantou!" screamed Xi.

"Sujing Cha!" yelled Doug.

Just then the iron door at the end of the chamber rumbled open and they were driven forward into a long stone passage, the water powering them along at great velocity. They shot out onto a drainage grille set in the floor of the next room. Doug sprawled in a tangled heap next to Master Aa, who pulled him out of the way just as a pair of huge Sujing fighters flew out and landed next to them.

Wiping the salt water from his eyes, Doug saw that they were back in the banqueting hall – and that they were surrounded by a hundred or so of Sheng-Fat's men, with their weapons drawn. Master Aa stood slowly and surrendered, throwing his swords and discuses to the floor. There was no other way.

CHAPTER SEVENTEEN

Captain MacKenzie strode through the gates of the fortress at the head of *Expedient*'s remaining crew, swinging his walking stick as if he were on a country walk.

Following the captain's surrender, Sheng had dragged, pushed and cajoled Becca and Linen Suit down the long spiral staircase from the gatehouse gun platform to the courtyard below. He was in a state of wild joy: laughing, then murmuring, then shouting about his victory. Once in the courtyard, he shoved them towards the other captives.

"Rebecca!" said the captain, spotting his niece. Becca ran over to her uncle, glad to see him whatever the dire circumstances of the reunion. She was still shaking from the terror of being hung over the battlements. Then the captain saw Linen Suit and stopped short. "Julius Pembleton-Crozier. Of course … the linen suit. This is a rare night for ghastly surprises."

"Good evening to you, Fitzroy. How's the leg?"

The captain lifted his chin and stared down his nose, then turned to Becca and said in a soft voice, "I thought I'd bought you a ticket to San Francisco? This nest of vipers is not on American soil, by my reckoning. I imagine that your hapless brother is about here somewhere?"

"Yes, Uncle," Becca muttered; she wanted to tell him everything, but couldn't find the words.

The pirates started shouting and jostling the prisoner column forward towards the banqueting hall entrance. Pembleton-Crozier was pushed in line behind the captain.

"We've found out plenty of information about Sheng-Fat," whispered Becca to her uncle.

"Silence," ordered a female guard, brandishing a rifle.

The captain glanced at Becca. "What information?"

The conversation was cut short as the guard cracked him across the shoulders with her rifle butt. They descended the stone steps to the dank subterranean hall. Sheng-Fat led the way, striding towards his makeshift throne. The Duchess was still chained to the column and roared when she saw the captain approach, pacing to and fro with her ears pinned back. She snapped at a guard who got too close, sending him scurrying away.

Becca caught sight of Doug standing beside the huge Sujing fighters. He grinned at her, held up his hand to prove he still had a full set of fingers, then pulled his socks up in an exaggerated movement. When he saw his uncle, he shrank away, turning his face as if trying to hide. The captain picked up his nephew's guilty eyes with a stare so hard it could have bored through tempered steel, then dipped his head at Master Aa.

"Ah, the tunnel rats," sneered Sheng-Fat. "And the MacKenzie boy who escaped. Bring him and the Sujing Quantou leader closer."

"You will all kneel before the great Sheng-Fat!" called Chung-Fat with false ceremony.

Becca knelt beside the captain, wondering how she could tell him what she knew. Then she noticed her uncle was tapping his fingers on his knee, in short and long bursts. Morse! His message read: REBECCA. SEND INFO IN MORSE.

Becca began tapping out the message on her own knee, a movement which looked like a nervous twitch. SHENG FAT HAS BEEN SHIPPING HIGH OCTANE BOAT FUEL TO THIS ISLAND.

The captain looked up as if some revelation had struck him. "Of course. High-octane fuel! He must have a torpedo boat," he mumbled.

Suddenly Sheng-Fat barked, "You too, Englishman! Kneel!"

"Don't double-cross me, Sheng-Fat," exclaimed Pembleton-Crozier. "I'm warning you."

Sheng-Fat laughed. "You view me as your puppet, not as your business partner. But look at you now, kneeling before me. You think I do not see your true purpose, your shrouded schemes... Did you think you could hide your other ventures from me – disguise your plans? We are in the South China Sea. Information flows as fast as the currents. I know you use your money to hunt for an ancient ship."

"What I do with my money is none of your business."

"Ah, but it is. This attack has made me suspicious. You and this captain know each other. And there is the matter of the Daughter of the Sun. Its source is the best-kept secret in China. My belief is that the Sujing Quantou are in league with you too. They gave you the sample in the first place, to bring it here to me. You are all in this together!"

"Rubbish!" snorted Pembleton-Crozier. "You've been at the opium, old boy."

"No. I see it all. This plan was an attempt to deceive me. To attack me here and destroy me. To take control of the torpedoes and my island so that you could cut me out of the hijack revenues."

"You're insane!" yelled Pembleton-Crozier. "Your mind's addled, man!"

The captain stood up slowly, leaning on his stick, until he towered over Sheng-Fat. "I would have fought to the last if you hadn't held the girl over the battlements. Your men are a disorganized rabble! And as for Pembleton-Crozier, he's a low-down crook. He is nothing to do with me."

"Silence!" snapped Sheng. "No matter who you are in league with, you are trespassing on my island. And I'll kill you all!"

Sheng's shouts turned to wild laughs as he slumped down on his chair. Then he looked thoughtful for a moment.

"I have the torpedoes and now I have the Sujing Quantou. What a piece of good fortune. Brother, how long do you think it will take to torture out of them the source of Daughter of the Sun?"

Chung-Fat slowly sized up Master Aa. "They will crack in the end."

Surveying his prisoners with satisfaction, Sheng-Fat suddenly spotted Chambois hiding in the shadows. *"What?"* he screeched. "The Frenchman? You are still *alive?"* The warlord leapt up and bounded towards Chambois, seizing him by the throat and pinning him against a stone column. Chambois cowered beneath his grip.

Sheng-Fat spoke in a venomous whisper. *"You. Chambois...* You are worse than scum. You killed my brother Li-Fat with your trickery. And you *dare* to return to my island? You dare to even breathe the same air as me? Look me in the eye, cowardly scum! To see you alive when my brother has been vaporized cuts me to the heart. His death must be avenged!" The blade of Sheng's parang pressed hard into Chambois's chest.

"Kill him, brother," hissed Chung.

"Kill, kill!" echoed one of Sheng's men. And the other pirates began to join in a menacing chorus, surging forward to get a better view.

But Sheng-Fat held back. He raised his hand for silence.

From Doug's sketchbook (DMS 2/59)

"No, my friends. Death by sword would be too easy. A death of equal scale to that suffered by Li-Fat is the only fitting vengeance." Sheng released Chambois and threw him to the ground, becoming thoughtful for a moment. "Warp the captain's ship off the mudbank. She is about to make her last journey."

The captain's voice cut through the smoky haze. "What do you intend doing with my ship?"

"Revenge, Captain." And to one of his men he barked, "Fetch manacles from the prison cells – and the welding torch." Turning back to the captain with an evil leer on his face, Sheng continued. "We are going to play a little game, Captain. I will let you go, but before I do, my men will manacle Chambois to the side of your ship. Then I'm going to come after you. I will show you how straight my torpedoes are running. And this time Chambois will not swim away. Prepare the torpedo boat for target practice!"

"But the *Expedient* has torpedoes too," said Chung.

"That crippled ship is no match for mine. Especially without any crew – except for the honourable captain." Sheng-Fat nodded at Captain MacKenzie with a sneer.

The captain looked appalled by Sheng-Fat's scheme. "If I'm to play your evil game, I must have a crew," he demanded.

"Well, let me see… Shall we make this a family trip? I'll give you the boy and the girl!" chortled Sheng, flicking his crazy eyes at Becca and Doug.

"And my chief engineer," argued the captain. "I need my chief engineer. Otherwise kill us all here and now, and to hell with this madness."

Sheng, bored with the discussion, waved his hand as if swishing away a fly. "Have the engineer as well. What is it to me? You have no hope."

"What will happen to the rest of my crew?" the captain asked.

"They will remain here, in case you have any ideas about trying to escape. Once I have avenged this particular debt, I will decide their fate – and the treacherous Englishman's."

"But Sheng old boy, surely I can go free?" pleaded Pembleton-Crozier.

"Oh, no. I have other plans for you, *old friend*."

CHAPTER EIGHTEEN

Becca's diary: April/May 1920
Since leaving Shanghai on Chung's junk I've lost track of the days.
Aboard the Expedient

From Doug's sketchbook: The Expedient *after the battle of Wenzi Island.* (DMS 2/66)

I can hardly believe it. My diary has survived, hidden deep in the
lining of my sea coat!

We found Expedient *moored in the deep channel of the estuary
in "a reasonably seaworthy manner" according to the captain. She's
in a terrible state. Her disappearing guns are still raised in the
firing position. Her decks are blackened from battle and all around
lie brass cartridge cases, grappling irons and bamboo ladders from
the final assualt. We watched as Sheng's men welded four manacles
to the hull and locked Chambois into them – it seems Sheng's
intention is to line up a torpedo on him and destroy us all.*

Once aboard the captain did a quick inspection of the ship with
Doug and me in tow, while Herr Schmidt hurried off to the engine
room. We returned to the bridge through the empty companionways

– I kept expecting to see people at every turn, but there were none. We are the only crew. What a terrifying thought.

The worst damaged area is the wireless telegraphy office, so there is no chance of radioing for help.

Herr Schmidt, or the Chief as our uncle calls him, has brought the boilers back up to temperature and we are limping along with the captain at the wheel and Doug and me as lookouts. Sheng-Fat has provided a pilot in a sampan who calls out the navigable channel. Dead ahead we follow a swinging lantern lashed to the sampan's stern, which guides us on our last voyage.

Chambois was manacled to the hull of *Expedient*, amidships and just above the waterline.

"Monsieur Chambois, the captain says to hang on," shouted Doug as he shone his torch down. The early dawn light made the beam very faint; the Frenchman was easily visible, trapped and unable to move.

"Do I have any choice?"

"Can we get you anything?" asked Becca.

"A glass of champagne would be nice, but in the circumstances…" He rattled the manacles and gave the ghost of a smile. Becca and Doug watched for a few moments, unwilling to leave him but unsure how they could help.

The captain called them both into the wheelhouse as he spun the ship's wheel and made for deeper water.

"Now, we've had our differences, that's for sure. But our only chance is to pull together, to work as a team to save our friends and shipmates. You must trust me and have confidence in my plan."

1920

From Doug's sketchbook: Chambois manacled to the Expedient. (DMS 2/70)

"What plan?" asked Doug.

"Sheng-Fat thinks this is a game – albeit a deadly one. A quick piece of target practice. But in his eagerness to avenge his brother's death, he has left himself wide open to failure. He thinks we have no chance, but we've *got* to defeat him. We must find a way to sink his torpedo boat, before he kills us all."

"But do you think we can beat him, Uncle?"

"Why not? He's a chancer. He's impulsive, ill-disciplined, and his weakness is that he has to impress his men. Though I'll grant you, he holds all the best cards."

Becca put her binoculars down on the chart table and tried

her luck. "If we get out of this, will we get a reprieve from Aunt Margaret?"

The captain smiled grimly. "Blackmail, is it? You've been spending too much time around pirates." He nodded slowly. "I may consider it."

"I won't forget you said that."

"What about a trick?" Doug schemed. "Can we lure Sheng-Fat into a trap?"

"My thoughts exactly," agreed the captain. "This ship is hardly fit to float, let alone fight. We've got to be cunning. We must find his weak spot."

"Might his speed be a weakness?" wondered Doug.

"Speed is not traditionally seen as a weakness in a fighting vessel," reasoned the captain. "But I'm open to ideas."

"If I were Sheng, if I had a really fast boat, and a tong to impress, I'd show off a bit ... you know, go flat out," said Doug, "before launching the torpedo to finish us off."

"An interesting thought, Douglas," said the captain as he cleared the sea chart of spent cartridges from the battle and inspected the scattering of small islands marked around the estuary. "He'll want to play cat and mouse with us for a while. We need to work ourselves into a good position. Now let's see. We need an island with deep water to one side..."

"How about this one?" suggested Becca.

"Ah, yes," he said in a steady voice. He took a pencil from a drawer and ringed the island. "We have six fathoms there, which should be ample." He turned and gave them both a stern look. "One last point. You must obey every order I give you. Do you understand?"

Becca and Doug nodded.

"Right, Douglas, take the wheel. Keep her heading due

east. Don't oversteer her. The engines are giving just enough steerage way to hold her against the tide."

Doug stepped up and for the first time gripped the ship's wheel.

Expedient was all his.

Despite the captain's order he turned the wheel a fraction just to check he wasn't dreaming. The ship responded and the compass card swung slightly to starboard. He gently brought her back on course with enormous satisfaction. The only problem was that he had to stand on tiptoe to see where he was going.

"Due east it is, Captain."

Suddenly they heard a voice behind them, making them all jump. "Wireless Operator Watts reporting for duty, sir," barked Sparkie. He appeared with a bandaged arm and smoke-blackened face covered with small cuts.

"Good God. Watts! How did you…?"

"The last thing I remember was walking through to the wheelhouse to give you a message and there was this almighty crash. When I woke up I was in the secret cabin, sir, with my arm injured. There were a lot of Sheng-Fat's crowd everywhere, so I stayed put when I realized you'd surrendered. I bandaged up my arm and thought I'd keep quiet just in case…"

"You did the right thing. Are you fit for duty?"

"Aye, Captain, my right arm is fine, and the left is just grazed."

"Excellent news. Now, Rebecca and Sparkie, follow me. Douglas – due east into the rising sun. You have the ship."

Doug took a deep breath and stared ahead. The captain's voice drifted back to him. "What we need is the light kedge anchor, some buoys and a steel cable. We must find some bolt cutters and a bosun's chair too, so we can cut Monsieur Chambois free at a moment's notice."

"Right, I want you to be my eyes. I want you to tell me everything Sheng-Fat is doing, every change of direction, speed, every last detail."

The captain moved back to the chart table. "Sparkie, get below to the torpedo room. Rebecca, take the starboard side; I'll cover port. Here are your binoculars. Keep close so you can hear my orders."

Captain MacKenzie rested against the port door jamb observing the estuary and fortress; Doug was at the wheel; and Becca was fifteen feet away at her lookout position on the starboard side. The captain walked two paces forward to the brass voice pipes beside the wheel. "Bridge to engine room. You ready down there, Chief?"

"Jawohl, Captain. Just about."

Doug, now over the initial shock of steering the mighty vessel, gazed out, looking for signs of Sheng-Fat. At first he saw nothing. Then gradually, as light began to flood the horizon, the red of the dawn sun caught the flotilla of junks' sails. About half of Sheng-Fat's tong had set sail in five junks to watch their master exterminate Chambois and the crew of the *Expedient*.

"Captain, they're on their way!" called Becca.

The low burble of a powerful engine rippled across the water and Sheng-Fat's motor torpedo boat emerged from the estuary. The MTB was an impressive craft; she had two torpedo tubes, and two heavy machine guns mounted fore and aft.

It was a ridiculously unbalanced contest. Suddenly Doug wanted to forget any ideas of trickery and instead steer as erratic a course as possible to confuse Sheng-Fat. He adjusted his grip on the wheel and checked the compass again. Due east.

"Head due south. Ninety degrees to starboard, Douglas. Let him zero his sights on Chambois. We must make a nice fat target."

"Nice fat target?" Doug repeated with incomprehension. He wavered, fighting every instinct in him to ignore the captain's command.

"That's my order," said the captain.

Should he obey his uncle as he'd promised? What about Chambois? Why not steer away from Sheng-Fat? It made much more sense.

"Do as he says, Doug," urged Becca. "Now!"

Doug met his sister's glare. He didn't want to obey. Then he pictured Xu and Xi and the rest of the crew and the Sujing Quantou back at the fortress. Running away would not defeat Sheng-Fat. He had to follow orders; it was the right thing to do. After all, the crew trusted the captain and obeyed him without argument, so why shouldn't he, Douglas MacKenzie, do the same?

"New course, due south, Captain!" Doug shouted out with resolve. "Turning now!" He knew that the coxswain spun the wheel spokes twice to turn the ship, then stopped and spun them back again when the bow was halfway to her new course. He tried it, and the ship turned immediately. He watched the compass card swinging through south-east, the

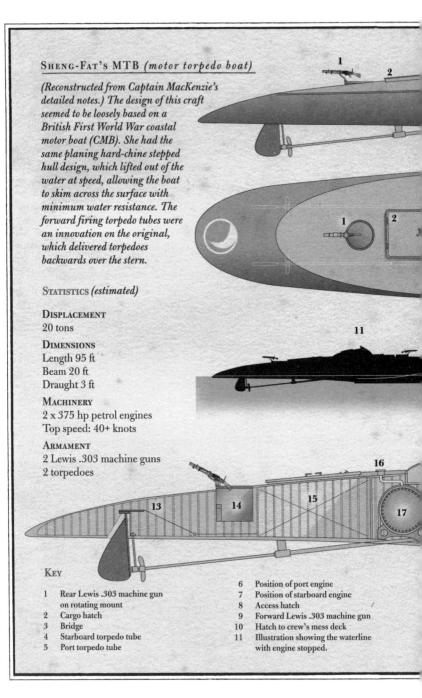

SHENG-FAT'S MTB *(motor torpedo boat)*

(Reconstructed from Captain MacKenzie's detailed notes.) The design of this craft seemed to be loosely based on a British First World War coastal motor boat (CMB). She had the same planing hard-chine stepped hull design, which lifted out of the water at speed, allowing the boat to skim across the surface with minimum water resistance. The forward firing torpedo tubes were an innovation on the original, which delivered torpedoes backwards over the stern.

STATISTICS *(estimated)*

DISPLACEMENT
20 tons

DIMENSIONS
Length 95 ft
Beam 20 ft
Draught 3 ft

MACHINERY
2 x 375 hp petrol engines
Top speed: 40+ knots

ARMAMENT
2 Lewis .303 machine guns
2 torpedoes

KEY

1	Rear Lewis .303 machine gun on rotating mount	6	Position of port engine
2	Cargo hatch	7	Position of starboard engine
3	Bridge	8	Access hatch
4	Starboard torpedo tube	9	Forward Lewis .303 machine gun
5	Port torpedo tube	10	Hatch to crew's mess deck
		11	Illustration showing the waterline with engine stopped.

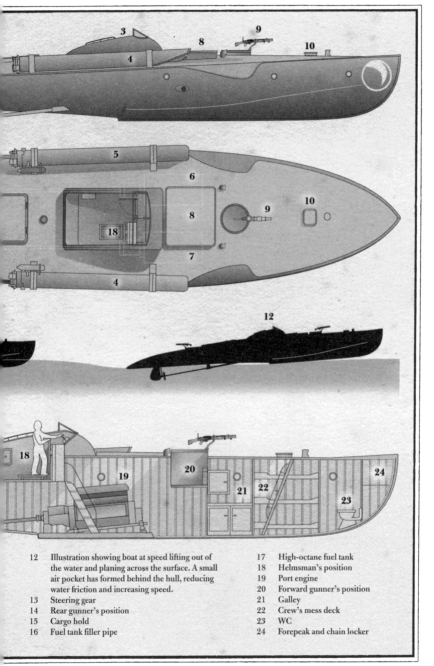

12	Illustration showing boat at speed lifting out of the water and planing across the surface. A small air pocket has formed behind the hull, reducing water friction and increasing speed.
13	Steering gear
14	Rear gunner's position
15	Cargo hold
16	Fuel tank filler pipe
17	High-octane fuel tank
18	Helmsman's position
19	Port engine
20	Forward gunner's position
21	Galley
22	Crew's mess deck
23	WC
24	Forepeak and chain locker

halfway point of the turn, and spun the wheel back. *Expedient* turned and straightened out heading due south, with only a fraction of oversteer.

"Very good, helmsman. Nice and steady now."

Doug wiped beads of sweat off his brow and checked the position of the MTB, which was accelerating to meet them.

"Surely he'll just come out and sink us?" said Becca.

"He can't miss," added Doug.

"Know your enemy!" cried the captain. "Sheng-Fat won't fire at us straight away. He'll play with us before coming in for the kill. He'll want to put on a show for all those spectators."

Sheng-Fat's boat threw out two large bow waves as he piled on more engine revs.

"He's going to ram us, Captain!" called out Doug.

"Steady, now. He'll not be wanting to ram anything with that new paintwork. When I give the order, turn hard a'port."

"Aye aye, Captain," replied Doug, glad that his uncle was at last making some sense.

The MTB stormed across the sea with her engines at full power. Her planing hull lifted from the water so that she seemed to be skimming the surface.

"Now, Douglas! Hard over."

Doug spun the wheel until it stopped. The steering gear creaked and groaned ominously and *Expedient* lurched to port.

"Midships!"

Doug straightened up and tried to spin the wheel back. It stuck, and he had to pull it with both hands to start it spinning again. "The steering is a little heavy, Captain."

"Grounding on the mudbank must have damaged her steering gear. Is the wheel still turning?"

From Doug's sketchbook: Sheng-Fat at the helm of his MTB. (DMS 2/74)

"Just about." Doug straightened her up, but with more oversteer this time.

The MTB was gaining on them, the detail on her decks hardening in the early light.

"Steady on that course. We'll make for that low-lying island dead ahead."

Sheng-Fat was racing close to the ship, standing up in the MTB and laughing like a maniac as he carved a long loop around her, cutting across her bow. The junks were some quarter of a mile distant, crammed with men. Doug could hear their shouts and whistles as they urged their leader on.

Expedient now offered a perfect target, and the captain knew it. Sheng-Fat was aiming up his first shot at Chambois.

"Douglas, alter course twenty degrees to port."

"Port twenty, Captain," replied Doug.

"Sheng-Fat is preparing to fire any moment … NOW!"

"Enemy torpedo running!" called Becca.

"Hard a'port – turn in towards her."

The wheel was suddenly much more difficult to turn in either direction, and had started making a grating noise. Doug used all his weight to start it spinning, and finally it moved.

"Keep her hard over, Douglas… Midships. Steady."

The torpedo missed by some twenty feet, and the MTB banked away. The torpedo ran on and struck a large junk in the pirate fleet. The bulk of its hull was lifted over a hundred feet in the air on a rolling, boiling half sphere of sea water as the zoridium warhead exploded. Doug watched in awe at the extraordinary power of Chambois's creation. The captain barely gave it a second glance.

"Hard a'port. Stand by to fire starboard torpedo!"

Sheng-Fat overtook on a parallel course to the *Expedient*.

The captain spoke into the brass voice pipe. "Wheelhouse to torpedo station. Prepare to fire torpedo to starboard. Set depth for one foot."

"Aye, Captain." Sparkie was one deck lower, directly beneath the wheelhouse. With a clatter, the false walls around the torpedo station collapsed, revealing the launch tubes.

The captain hinged down a sight from above the wheel. It looked like a brass telescope, but had many more dials and levers attached to it. He adjusted them then said with a steady voice, "Target in range."

"Torpedo loaded and ready to fire. Tube locked in firing position, forty-five degrees to starboard, Captain," shouted Sparkie.

The MTB was still at full speed, switching back across their path on a straight course.

The captain leant forward. "SHOOT!"

With a whoosh the torpedo was ejected from the launch tube by a burst of compressed air.

"Torpedo gone!" came the reply.

The captain headed for the door and lifted his telescope. "It's running straight and true."

"Go on!" encouraged Doug.

The torpedo raced for the MTB, cutting a fine line through the water. Sheng-Fat's coxswain spotted the telltale streak coming towards them. Sheng took control of the wheel and altered course. The torpedo skimmed by, just inches from the hull.

"Bad luck, Captain," said Doug.

"Well, it was worth a try."

Sheng-Fat made a pass of his junk fleet, his arm held high in anticipation of certain victory.

"Alter course. Steer for those junks," ordered the captain.

Sheng-Fat had now rounded and stopped on the other side of his fleet, waiting for the *Expedient*. His next move was unexpected, and it was only Becca's keen eyes that saved them. As they crossed in front of the leading junks, which lay some four hundred yards off their bow, she caught sight of three puffs of smoke.

"Captain! Torpedoes launched from three of the junks!"

"The cheating swine," muttered the captain. "Hard a'port, Douglas. Well done, Rebecca!"

Doug wheeled *Expedient* round, leaning hard as the ship turned. He could see that two of the torpedoes would miss easily, but the third looked more dangerous. He braced himself for the explosion.

The torpedo struck but at such a low angle that it ran along the ship's waterline with a scraping metallic squeal. Chambois could be heard screaming as it passed by, then raced off towards Wenzi Island.

"Enough is enough!" fumed the captain. "Let's finish him." He was thinking hard, calculating the various distances and speeds of the two vessels. "Sparkie, Rebecca! Get aft as fast as you can."

"Aye, Captain." Becca hung her binoculars on the door handle and made for the bridge ladder.

"Are you scared, Douglas?"

"Well, yes, to be honest."

"Mm. I have to compliment your coolness under fire. You are much more like your father in battle than I would have given you credit for. He'd be proud."

Doug thought about his father for a moment. He was a rather quiet man and difficult to picture in any sort of battle other than straightening out a newspaper. A thousand questions sprang to mind, but this wasn't the time to ask them.

The aft twelve-pounder speaking tube suddenly echoed to Becca's voice. She was out of breath. "I'm here, Captain, and Sparkie is on his way. I'm standing by."

"Douglas, steer as close to the seaward side of the last small island as you can. She'll not ground: there's plenty of water. We'll give Sheng-Fat a shot he cannot miss! Stand by aft. Here he comes."

The captain watched the activity on board the MTB intently through his telescope. Sheng-Fat was now approaching at full speed. His coxswain was readying the last torpedo tube to finish off *Expedient*. Sheng gave the order to fire.

"NOW!" bellowed the captain down the speaking tube. Sparkie and Becca cut the line releasing the kedge anchor, then leapt away as the buoyed steel cable paid out over *Expedient*'s stern.

"Hard a'starboard!"

Doug spun the wheel hard to the right, struggling to turn it quickly. The ship curved round, the steel line following the arc of their course. The anchor bedded in and bit on the seabed. The *Expedient* turned into Sheng-Fat's path.

Sheng was trapped. The MTB was already turning as fast as she could. In a split second he had to decide whether to smash into *Expedient*'s solid side, rip his rudder and propellers off on the tightening steel cable, or run ashore on the low island. His torpedoes missed and carved up the beach at the end of the island, exploding in a huge blue flash.

At the same time, the MTB roared up the rockstrewn beach, tearing the bottom out of her hull. She was caught by the pressure wave from the explosion and flipped over like a leaf.

"Herr Schmidt, stop the engines," called down the captain in a subdued tone. "Sparkie, release the block securing the steel cable, or we'll rip our stern off. All ahead slow. Doug, bring me in as close as you can to the island."

Sheng-Fat staggered out of a gaping hole in the side of the wrecked MTB, clutching a spreading scarlet wound on his arm. The captain looked on at the scene of devastation.

Becca and Sparkie raced back up to the bridge.

"You did it, Uncle!"

"With your help, yes. But I'm afraid it isn't over yet. Did you see any other survivors?"

"No, just Sheng-Fat."

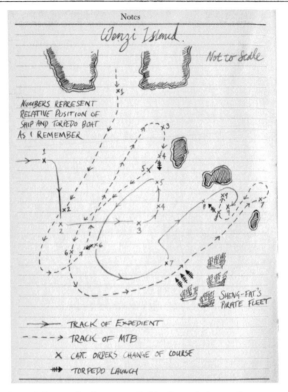

Plan of the sea duel as recorded in Becca's journal. (RMD 1/129)

The warlord cut a lonely figure as he stood watching his burning torpedo boat.

"Sparkie. Get the bosun's chair and cut Chambois free. Becca – throw a line over and prepare to pick up Sheng-Fat."

CHAPTER NINETEEN

Doug steered the *Expedient* up the deep channel of the estuary to Wenzi Island. Smoke from the night's battle still hung over the fortress and the sweeping arm of the harbour wall. A muffled *crump, crump, crump* of detonations and the crack of rifle fire made him tense.

The captain snatched up his telescope and fixed on a heliograph Morse signal flashing from the harbour path.

LIBERTY DA VINE LAUNCHED ATTACK TO RESCUE SUJING QUANTOU AND CREW FROM BANQUETING HALL. GENERAL BATTLE ENSUES. IVES.

The captain deciphered the message aloud, but both Becca and Doug had read it well enough.

"Who is this Liberty da Vine?"

"She's a pilot," said Chambois. "She was kidnapped by Linen Suit and Sheng-Fat so her father, who's high up in the shipping world, would sign the shipping treaty. With no ships in the South China Sea there was nothing to hijack, no money to be made."

"Sheng's tong clearly wish to slug it out to the bitter end," the captain considered. "We must prepare ourselves. Here is the key to my day cabin, Rebecca. Please bring my boarding cutlass. You know where to find it."

Finishing her errand, Becca returned to the wheelhouse just as Doug and Sparkie were mooring the *Expedient* to the harbour wall. Chambois leapt ashore and headed towards the fortress in search of Liberty.

A second Morse signal flashed out from near the gatehouse.

TORPEDO STORE SABOTAGED. SUGGEST EXPEDIENT SAILS IMMEDIATELY. MASSIVE ZORIDIUM EXPLOSION IMMINENT.

Suddenly they saw figures sprinting out of the fortress. Liberty, her scarf flapping behind her, led the retreat at the head of the shabby-looking gaggle of ransom hostages. *Expedient*'s crew covered them with weapons acquired from the fortress. They were making for the harbour. The remainder of Sheng's tong fired furiously from the courtyard and defensive walls. The Sujing fighters retaliated by spinning their deadly discuses back into the fortress, which rocked with huge explosions and bursts of intense light.

"Do we turn the ship about, Captain, and head out to sea?" asked Sparkie.

"Not yet!" The captain flicked the cover off the engine-room voice pipe. "Herr Schmidt, stand by to give me all she's got in reverse. Sparkie, take the wheel. You're in no fit state to fight. Rebecca and Douglas – stay here out of trouble. I'm going ashore to look over Sheng's armoured junk."

The harbour wall was protected by a watchtower at the landward end, some four hundred yards distant. This guarded the harbour approach, the moored junks and the path up to the fortress. At present it seemed unoccupied.

Doug stood outside the wheelhouse, following the captain's progress through powerful binoculars. Panning over the rocks to the dusty line of the path above, he fixed on the dual blades of a Sujing fighter, flashing and glinting in a whirl of hand-to-hand combat with three pirates. She kicked and barged, then engaged each of their parangs, left then right. She finished with a kicking, slicing combination which floored all three of her opponents simultaneously.

Switching his focus, Doug sighted Mr and Mrs Ives lower down the path, much nearer the harbour wall. Mrs Ives looked grimly determined as she loaded a Martini-Henry single-shot rifle and handed it to her husband. He had just fired an identical one, keeping up an almost constant barrage directed up the path towards the gatehouse. The Duchess guarded their rear, the white fur around her mouth scarlet with fresh blood.

Doug watched as the captain clambered aboard Sheng-Fat's armoured junk, walking stick in his left hand and cutlass in his right. This was the ship they'd seen attacking the *Rampur Star*, he was sure of it.

"Look at the sea cave! There's a sampan making for Sheng-Fat's junk," he shouted.

"That junk has three stern cannon," added Sparkie. "Ideally placed to cover the harbour path."

"If the pirates can board her, they'll be able to stop anyone reaching the harbour wall!"

"Her other cannon could hit the wall at point-blank range," cried Becca. "Anyone trying to reach the *Expedient* would be cut to pieces! We must warn the captain!"

"You're meant to stay—" Sparkie turned, but Becca and Doug were already running towards the bridge ladder.

Becca grabbed Doug's shoulder as they reached the shelter deck seconds later. "Wait. I borrowed these – just in case." Behind the door were the Bavarian rapier and a boarding cut-lass from the captain's cabin. Doug raised his eyebrows and grinned at her, then tucked the cutlass into his belt.

They vaulted the *Expedient*'s gunwale together and landed on the harbour wall. Doug thought he heard Sparkie shouting after them, but didn't turn round. They sprinted to the junk and clambered aboard, drawing their swords as they hunted for their uncle.

"Captain!" cried Doug, searching the decks.

A single door gave access to the after section of the ship; the lock had been blown with a gunpowder charge. Doug nudged it open and crept into Sheng-Fat's cabin, raising his cutlass. Becca followed, rapier at the ready. Inside were sounds of movement, muttered curses and furniture being overturned. They pressed themselves against the wall, hardly daring to breathe. Someone was ransacking the cabin – the captain! A box lay on a low table with its lid smashed open. It contained eight gold bars marked with Sheng's dragon's tooth emblem. They watched their uncle as he stuffed a sheaf of papers inside his sea coat. Sensing some-one behind him, he froze. With astonishing agility he swung round and knocked Doug's blade away with his walking stick, lodging it firmly in a deck beam.

"Uncle, quick! There's a sampan approaching. It looks like the pirates are going to board this junk and cut off the line of retreat along the harbour wall."

"Curses! We must act immediately." He made for the door, crashing past Doug, who was still extracting his blade from the woodwork.

The pirates in the sampan were now closing in on the junk. "Let's see if Sheng keeps his powder dry," said the captain. He found a cannon on the starboard side and angled the barrel down and onto the target.

"Stand by to fire! Firing now!"

Doug gripped his cutlass tighter and squatted down for cover beside his sister. The captain took matches from his pocket, lit one and touched it to the vent located at the can-non's breech. The barrel had been loaded with pieces of metal and chain which tore into the water around the sampan, upturning the small boat and puncturing the hull in several places. The screams of the pirates cut through the billowing gun smoke. Their attack had been stopped dead.

The captain didn't linger to savour his victory. Instead he hurried Becca and Doug back inside Sheng-Fat's cabin. "That's stopped them from the sea, but now we must slow their land attack with these stern guns."

Becca noticed the elaborate decoration and worn Spanish lettering cast into the breeches. "But these things look like they're from the eighteenth century, Uncle."

"They are," the captain snapped, squinting down the barrels at the path.

Doug leant out of a gun port. He could see Posh Charlie shooting his Purdey from the hip at a duo of approaching brigands. "The pirates are about to make a charge, Captain!"

"Numbers?" his uncle asked, taking out his matchbox again.

Samples of Sheng-Fat's rough-smelted gold bullion.
The gold was extremely impure. (MA 00.1049 SHENG)

"Thirty I'd say. Perhaps more."

The captain found a taper beside one of the guns and lit it with a match. "Stand against the bulkhead and put your fingers in your ears, both of you."

The captain fired each of the cannon in quick succession, their great weight bucking back with a resounding crack. They all coughed and blinked at the foul white smoke, their ears ringing. These guns had also been loaded with grapeshot; fragments of metal tore up the track in a blast of smoke, making it impossible to tell if anyone had been hit. Beneath their feet the junk rocked and then steadied against the recoil.

"We've taken the wind out of their sails, but they won't be held back for long," yelled the captain. "Make for the harbour tower."

Doug was first out on deck. Gunpowder smoke swirled around the junk, confusing the scene. A figure charged towards him. Doug instinctively parried a blade with his cutlass and jinked to one side. Seeing he was in trouble, the captain and Becca burst out of the door at a run. The smoke thinned a little, and Doug laughed – the adversary was none other than Xi. They lowered their weapons and shook hands.

"Surprised to see us?" Doug shouted.

"With a sword in your hand, well … I hardly recognized you. I am glad you decided to join the fight at last," joked Xi. "Your sister too? Gods! This day will be fêted for eternity and remembered with thanksgiving, feasts and fireworks!"

"Just shut up," said Becca, looking around to see if any more surprises were lurking in the smoke.

Xu approached the captain. "Greetings from the eastern chapter of the noble Order of the Sujing Quantou," he began in a formal tone between gasps of breath. "Master Aa sends his compliments and a message. He says we are outnumbered and short of ammunition. He is planning to regroup at the harbour tower before making a run for the ship. He invites you to join him."

Suddenly Doug spotted something out of the corner of his eye. Without hesitating he pushed Xi aside as the blade of a parang sliced towards them. It was a survivor from the sampan, soaked to the skin from swimming, blood streaming down his face from a head wound. Becca attacked. She found his blade with her rapier and released the parrying dagger. Within a moment her opponent's blade was locked between the dagger and her sword's hand guard. She ripped the parang from his grip and sent him sprawling. He tripped, catching his foot on the coaming of the central powder magazine. Xu issued a swift high kick that knocked him backwards overboard.

Sis and Xu fighting a pirate
DM 1920

From Doug's sketchbook (DMS 2/83)

"Enough," called the captain. "To the harbour tower. Follow me!"

The barrage of shrapnel from the stern of the junk had bought some precious minutes for their friends on the path. The pursuing pirates seemed to be hanging back, reluctant to be caught in the open a second time.

This pause had given Liberty and Chambois the opportunity to lead the bedraggled prisoners to the safety of the harbour tower, where they had collapsed in exhaustion. Most looked too tired and sick to make the final dash for the *Expedient*, but Liberty was berating them, reminding them that they could soon be free. The rest of *Expedient*'s crew reached the base of the tower and took up defensive positions.

"It's no good, Captain," yelled Ives over the roar of the battle. "We can't hold them off."

"Where's Pembleton-Crozier?"

"No idea, Captain. He must've escaped in the confusion."

"How long till the torpedo store explodes?"

"Any time now."

"Is everyone here?"

"Yes. The Sujing are holding the base of the path. They're just waiting for your word."

"Hey!" came a shout. "Are you the skipper of that beaten-up hulk tied up over there?"

The captain spun round. Liberty ran over and hunkered behind the safety of the wall, reloading her blunderbuss as she talked.

"Miss Liberty da Vine?"

"You got it, bud. Are you bound for civilization?"

"We're bound for oblivion if we can't stop their advance. At this rate they're going to wipe us out and take the *Expedient*."

"Oh, come on now, Skip. You forgot to add me into your ugly little equation."

Master Aa joined them. "Captain. Have you defeated Sheng-Fat?"

"Yes. He's a prisoner aboard my ship."

"Then our work is done," said Master Aa. "We will lay down a smokescreen and pull back to the *Expedient*. Between the Sujing Quantou and your crew we can carry the ransom hostages."

"An excellent plan. Ives, have the men carry the ransom prisoners to the ship. Rebecca, Douglas, stay close to me."

Master Aa adjusted the controls on his last discus and hurled it towards the pirates, filling the path with thick white smoke.

"Fall back to the *Expedient*!" ordered the Captain.

They all started to run: Ives, Mrs Ives, the Duchess, Posh Charlie, Chambois … everyone making along the harbour for the safety of the ship.

Doug sprinted beside his sister, flanked on either side by Xu and Xi. They pounded down the stonework of the harbour wall neck and neck, faster and faster, each of them matching the others. Halfway to the ship their escape changed into an impromptu race. Doug drew on his last reserves of strength and pumped his legs even harder. All the fear and dread of the last few days was suddenly converted into boundless energy and exhilaration. He'd never felt so fiercely alive as he did at that moment, finding within himself a speed he hadn't known he was capable of. He glanced to see Becca, Xu and Xi, heads thrown back, equally fearless and determined to win. Anything was possible. Everything was suddenly within their grasp. Doug felt like he could run for ever in the company of his new-found friends.

Then somehow they were back on board the ship, choking for breath as they collapsed onto the deck. They were joined a minute later by the Sujing fighters and crew carrying the half-dead ransom prisoners between them. Master Aa and the captain were the last aboard.

As the final wisps of the discus smoke cleared, Doug could see the pirates realizing what was happening. The remains of Sheng's tong began to surge forward in a last attempt to stop the *Expedient* leaving harbour.

"Coxswain, take us away from this ghastly island!" ordered the captain.

There was a shout – a scream of desperation. It was Chambois. "LIBERTY! We don't have Liberty. Hold the ship; she must still be on land!"

Then they saw her. She was standing on the roof of the harbour tower with one foot up on the battlements. The mass of pirates was spilling down the path and onto the wall below her. Liberty watched and waited until they were passing Sheng's junk. The pirates had seen her now and were raising their rifles to take aim. She gave a mock salute, pulled down her flying goggles and cocked the flintlocks of her blunderbuss, then fired directly at the central powder magazine of Sheng-Fat's junk. A blinding white flame thirty feet long belched out of the barrels as the Sujing gunpowder additive ignited, lifting Liberty off her feet and hurling her backwards with the recoil.

"She has used the whole bag!" exclaimed Master Aa.

His words were lost as the junk shuddered and then erupted in a cleaving explosion that ripped it in two. Great chunks were blown upwards and outwards – in no time at all Sheng's ship and his tong were destroyed.

But this was just the beginning. As the flare of Liberty's explosion withered, a second eruption rocked the island.

It was the zoridium torpedo store.

As the zoridium exploded deep in the tunnels beneath the fortress, the energy released was like a movement within the earth's mantle. The shock waves vibrated up and burst out through every crack and fissure in the bedrock. The *Expedient* shuddered and lurched. Great waves swept out across the estuary. The fortress erupted in a vast rolling fireball that consumed the remains of the ancient walls and tower and shook the island with wrathful violence. In the final phase of the detonation forks of jagged lightning shot into the sky with the primitive power of an electrical storm.

In a blinding blue flash, Sheng-Fat's fortress ceased to exist.

Dear Sis. Not my best effort, I fear. It's painted
half from memory and half from imagination, but I hope
it reminds you of that extraordinary adventure.
                    With love. Doug. Christmas 1926

WENZI ISLAND AFTER THE ZORIDIUM EXPLOSION

The skies over the *Expedient* were dark with purple-black clouds that bulged like overripe fruit. As the dust dispersed on the strengthening south-westerly wind, the last echoes of the explosion rumbled down the estuary and out to sea. A large chunk of carving from the gatehouse tower had crashed onto the fo'c'sle. Almost everything on deck was damaged. Twisted fittings and stanchion railings hung as if they had been melted; the funnel was stooped over like an old man; and all of the ship's boats had been holed or smashed to firewood.

Expedient was still floating, but she looked ready for the scrapyard.

Doug surfaced first. Like many of the others the blast had lifted him bodily and dumped him in the water.

"Are you all alive?" shouted the captain.

Doug checked the faces as they bobbed up: Becca, Chambois, Xu and Xi were all there. He gave a thumbs up.

Xu and Xi began to laugh. "Did you see those pirates try to fight? What a disgrace!"

"I saw Master Aa dispatch five with only two sword strokes. Just two strokes!"

"Are you all right, Doug?" asked Becca.

"My lucky socks came through for me. My ears are ringing a bit, though."

"Mine too."

They swam round the ship and scrambled up the worn

steps at the end of the harbour wall. Through the settling dust clouds they saw the figure of a woman strolling casually towards the ship with a twin blunderbuss slung over her shoulder.

"Liberty?" shouted Chambois. "You're ... you're still alive?"

"Looks that way, doesn't it? Boy, this scattergun kicks harder than a jackass mule."

"You stopped Sheng-Fat's tong!"

"Well, you know, Chambois old pal," she said, putting an arm round him and steering him back towards the ship, "sometimes it takes a woman's touch to get a job done properly. Where's that skipper? I want a first-class cabin and a long soak in the tub."

The captain stepped out on deck and led Sheng-Fat onto the harbour wall. For a long moment the defeated warlord stared up at the ruins of his fortress.

Master Aa dusted himself down. "A simple raid on some tunnels, Captain?"

"My apologies, Master Aa. A satisfactory result for the Sujing Quantou?"

"It nearly cost us everything!"

"Hey! There he is!" yelled Liberty. "Hey, you. Sheng-Fat. You butchered my little finger! Now I want yours – and that's just for a darn start-me-off!"

Chambois hurried over. "Stop it, please, Liberty. I insist."

"I've every right to treat you like the rattlesnake you are, Sheng-Fat. And you darn well know it."

"Miss Liberty, I must also insist that you do not," added the captain.

"Look here, Skipper, I don't take orders from you or anyone else."

"Please – drop your weapon."

Liberty raised the blunderbuss and aimed it at Sheng, nudging him backwards with the barrels.

"Give me that darn necklace, you sick dawg."

Sheng lifted the gruesome garland very slowly over his head and handed it to her, never once severing eye contact. Doug noticed that the hand of this once terrifying man was shaking.

"I wouldn't come any closer if I were you, Captain," warned Liberty. "This thing isn't very accurate but it is deadly, I assure you."

"Again, I demand that you drop the gun. There is no need to descend to Sheng-Fat's level. He is defeated."

"I've a score to settle, Skip. I've a score of scores to settle with this creep. Where's my plane? Where's that English guy with the suit?"

Liberty gets the better of Sheng Fat
Dm 1920

From Doug's sketchbook (DMS 2/91)

"That is exactly what I'm trying to find out," said the captain. "And Sheng-Fat was about to tell me before you started waving that gun about."

"So why doesn't he tell us now?"

Sheng-Fat's shifty eyes flicked up at the smoking pile of rubble. "You think Pembleton-Crozier survived that, Captain?"

Liberty pulled back the hammers on the flintlocks. "He's double-crossed you, hasn't he, Sheng? We've blown your fortress sky-high. Your torpedoes are gone. So are your prisoners. I must say that goes fifty per cent towards makin' me feel a darn sight better."

Sheng-Fat focused on something on the estuary bank opposite and laughed. "It makes no difference now. You're too late. All of you…"

Liberty tensed, her face fixed and resolute. Her finger tightened on the trigger and a shot rang out. The bullet clipped the shoulder of the captain's sea coat and tore into Sheng-Fat, sending him sprawling to the ground. Everyone instantly ducked for cover.

"But I didn't fire!" screamed Liberty.

They heard the sound of an engine cracking into life, and watched as a red seaplane broke cover from across the river. The pilot raised his hand in a mocking farewell as he lifted off the water and thundered overhead with the engine gunned to full power.

"Julius Pembleton-Crozier," breathed the captain, clenching his walking stick until his knuckles whitened.

"I knew it! I knew it when I heard her engine from the tide cages. That thievin' rustler's got Lola! He tricked me into gettin' kidnapped and took my plane as well!" Liberty watched Lola roar overhead. She ran forward three paces, then lifted the blunderbuss and aimed into the sky. But she couldn't shoot. "Darn it!" she cursed. "I can't shoot my own bird." She let the weapon drop. "I've gotta get off this stinkin' rock. He may have Lola, but he didn't get—" She gave a secretive smile. "Well, Skipper, if I hadn't spent so much time shootin' the breeze, I promise you I'd have pulled that trigger eventually."

But the captain wasn't listening. He was kneeling down, lifting Sheng-Fat's head to make him more comfortable. "Mrs Ives, your first-aid kit immediately. Frankie, Charlie, get a stretcher."

Sheng-Fat's face had drained of blood and his eyes rolled in excruciating pain. A red bloom darkened his shirt. It was clear that he was dying.

"Why did Pembleton-Crozier need the money from the protection rackets?" questioned the captain.

Sheng-Fat gurgled and closed his eyes.

"What was he doing? Why did he shoot you?"

"I knew ... too much..."

"Too much about what?"

"The ship ... the ancient ship..."

"Has he found it?"

"Yes. He has to dig it out of a mountainside... Very expensive ... very many people... The money would have paid for..."

Sheng seemed to fade, then woke for a second with a startled look.

JULIUS PEMBLETON-CROZIER

A former, dishonoured luminary of the Guild, Pembleton-Crozier's connections with the international underworld ran deep. A corrupt genius, endowed with dangerous knowledge of Guild secrets.

"I can avenge your death, Sheng-Fat, if you tell me where Pembleton-Crozier is bound."

"I am a dishonourable man – why would you avenge me?"

"Tell me where he's gone, I beg you!"

Sheng-Fat gave one last snarling grin – and died.

Drawn from life. DM.
May 1920

From Doug's sketchbook:
Sheng-Fat dies. (DMS 2/93)

CHAPTER TWENTY-ONE

The explanation took fifteen hand-wringing minutes. The captain sat in silence as his niece and nephew told him everything that had happened to them up until the moment when they were all reunited in the banqueting hall.

The captain's face was emotionless. "You can't help yourselves, can you? You disobey every order you're given. You think you know what's best, rather than deigning to do what people ask of you."

"We are just searching for the truth, Uncle. We want to know what's happened to our parents and exactly what we're involved in," Becca retorted angrily.

"Oh yes, you two certainly have an inquisitive nature."

"Did the Guild force Mother and Father to go to the Sinkiang, the way they forced you to go after Sheng-Fat?"

"The Guild is a voluntary organization," the captain answered. "We are not forced to do anything."

"What were they doing in western China?"

"You have to believe me when I say I do not know."

"You must have some idea," pressed Doug.

"I have theories. But nothing I could prove."

Becca and Doug were silent for a moment. Then Becca spoke again. "You promised us we wouldn't have to go back to Aunt Margaret's if we defeated Sheng-Fat."

"So I did," agreed the captain.

"Are we still going to San Francisco?"

"Well, you've missed your steamer."

Becca turned and stared out of the scuttle. "Are we to stay with you, then?"

The captain tapped his walking stick on the desk as he considered his reply. "I will honour my promise. You can stay aboard *Expedient*. I have no time to return you to Shanghai, or any other port, so necessity plays no small part in this. I cannot lose Pembleton-Crozier now that I'm back on his trail. The papers I discovered on Sheng-Fat's junk have grave implications. I must hunt him down without delay."

"What implications?"

The captain hesitated. "You two are not as stupid as I'd assumed when I put you ashore in Shanghai. You were foolish to go after Sheng-Fat on your own, but I admire your motives and your dogged persistence. You have proved yourselves capable in the face of adversity. So, I have decided that you should join the Guild – if you pass the Firenze examination papers, of course. I now feel confident to entrust you with some of our secrets, though I must first put you under oath. Do you swear never to divulge any of the information I am about to tell you?"

Becca and Doug, both slightly stunned, swore their oaths solemnly.

"Excellent," said the captain, with the briefest hint of a smile. "You should know that the Guild is on the threshold of leading mankind into a new scientific age. But it is imperative that Pembleton-Crozier does not get there first. And he's getting close – using information stolen from the Guild, he has almost located the southern gyrolabe."

"Gyro-what?" asked Doug, looking puzzled.

"Gyro*labe*. It's an initiator – a key, if you like – to an extraordinary machine believed to be over six thousand years old. Perhaps it will be easier if I give you a demonstration."

With the air of a magician about to perform a trick, he pressed two false rivets on the bulkhead causing a bookcase to drop and reveal a safe. He unlocked it with a key on his watch chain and removed a mahogany box, which he placed on the desk.

"This is an exceptionally old piece of apparatus from northern India."

The captain lifted out a silver sphere mounted on an axis spindle. It was surrounded by what looked like longitude and latitude lines made of gold; these were attached to the spindle in such a way that they could rotate independently of the sphere.

The captain lit the oil lamp on the bulkhead and put the deadlights over the scuttles, darkening the cabin. "It was given the name gyrolabe by the Guild because it looks like a cross between an astrolabe and a gyroscope. There are four of them in existence, each associated with a different point of the compass. During the Greek conquest of northern India in 326 BC they were looted from an eccentric sect of cosmologists, along with a book of collected ancient texts called *The 99 Elements*. After that the gyrolabes became separated and scattered.

"This one turned up in London in 1533, along with several chapters of *The 99 Elements* translated into ancient Greek. They were the property of an Egyptian spice trader, who sold them to a French diplomat named Jean de Dinteville. It is this gyrolabe and the ancient texts that form the very foundations of the Guild. To understand what we are trying to do, you must first witness the radical nature of the science we are dealing with."

The captain handled the gyrolabe with great care. Normally so self-assured, he seemed a little hesitant in the presence of this curious device; his voice had become tight and slightly anxious.

"At each pole I shall insert a single grain of zoridium, or Daughter of the Sun."

"You have some?" asked Doug.

"Yes, a small phial of twenty grains collected by the Guild during the wars between the Sujing Quantou and the Ha-Mi two hundred years ago. Help me, would you ... get it from the safe there."

Doug jumped up and went to the safe, keen to get his hands on the substance he'd heard so much about. He saw the phial immediately – a metal tube about the size of his thumb mounted upright on a brass stand – and tried to grab it. But the phial wouldn't move.

"It's stuck down."

"Try again."

This time Doug managed to shift it a fraction. "It's almost impossible. It's so heavy."

"Allow me," said the captain, lifting the phial out of the safe with some effort. He unscrewed the lid and tipped out two small grains into the palm of his hand. It looked no more exciting than lead shot. "Daughter of the Sun. Now you know why the Sujing are heavily built. I shall load it into the gyrolabe."

The captain inserted one grain into a small receptacle at each pole, and attached a thin watch chain. He twisted the oval outer band and set the device spinning on the desk. It danced momentarily, then settled.

The Duchess growled and slunk off with her tail between her legs.

"Lethal!" enthused Doug, wrinkling his nose as he took a closer peek at the gyrolabe. "Look, it's getting faster. It's burning into the wood of the desk!"

A wisp of smoke appeared. Delicate blue forks of electric charge began arcing up between the bottom and top of the axis spindle.

"Now watch." The captain took a pencil and placed it on the desk. It began to roll towards the spinning sphere.

"The motion of the ship?"

"No. Have another guess."

"Magnetism?"

"No. The pencil is just wood and graphite."

At that moment, several sheets of paper fluttered and circled in orbit around the desk.

"Gravity?"

"Now you're on the right lines. As the gyrolabe speeds up, its pull on objects around it increases. It generates its own gravitational field."

First encounter with the gyrolabe

DM 1920

From Doug's sketchbook (DMS 2/98)

This enigmatic gravity device has given up few of its secrets in the last four hundred years. The inscriptions (figs. 3–6) are Indus Valley script, a language undeciphered to this day. Guildsmen researching The 99 Elements *believed the marking at the top of the gyrolabe (figs. 2 and 7) referred to a*

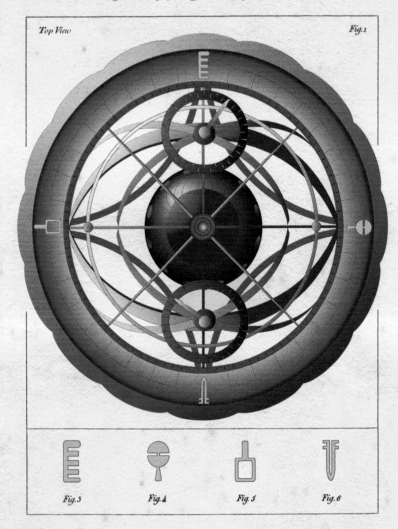

Top View   Fig. 1

Fig. 3   Fig. 4   Fig. 5   Fig. 6

point of the compass, in this case north. The western gyrolabe bore the marking in fig. 10. When turned on their side, both gyrolabes were attracted to the relevant point of the compass. In 1720, a third gyrolabe, marked with the east symbol (fig. 8), was observed to react consistently, reinforcing the theory that four devices existed – assuming a missing southern gyrolabe.

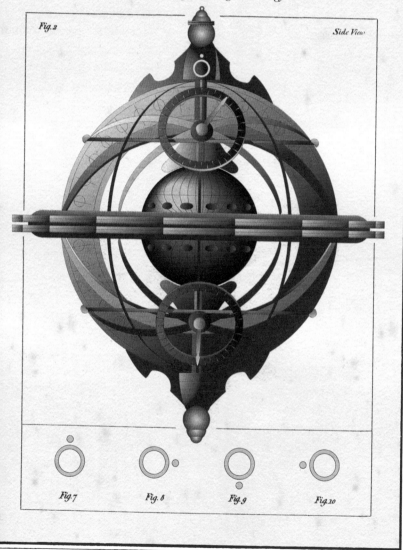

Fig. 2

Side View

Fig. 7   Fig. 8   Fig. 9   Fig. 10

As the captain spoke the mahogany box began to shift, then a glass of water, then Doug felt himself being pulled towards the gyrolabe as if he was falling. He braced himself against the desk, pushing away with all his might to lock his arms out straight. A low oscillating hum began to emanate from the sphere, now spinning so rapidly that the longitude and latitude lines had merged into a blurred halo, lit by the arcing sparks of electricity.

Becca gripped her chair tightly as it began to slide across the floor. She halted her progress by jamming her feet against the edge of the desk and had a strange feeling that, although she was almost horizontal, she was standing. The Duchess roared and howled as she was dragged across the cabin too – her long claws dug deep into a Persian carpet that slid along the deck beneath her.

"Enough!" The captain jerked the watch chain, dislodging the uppermost receptacle and breaking the gravitational field. The spinning sphere slowed immediately and after a few seconds he was able to catch the gyrolabe with his left hand. He gently returned it to the mahogany box and closed the lid. "If I'd left it any longer all my books would have been pulled from the shelves, and the cabin wrecked."

"But what is it for?" asked Becca.

"From our study of *The 99 Elements*, we believe the gyro-labes to be a key ... that they help to start a much more powerful machine, the location of which is still a mystery. Our work in Firenze suggests that this machine, fuelled by zoridium, could unleash colossal energy sources.

"If this energy could be harnessed, it would lead the way to a leap in scientific development as radical as the Industrial Revolution. We would begin a new, higher level of scientific understanding. But by the same token, it could destroy the planet and all mankind with it. When we find the machine, it will be a test of man's higher resolve. Such unquantified power could be used for good or evil."

"Surely you could just build your own machine," said Becca.

"Sadly, no. Our translation of *The 99 Elements* is incomplete – we do not possess all the chapters. It has also been transliterated through at least two languages using ancient terms for which there are simply no translations. Our knowledge is very far from complete."

"So you need to get hold of the original," said Doug.

"Exactly. And this quest has taxed some of the best minds since the Guild was founded by Jean de Dinteville and Georges de Selve in 1533. Our sole purpose has been the exploration and research of all subjects related to this revolutionary branch of science, the gyrolabes and *The 99 Elements*. We have striven for centuries to understand the meaning of the texts, to hunt for the gyrolabes, and to discover the source of Daughter of the Sun.

"We have also been scouring the planet for the unknown machine. Information on its precise location is encoded in a cipher engraved on the four gyrolabes. We need all of them to crack the cipher, but the fourth gyrolabe is lost. The Guild possesses two of them, and we have the information from the third. But Pembleton-Crozier made copies of these when he was a member of the Guild. If he finds the missing gyrolabe before us, he will be able to locate the great machine and unleash the full potential of Daughter of the Sun. In comparison, Chambois's torpedoes will look like firecrackers.

"You can see my need to pursue him."

Becca's features looked pinched, as if she was readying for

an argument. "So ... is that what our parents are looking for? A gyrolabe?"

"It's possible, Rebecca. But—"

"—you'll never bother to try and find out!" she yelled. "The Guild has done precisely nothing to rescue our parents since the day they went missing. And we're sitting here playing spinning tops!" She ran from the cabin, slamming the door behind her.

"Aren't you going after her, Douglas?" asked the captain.

"*Has* there been a rescue party sent to the Sinkiang, Captain?"

"There has. I received a message before the attack on Wenzi Island. I'm afraid the search party could find no trace of your mother or father. I'm sorry, Douglas."

Doug stood up.

"You understand what I've just said, Douglas? They are lost."

"Yes, Captain. I heard."

"You are remarkably calm, nephew."

"Everyone keeps telling me how big the Sinkiang is. Perhaps the search party looked in the wrong place."

"A scientific deduction rather than an emotional one." The captain smiled.

Doug walked towards the door, then stopped and turned back as his mind gave shape to an idea that had been niggling at him. "The Sujing Quantou. They're not Chinese, are they?"

"No. Not at all."

"They're Greeks," deduced Doug.

"Indeed they are. Where was Alexander the Great in 326 BC?"

"India?" guessed Doug after a moment's thought.

"Very good. He'd reached the River Hyphasis but his army was in virtual mutiny. Morale had reached rock bottom. They'd conquered every country from Egypt to India, and the surviving soldiers wanted to return home after years of fighting. Then the gyrolabes were discovered. It seems Alexander was not told about them, as some of his high-ranking officers feared the discovery would prolong the campaign. A decision was taken to send the gyrolabes as far away from Alexander as possible, in case he should be tempted to put their radical science to military use. The finest reconnaissance troops were selected for this mission, divided into four teams and each given a gyrolabe and a quarter of *The 99 Elements*. They were ordered to take these to the furthest reaches of Asia and hide them.

ALEXANDER THE GREAT (356-23 BC)

King of Macedonia and military genius, he conquered much of the then civilized world, taking his troops through Persia, Egypt, Afghanistan and India.

Photograph © The British Museum/HIP

"When Alexander heard his men had left without any explanation, he assumed they had deserted. They were officially disgraced, and therefore doomed to wander the continent without hope of ever returning to Greece. The Sujing Quantou are the direct descendants of these four ill-starred military sects. How did you guess?"

"The discuses ... the downturned ram's horns on their helmets. That's Alexander's personal emblem – it's on his coins; I've seen it in a book. Is it the Sujing who have the third gyrolabe?"

"Yes, they keep it at their headquarters in Khotan."

"But their name is Chinese, not Greek."

"After many centuries in their adopted country, they assumed Chinese ways and became known by the name of Sujing Quantou."

"Can't they ever return home to Greece?"

"Of course they could now. But home is in the heart, Douglas."

"They must have discovered the source of Daughter of the Sun, though?"

"Yes, and they guard it jealously."

Doug made to leave, deducing from the captain's tone that the interview was over. "Thank you for not sending us back to America, Uncle."

"Wait. There is another reason for letting you stay on board – you and your sister have made good friends here. A ship's complement has ways of letting a captain know when he's made a decision they do not like."

Doug clambered down to his cabin. Through the open connecting door he could see Becca slumped on her bunk, her gaze fixed on the pipe bracket above her desk. Neither spoke, lost in their own worlds.

Caught between exhaustion and utter confusion about his future, Doug had never felt so disorientated or uncertain. After all that had happened, the fate of their parents was no clearer than it had been a year ago. He told himself again that no trace didn't mean they were dead.

It wasn't much of a comfort.

Both Becca and Doug were snapped out of their reveries by a rustle from the luggage locker at the end of Becca's bunk. She put her finger to her lips and in three quick steps reached the locker door. Doug bounded through and wrenched it open, ready to tackle any rogue member of Sheng-Fat's crew hiding in there.

Two slight figures sprang out shouting "Sujing Cha!" Xu and Xi looked at Becca's grimace and burst out laughing. Despite herself, Becca couldn't help laughing too.

As they were all settling down and making themselves comfortable – Becca perched on the edge of her desk, the Sujing twins on the bunk and Doug on the chair trying to fish his silver pocket compass from the lining of his sea coat – Xu produced a treacle pudding and four spoons from the locker.

"Are you staying aboard the ship?" asked Xi.

"For as long as we need to. I've got a plan to mount an expedition," revealed Becca.

Doug frowned at her. "You mean *we've* got a plan," he said.

"What is it?" asked Xi curiously.

"To go to the Sinkiang to look for our parents."

"The Sinkiang is a dangerous region," noted Xu, his cheeks bulging with pudding.

"More dangerous than Sheng-Fat's island?" retorted Becca.

"Didn't anyone ever tell you? Sinkiang is the worst place in the world. You might need some help."

"Are you interested in coming?" said Doug.

"Of course!" Xu and Xi seemed to sense the desperation in Doug's voice. "As we have fought in battle with you, so we are for ever bound to you by honour. This is the Sujing Quantou way."

Becca sighed. She looked at each of the three pairs of eyes in turn and saw their resolve. "It's settled then. A secret pact."

"These might come in handy." Doug pulled out eight slender gold bars, each marked with a dragon's tooth motif. "They can pay for any crankshaft problems we may encounter along the way," he said, grinning.

Becca's diary: 2nd May 1920
Aboard *Expedient*, off Wenzi Island

The Guild has its secret purpose. Xu, Xi, Doug and I have ours. For the moment my ship is the Expedient, *my employer the Honourable Guild of Specialists. It is better to be part of something than part of nothing. Doug and I have set our course.*

I am to report on watch in five minutes. Doug has four hours to catch up on some sleep – if he can stop eating. I pull on my sea boots, pack up my books and prepare for my first watch as deckhand on the Honourable Guild of Specialists research ship Expedient.

Captain MacKenzie tapped the point of his dividers against the chart laid out on the desk. The thousands of East Indies islands looked like rain splashes on glass. Outside on deck, he could hear the sounds of the *Galacia* being shipped by his fine crew. "Somebody's had me pudding!" squawked Mrs Ives, not much muffled by the armoured deck above him. "Own up! I bet it's those Lapsang Souchong twins. Trouble, they are, and no mistake!"

The Duchess yawned, then let out a stifled roar.

"What are you making all that noise for?"

The tiger cast a lazy look at the barometer and raised her head to sniff the air: the needle was dropping like a stone. The captain could be in no doubt of the weather. With a rueful smile he opened his desk drawer and filed the extremely useful papers and charts he'd discovered on Sheng-Fat's junk.

"Wheelhouse?" he said into the speaking tube.

Ives's voice echoed down the pipe. "Wheelhouse, Captain. Ives here."

"Set course for the Celebes Sea."

"Celebes Sea it is, Captain. Have you seen the sky? It sure is a strange colour. I don't like the look of it."

"Have the hatches battened down. Rig the ship for dirty weather. We're in for a full typhoon."

END OF BOOK I

Appendices

THE HONOURABLE GUILD OF SPECIALISTS

The Honourable Guild of Specialists (HGS) was an eccentric group of scientists and explorers founded in 1533. Membership was by invitation only. By 1920 the Guild was troubled by mounting debts, and the question of its future direction and purpose had split the twelve board members into three factions.

The first remained solidly behind the search for a solution to the ancient Indus mysteries of *The 99 Elements* and *Daughter of the Sun*. The second believed the Guild should sell some of the knowledge it had gleaned through centuries of exploration and scientific research. The third faction, considering the Indus quest to be a waste of time, wished to abandon the high ideals of the Guild in favour of the lucrative confidential missions for governments which had become its primary source of income. The criminal activities of Julius Pembleton-Crozier were to force each member of the board to consider their position very carefully.

The crest of the HGS. The Latin motto translates as "With skill and honour". The device at the centre of the shield represents the four points of the compass, and the skull is a reference to Holbein's painting The Ambassadors. *The hand clutching the arrow represents readiness for battle in a just cause; the arrow also stands for the compass needle, a symbol of the Guild's fascination with the forces of nature.*

"THE AMBASSADORS"

Jean de Dinteville and Georges de Selve are best known for their appearance in this celebrated yet beguiling painting by Hans Holbein the Younger. The two men stand next to a variety of scientific apparatus, musical instruments and collected objects all painted at near life size. With its famous distorted skull and many intriguing visual references, the picture seems to hint at some secret meaning which has defied definition by centuries of scholars.

Research papers uncovered in Rebecca MacKenzie's archive may cast some light: she claims the painting's original title was *The Founding of the Honourable Guild of Specialists, 1533*.

The Ambassadors by Hans Holbein the Younger, oil on oak, 207 x 209.5 cm, National Gallery, London
© *National Gallery Company Ltd*

LUC CHAMBOIS'S INVENTIONS

THE MOLECULE INVIGORATOR

Mystery has always surrounded the workings of the molecule invigorator. Chambois maintained that Pembleton-Crozier's agents stole all of his research papers on the night of his kidnapping in Paris, and no drawings or notebooks relating to it have been found in the MacKenzie Archive.

Fragments of a lecture transcript survive, one of a series attended by Rebecca, Douglas and their parents. But Chambois gave this and other lectures purely to raise funds for his research and he was careful not disclose the secrets of his invention, never describing the precise workings of the machine.

One documentary insight into the mechanics of the invigorator does exist: the MacKenzie Archive contained a single page of a longer letter written by Chambois to Hamish MacKenzie (Rebecca and Douglas's father). Though far from giving a technical explanation, Chambois writes enthusiastically about tuning steel with his molecule invigorator "almost as if playing a musical instrument". There is a passage about harmonics and the unified laws of nature – a particular interest of the Guild's – and it is known that the Guild funded the final development of the invigorator.

But why the absence of this machine from the modern world? The solution seems obvious, though unprovable. Chambois's invention may have been realized not only by the Guild's financial backing, but also through their knowledge of a more advanced science. In this instance, he would have been bound by their uncompromising secrecy laws.

THE FOG GENERATOR

Six wire grids were arranged around the ship. Each grid was structured as a group of hexagons and each hexagon had a steam nozzle at its centre. This nozzle was fed from the ship's boiler via electrically insulated pipes.

Since sea water is mildly alkaline, the steam that emerged from the nozzles was negatively charged. A circuit was set up between the wire grids/boiler (positive charge) and the steam (negative charge), causing the "curtain" of steam to be attracted out towards each grid. The effect was amplified by connecting the grids to an electrostatic device.

Chambois observed that the steam needed to be "wet" (containing some condensed water) and at 100°C. The steam from the ship's boiler would have been "dry" (superheated), and well over 100°C. It appears that it was merged at the control box with fresh steam from the auxiliary boilers to produce a suitably charged "wet" mixture.

(Compiled from Luc Chambois's notebooks – see page 185 for sketches.)

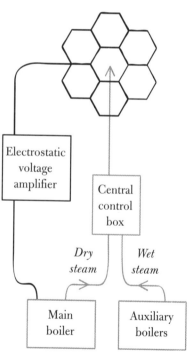

CAUTION: under no circumstances should electricity be mixed with either steam or water in an attempt to recreate Chambois's invention. Doing so may result in electrocution and death.

COVE COTTAGE

One of the main chambers of the archive.

These photographs show the MacKenzie Archive at Cove Cottage, Rebecca MacKenzie's home in Perenprith, Devon.

It is believed to house the collected documents and artefacts of the Honourable Guild of Specialists, including material relating to expeditions, scientific inquiries and confidential missions undertaken by the Guild since its inception in 1533. Originally kept in Florence (Firenze), Italy, the archive was moved to its current location sometime in the last century. The reason for this relocation is thought to be concealed among the estimated fifty thousand files which have yet to be read and assimilated.

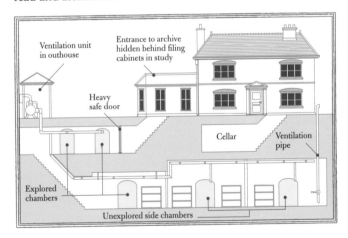

The archive's entrance is hidden behind filing cabinets in the study, beyond which a set of concrete steps leads down to a heavy safe door. The subterranean complex is well ventilated and dry. At present several sealed side chambers have yet to be explored.

Top left: The sealed entrance to the archive.

Top right: Rebecca MacKenzie's study.

Left: Portrait of Hamish and Elena MacKenzie (Rebecca and Douglas's parents) with an infant Rebecca.

Far left: Cross section of Cove Cottage showing the position of the secret chambers.

(MA 239.44 MAC)

WENZI ISLAND

The fortress at Wenzi Island had a long and infamous history. Built in 1410 by two exiled generals of the Ming Dynasty army, its fortunes waxed and waned with the succession of blood-thirsty warlords and criminals who claimed it as their own. Its discreet proximity to China made the island an ideal base for pirates preying on ships sailing the South China Sea, Pescadores Channel and Formosa Strait.

Occupation was sporadic, however. In 1796, Captain William MacKenzie's HGS expedition reported only a handful of fishermen using the harbour for repairing junks and nets, and he was able to conduct his survey without obstruction.

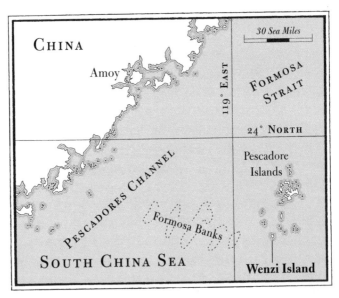

Wenzi Island in relation to the China coast and neighbouring islands. (MA 809.80 WEN)

(MA 00.298 SE)

Above: Rare example of The Scientist & Explorer, *which documented the Guild's public expeditions and discoveries. The confidential missions which funded the HGS were never mentioned.*

FULL CREW LIST OF THE EXPEDIENT

MacKenzie, Fitzroy	*captain*
Ives, Erasmus	*coxswain*
Watts, Stephen (Sparkie)	*wireless telegraphy officer*
Schmidt, Wolfgang (The Chief)	*chief engineer*
King, William (King Billy)	*chief petty officer*
Lincoln, Robert (Ten Dinners)	*petty officer/diver*
Denyer, Harold (Arrow)	*chief armourer/diver*
Steinhauer, Konrad (Bullets)	*armourer's mate*
Lange, Anton (Shortie)	*gun-layer first class*
Bray, Sam (Slippery Sam)	*gunner's mate/diver*
Vasto, Giuseppe (The Gondolier)	*diver/leading torpedoman*
Hoshino, Kiyoshi (Leaky)	*mechanician (for* Galacia*)*
Wilhelmsson, Axel (Grease)	*leading seaman*
Charles (Posh Charlie)	*able seaman/diver*
Fukuda, Kinsaku (Lucky)	*carpenter*
Smola, Frank (Fast Frankie)	*mechanician/diver*
Draycott, Gerald (The Priest)	*chief stoker*
Donne, François (Grappa)	*leading stoker*
Messop, John (Laughing Boy)	*stoker*
Teng, Mr (The Professor)	*ship's steward*
Ives, Faith Hope Anne Charity	*cook*
The Duchess	*ship's cat*

SELECT BIBLIOGRAPHY

Barrouillet, Stéphanie: *Voyages archéologiques et géographiques à travers les déserts de Sinkiang* (Paris, 1901)

Beak, Catherine: *Underwater Geological Anomalies: A Study of the China Coast* (Badger, London, 1934)

Blazeby, Commander Crispin, RN (Retd): *Sailing Explained: With Strategies for Avoiding Disasters at Sea* (Gibber Books, Salcombe, 1952)

Bullen, Benjamin: *In the Company of the Sujing Quantou: With Canvas and Brush Across China* (Erskine, London, 1903)

Chambois, Luc: Extracts from the 1918 lecture "Renforcer la chaîne moléculaire de l'acier par stimulation électrique" ("Strengthening the Molecular Bond of Steel by Electrical Invigoration"), trans. Monica Perez for her monograph *New Directions in Science* (Candlewick, Texas, 1919)

Conroy Scott, Kevin: *On Secret Societies and Other Related Discoveries* (Chicago, 1911)

Drasar-Schmidt, T & E: *Duelling and Swordplay in the Bavarian Manner* (London and Munich, 1810)

Earley, Lucy: *To the Source of the Yangtze Solo: An Account of One Woman's Thrilling Adventures in a Sampan* (London, 1936)

Finnis, Anne: *Alexander: Decision at the River Hyphasis* (Chapter 21 Publishing, Calcutta, 1941)

Gurney, Stella: *Villains and Rogues of the South China Sea* (London, 1931)

Heller, Julek: *A Brief Sketch of Shanghai Society* (HB Books, Shanghai, 1922)

Hookings, Georgina: *Ancient Texts of the Silk Road* (St Mawes, Sydney, 1931)

McDougall, James: *Monarch Class: The Riddle of the Q Ship* (St Duthus, Edinburgh, 1938)

MacKenzie, Rebecca: "The Ambassadors: A New Interpretation" (*Bulletin of the Royal Guild of Artists and Craftsmen*, vol. 258, no. 7 [1975], pp. 121–66)

Morgan, Linda: *A Traveller's Guide to Shanghai's Ancient Chinese City* (Shanghai, 1925)

Morrison, Alison: *A Compendium of Chinese Warlords* (Krakow Lobes, London, 1924)

Muir, Caroline: *Shipping Contracts and Treaties in Asia, 1900–1925* (3 vols., Krakow Lobes, London, 1928)

North, Sam: *Robina Hood and Other Lost Films of the Silent Era* (Academy, London, 1961)

Northrop, Captain Martin, RN: *Naval Gunnery* (3rd edn, Bellarose Press, Margate, 1908)

Oldfield & Gray: *A Guide to the Finest Hotels, Restaurants and Attractions of Shanghai and Hong Kong* (Kensington Press, London, 1928)

Puttapipat, Niroot: *Notes and Sketches on the Ancient Martial Arts of the Tarim Basin* (Rangoon, 1890)

Stannard, Gavin: *Chinese Fighting Orders and Mercenaries: With Appendices on Reliability and Rates of Pay* (Munjati Press, Bangkok, 1880)

Tothill, Christopher: *A Scientific Revolution: Twenty Astonishing Advancements Within the Realm of Physics* (Linacre, London, 1920)

Wedderburn & Insole: *Hydraulic Gun Carriages: New Advances Described, and Some Observations on Installation* (London, 1913)

About the Author

Joshua Mowll was sent to boarding school aged eight.

He says, "It was a draughty gothic pile atop a remote hill on the Welsh borders where we had porridge for breakfast every day. It was more like 1878 than 1978." His family later moved to Kent, where he claims he spent his school years "achieving not very much, on the whole", choosing to pursue his musical ambitions in a number of under-rehearsed and unsuccessful bands.

However, he did love art lessons, and went on to study graphic design at Canterbury and Ipswich. On leaving, he began to work in newspapers and is now a graphic artist for a national Sunday paper. Operation Red Jericho *is his first book.*

ACKNOWLEDGEMENTS: I would like to thank: my agent, Clare Conville, without whose energy and unwavering conviction the HGS may have been lost to history for ever; Jane Winterbotham and David Lloyd for the box of fortune cookies; Gill Evans for her steadying hand on the tiller; and finally the quite remarkable and unstinting talents of Ben Norland.

First published 2005 by Walker Books Ltd
87 Vauxhall Walk, London SE11 5HJ

2 3 4 5 6 7 8 9 10

Text © 2005 Joshua Mowll

All illustrations © 2005 Joshua Mowll except:
Sujing warrior icon p.1, p.273 and cover;
Cove Cottage photos (appendix 4) © 2005
Benjamin Mowll and used under licence.
Doug MacKenzie sketches
© 2005 Julek Heller
Illustrations p.38, p.63 foldout
(diver only), p.143, p.144,
p.160, p.193 foldout
© 2005 Niroot Puttapipat

The right of Joshua Mowll to be
identified as author/illustrator of
this work has been asserted by him
in accordance with the Copyright,
Designs and Patents Act 1988

This book has been typeset in
Giovanni and Bulmer MT

Printed in China

British Library Cataloguing in
Publication Data: a catalogue
record for this book is available
from the British Library

ISBN 1-84428-625-8

www.walkerbooks.co.uk